The
Noel Coward
Murder Case

The
Noel Coward
Murder Case

George Baxt

St. Martin's Press   New York

Design by Judy Christensen

Library of Congress Cataloging-in-Publication Data

Baxt, George.
      The Noel Coward murder case / George Baxt.
           p.   cm.
      ISBN 0-312-08272-X
      1. Coward, Noel, 1899–1973—Fiction.   I. Title.
      PS3552.A8478N63   1992
      813'.54—dc20   92-24641
                                                        CIP

First Edition: November 1992

10 9 8 7 6 5 4 3 2 1

This book is for
American Express,
Optima,
MasterCard,
Visa, and
Discover,
without whom
it could not
have been
written.

The
Noel Coward
Murder Case

One

DETECTIVE Inspector Abraham Wang of the Shanghai police studied the corpse found floating amidst the flotsam and detritus of the Huangpu River. He asked his assistant, an ambitious young man named Matt Lee, "Now what's a black woman doing floating in a Chinese river?"

"What's a black woman doing in Shanghai?" countered Matt Lee.

The coroner, a chubby little man who sucked his teeth and made ugly little noises, told them, "She was dead before she hit the river. Garroted." He indicated the nasty bruises on her neck. "There's flesh under her fingernails. She put up a good fight."

"That wins her my admiration," said Wang. He stared at the bloated face. "Very heavy with the makeup, very theatrical. That French Music Hall show at the Opera House . . ."

"No black actresses. I saw the show last week."

"Check them out anyway. She might have worked behind the scenes. Also the clubs along the river. Her dress is very tight, very provocative. Maybe she's a nightclub artist of a sort."

"Maybe she was a whore."

There was an ankle bracelet on her right leg. Wang examined it. "Maxine Howard." Then he said, "Garroted. Imagine. Not just ordinary strangled, garroted. Very old hat. Dacoits garroted their victims." Dacoits had terrorized China for years, hired killers who came silently in the night to kill undetected.

Matt Lee grinned and said, "Doctor Fu Manchu."

"What about him?"

"He used dacoits. I've read all the books about him. Crazy wild, that writer Sax Rohmer."

"Appendix scar," said the coroner. He examined her left arm. "She's been vaccinated and had innoculation shots. They do a lot of that in America." He examined her teeth. "Gold fillings. Positively an American."

Matt Lee followed Wang back to his office. As they walked, Wang said over his shoulder to the younger man, "We'll send a cable to my friend Jacob Singer of the New York City police. He's a very good friend. I met him when I studied at Columbia University. Ten years ago. Maxine Howard. Five yen will get you one she's another of those so-called missing persons being shipped out here to work against their will in whorehouses."

His office was small and cramped. On one wall were portraits of his Chinese heros, Sun Yat-sen, Chiang Kai-shek, and Anna May Wong. He indicated a chair for Matt Lee, who took a pad and pen out of his jacket pocket. Wang dictated slowly.

In New York, the following day, detective Jacob Singer read Wang's cable and took action immediately. He contacted Missing Persons and gave them Maxine Howard's name. They were back to him in less than fifteen minutes. He took notes and then read them aloud to his associate, Abel Graham. "Maxine Howard, age twenty-eight, five foot seven . . . a big one that one . . . weight one thirty . . . singer and dancer . . . Negro . . ."

As he cleaned his nails with his gold toothpick, Abel Graham asked, "Now what's a *schwartzer* doing floating in a river in Shanghai?"

"That's what Wang wants to know. She was reported missing four months ago by her sister, Electra Howard."

"Electra?"

"Yeah, sure, what's wrong with it? Like that O'Neill play, *Mourning Becomes Electra*."

"Never heard of it."

2

"That's because you got no intellect. I've got a phone number here for Electra." He dialed. The phone rang eight times before Singer hung up. "Out to lunch."

"You got an address?"

"I got an address and a phone number and an address for her agent."

"She would be show business. Right up your alley. Send her a telegram."

"Good thinking," said Singer in a rasping monotone, "I'd never have thought of that myself." He wondered again as he wondered several times a day why a dullard like Abel Graham opted for a career in police work. But then, he doubted if Graham had the skill to be a dogcatcher.

The voice was pitched high. It was thin and reedy, and yet it was melodic. Noel Coward knew how to sell a song, especially the ones he wrote.

Yesterday was gray, the day before was blue,
I am in the pink, darling how are you?

The sun poured into the large, beautifully appointed living room as Noel entertained his audience of one, Millicent Headman, a handsome woman in her early sixties.

Monday was ecru, Tuesday I thought puce,
Wednesday was a flood, Of lovely orange juice . . .

Noel was doing a superb job with his latest composition. Millicent Headman's face was wreathed in an angelic smile. Thought Noel, she must have been a knockout thirty years ago in 1905 when she'd been in the musical theater with the likes of Lillian Russell and Mae West. She looked pretty damned good now, white hair carefully coiffed, a simple string of pearls to enhance her simple navy blue suit.

Life can be a rainbow,
When you let the pain go . . .

3

He adored listening to himself sing, and he adored Millicent Headman for obviously loving the way he sang. In that moment he had made his decision. He would rent this lovely furnished apartment. The monthly cost was reasonable, it was centrally located in New York City on West Fifty-eighth Street between Sixth and Seventh avenues, and it faced south. The sunshine was divine.

> Thursday might be black, Friday might be white,
> Put them all together, dear, what a colorful sight . . .

And it was not too far from the Fifty-ninth Street bridge, which led to Astoria, Queens, and Paramount's East Coast studios where he would soon be filming his first starring vehicle, *The Scoundrel*. Despite the title, it was not autobiographical. It was written by Ben Hecht and Charles MacArthur, coauthors of two Broadway hits, *The Front Page* and *Twentieth Century*. They were also producing and directing the film. They were wicked charlatans.

> Gray—blue—pink—puce—ecru—
> White and black . . . My darling how are you?

His hands were raised in the air and there was an almost flirtatious smile on his lips. Mrs. Headman clapped her hands together and said in her whipped cream voice, "How utterly marvelous, Mr. Coward. I'm so flattered to be your audience of one."

"As well you should be, dear woman. You're the first person to hear it. I dashed it off this morning between the grapefruit and the eggs. You can tell by the stains on the lead sheet."

"Oh Mr. Coward, Mr. Coward!"

"You must call me Noel and I shall call you Millicent, as I have decided to be your tenant."

"How delicious!"

"Really?" He moved away from the piano and was jamming a cigarette into his holder. "I had no idea decisions might be edible. What a magnificent table lighter. It must be Tiffany's."

"It is." He detected the sudden sadness. "It was my husband's favorite. I gave it to him on our twentieth anniversary." She found a small smile. "I think you two would have liked each other very much. Linus was a great anglophile. He doted on the British theater."

Noel was genuinely pleased. "Did he really? How nice."

"He loved you . . ." Noel rewarded her with a charming smile. "Beatrice Lillie, Miss Gertrude Lawrence of course . . ."

"Of course . . . or else."

". . . and Marie Tempest . . ."

"Dear Marie." He blew a smoke ring past the room's splendid chandelier.

". . . and Gerald du Maurier . . ." Noel wondered where the switch was located that could turn her off. ". . . and Ivor Novello . . ."

Noel winced but she didn't see it. She paused for breath and he leapt swiftly into the breach. "When would it be convenient for me to move in?"

"Why, as soon as you like. I've moved into my smaller apartment down the hall. Actually, it was kept as servants' quarters."

"Oh my dear . . ." He hoped he sounded suitably forlorn.

She held up her hand. "Oh no no no! It's quite pleasant and quite comfortable and more than enough for me. My daughter has her own place on Central Park West. Perhaps you've heard of her? Diana Headman. Lately she's been singing in supper clubs."

"Oh of course! They call her 'high society's sultry singer of sensuous songs.' Quite a mouthful, I suppose she is too."

"If I must say so myself, Diana is a very beautiful woman."

"And well she should be with you as her mother."

"You're too kind."

"Not too often. Is she singing in town anywhere?"

"Not at the moment. She's opening some time in the near future at a new club on West Fifty-seventh Street, somewhere near Tenth Avenue, on the fringe of the Hell's Kitchen area."

"How brave and daring of the owners. It's not by any chance the one that's called The Cascades?"

"Yes it is. Then you've heard of it."

"Heard of it? My dear woman, I am plagued by it. The three wretched owners are besieging me with all sorts of head-spinning offers to be their first headliner. I have every reason to believe in an earlier life they were gangsters. Now they're merely hoodlums. Yet they're quite a musical threesome. Vivaldi, Beethoven, and Bizet. At

5

least that's what they call themselves. I'm sure it was something else in an earlier incarnation. Come to think of it, I have a friend in the police department, a detective named Jacob Singer. I must ask him about them. I'm sure there are thick dossiers detailing rum running, gun running, and instant unsolvable assassinations."

"Noel, you have such a delightfully vivid imagination."

"Of course I do, my dear. Without it I'd starve to death." He was at the window staring out. "What a lovely view. I adore your skyline. It never ceases to thrill me when I'm aboard ship entering New York harbor, and of course that divine statue of Constance Bennett. Let me write you a check to cement the deal." He sat at a beautiful antique desk said to have belonged to Nathaniel Hawthorne, produced a checkbook from his inside jacket pocket, and wrote in his clear, concise hand. "First month's rent and a month's security, right?"

"Yes, that would be fine. I don't have much of a head for business."

"Oh come come," as he wrote carefully, meticulously, "the wife of Linus Headman not have much of a head . . . no pun intended . . . for business?"

"None at all. I'm afraid Linus didn't have much of one either. Poor dear. He struggled so hard all those years to build Headman Pharmaceuticals . . ."

". . . Marvelous aspirins . . ."

". . . but the market crash six years ago sent him plummeting. He had to sell out and for very little. It's what killed him."

"How very sad. Here is your check. All quite correct?"

"Oh quite correct."

"Um . . . if a bit more would come in handy?"

"Oh my dear Noel, how very kind of you, but no, no thank you. I manage quite well, I assure you. I own both these flats, and there are royalties I receive from the business. If I ever need assistance, I'm sure Diana would help me."

"Ah, then she's wealthy in her own right?"

"Oh yes. She divorced well."

"Good for Diana. How many times?"

"Three."

"Three!"

"They were brief marriages, at least the first two were. Diana, you see, has a short attention span. Her third marriage is where most of the money came from. He was a rancher."

"Ah! Way out west! Montana?"

"Africa. Rhodes."

"A scholar?"

"No. Nor a gentleman."

"But oh well, there's all that lolly to comfort her."

"Lolly?"

"Lolly, yes. Money. British vernacular. Possibly derived from lollipop, as it frequently requires someone to be a sucker." Her laugh tinkled and Noel found it pleasing.

As she put the check into her handbag she said, "Well, so far 1935 has been a pleasant year for me."

"I'm glad it was pleasant for someone." He was bristling. "I'm sure you're aware I've had two disasters in a row on Broadway."

"Oh I'm so sorry."

"Sorry isn't enough, Millicent. First there was *Conversation Piece*. I thought it was absolutely charming. It starred the enchanting French stars Yvonne Printemps and Pierre Fresnay. I suppose it didn't help that nobody could understand a word they said and God knows Noel Coward's words must be clearly enunciated. One critic wrote a paraphrase of the logo on Rice Krispies boxes . . . and I still adore them . . . Rice Krispies, dear, not the critics. He wrote"—Noel enunciated each word tinged with venom—"Snap! Crackle! Flop!"

"How rude!"

"Are you always given to understatement? Then came *Point Valaine*. It was cleverly sordid. I thought Lynn and Alfred would make it work. The Lunts, you know. They rarely have a box-office disaster. But with me they made an exception. One beastly critic wrote, 'All Lunts and no play make Noel a dull boy.' I wonder if critics have a sex life. Ah well. Some day I shall look back and laugh. The hell with the lot. I will not countenance anyone, let alone a lowly critic, upsetting the perfect symmetry of my life. That's why I stayed on to do the movie. The money, my dear Millicent, the money. Come to think of it, The Cascades is offering me tons of

7

money. I'm sure it would be a snap for me, filming by day and performing by night . . ." He was briefly lost in thought.

"Oh do consider it seriously," urged Millicent. "It would be such a thrill for Diana to share the bill with you."

"Share? With me? Oh well, I suppose that's one way to put it. Now then, I'm off to my hotel to put myself together and I'll move in later this afternoon."

"Here are the keys. These are two sets. I can arrange to share my housekeeper if you like."

"Oh that won't be necessary, thank you. I have a companion who travels with me as sort of chief cook and bottle washer. He's Jeffrey Amherst. Perhaps you've heard the song . . . ?" He sang reedily, *"Oh Lord Jeffrey Amherst . . ."*

"Oh of course," said Millicent.

"Of course. Well, my Jeffrey is a descendant of that Jeffrey. He's terribly charming. I'm sure you'll find him most engaging, especially since he's unengaged. *A bientôt,* dear Millicent, you are such a charmer." He took her hand and kissed it. His was a heady performance.

After he left, Millicent phoned her daughter. Diana was entertaining Nicholas Benson, her close friend and occasional lover. Nicholas was the scion of another wealthy family ruined by the market crash but had managed to make a profitable career for himself as a crime writer. Diana picked up the phone, said "Hello?" followed by, "Oh hello Mother." Then, "Noel Coward?" Her voice had risen an octave. Nicholas was interested. "Nick you'll never believe this, Noel Coward's rented Mother's place."

"How nice for Mother."

"Well now I can get to know him better, and convince him to open at The Cascades with me. Isn't that wonderful?"

"Noel Coward singing in a nightclub? I can't quite envision it."

"I can." She nailed both words to his ears. He listened to Diana babbling away and then turned his thoughts in another direction. Vivaldi, Beethoven, and Bizet. Hardly Wynken, Blynken, and Nod. The Cascades was the most talked about event on the Great White Way, and those three men had every intention of making the opening a spectacular one. Located in an old warehouse the size of half a city block, it had been redesigned and reconstructed with revolv-

8

ing stages that disappeared into the basement and then rose again at the touch of a switch. The centerpiece was to be a genuine waterfall, a cascade that roared from ceiling to floor, another modern mechanical marvel. There was to be a staff of fifty in the kitchen and double that in the main room. No expense was spared to make The Cascades what the newspapers already labeled the ninth wonder of the world. A day didn't pass that the world's leading gossip columnist, Walter Winchell, didn't have an item or a rumor or a press agent's puff in his column. He had mentioned it four consecutive Sundays on his 9:00 P.M. fifteen minutes on the NBC radio network. The Cascades' rivals were foaming at the mouth with anger and envy.

"Nick!" The sharpness of her tone startled him.

"What? What is it?"

"You're miles away!"

"Oh, sorry. Finished talking to your mother?"

"Obviously. What's preoccupying you so much of late?"

"Vivaldi, Beethoven, and Bizet."

"Don't concern yourself too much with them."

"Why not? They're the talk of the town. I think there's a good story in them. Anyhow, I suspect there is. I've got a hunch."

"Never trust a hunch."

"Coming from a woman, that's a laugh."

She caressed his cheek. "I like them. They're paying me a handsome salary. I'm society, I give them credibility."

"And they need Noel Coward to draw the customers."

"Mother's asking him in for a drink tonight. He'll be moved in by late this afternoon. And I shall be at Mother's. Want to come too?"

"I wouldn't miss it for the world."

The basement of this particular building in Harlem was dank and cold and smelled of evil. A goat tethered to an iron ring in the wall bleated with fear and frustration as it tried to break loose. Its eyes reflected terror as the tall black woman walked slowly toward the animal. In her right hand she held a carving knife. She chanted an incantation as she approached the goat. The poor animal leapt back and forth, sensing the fate that awaited it. A door opened and a shaft

9

of orange light spilled into the room. A tall, muscular, handsome black man who moved with a dancer's grace entered. In his left hand he held a yellow envelope.

"Electra!"

The upraised hand gripping the knife froze. She turned with a sinuous movement.

"You know better than to interrupt me when I'm casting a spell!"

"There's a telegram for you. Telegrams are always important."

She flung the knife to the floor. The animal behind her stood trembling, grateful for the brief reprieve. Electra went to the man and took the envelope. "It's bad news. I feel it through my fingers. Dan . . ." Their eyes met as she handed the envelope back to him. "You read it."

Daniel Parrish, dancer, choreographer, and in his spare time voodoo priest, tore the envelope open. He read the message and then linked eyes with her again. He spoke softly. "It's bad news. Maxine's dead. The wire's from the police department. You're to call a detective Jacob Singer. They found her body in Shanghai, in the river. She was murdered."

Electra flung back her head and emitted a howl that caused the building to tremble. "Maxine!" she cried. "Baby sister! They murdered you! They murdered you!"

She picked up the knife from the floor and hurled herself at the goat. She hit it with such force its knees buckled and it fell to the floor, bleating piteously, the eyes seeing death and the soul sensing it. Electra cut the animal's throat. It died instantly. Electra leapt to her feet and faced Daniel Parrish.

Her words struck lightning. "I'm going to kill them."

"Cool it, baby, and call Mr. Detective Man. Call Jacob Singer. And cut the dramatics. You loathed Maxine."

Two

THE Cascades executive offices were located in the basement. Although the three partners had offices of their own, like homing pigeons they chose to nest in the conference room, which consisted of a long, oval-shaped mahogany table with a dozen matching chairs, a bar, and a Frigidaire, the wall decorated with numerous framed photographs of nightclub celebrities. There was a thick fog of black cigar smoke hanging under the ceiling and Big Ike Vivaldi, sitting at the head of the table, looked like a defendant in a courtroom, a situation not unfamiliar to him. Big Ike was big indeed. He was almost six feet four inches in height with huge, ugly, powerful hands. A thin scar ran from his left nostril to his left ear, a souvenir of a boyhood encounter with a thug whose funeral he chose not to attend. He was forty years of age and entertained few illusions of ever reaching fifty.

Fat Harry Beethoven was a few years older than Vivaldi, not quite six feet tall, and shaped like a pear. He had a strong Bronx accent and weak eyes. He wore thick glasses that gave his face a menacing look. A former associate had suggested Fat Harry belonged in a tank of tropical fish, which is why he was a former associate. Harry's hands had been compared to anvils. Despite the enormous weight he carried, he was light on his feet and moved with the grace of an athlete.

11

Irving "The Weasel" Bizet was the shortest and youngest of the three. While his partners favored pretentious fat Cuban cigars, Irving preferred thin panatelas. His clothes, of course, were custom-made and exquisitely tailored to highlight his almost boyish, slender figure. He sought and adored the company of celebrities, fawning on them like a member of a royal retinue. His nose was long and thin and his eyes were narrow. His ears came to a point and it was Big Ike who nicknamed him "The Weasel." In addition to being uneasy partners, the three had one other thing in common—they favored tall showgirls.

Their mistresses, of course, were to be displayed onstage at the club. Vivaldi's girl was tall, blonde Edna Dore. Edna was a maverick. She read books. Beethoven's catch was tall, redheaded Trixie Bates. Trixie saved what money she could and was buying up lots in Brooklyn. She was smart enough to know that her exotic good looks couldn't be depended upon as a meal ticket forever. The Weasel's girl was tall, brunette Angie Murray. She'd been a public secretary in an office building in which Bizet's accountant had an office. She actually liked the Weasel. He'd paid for the furnishings of her apartment, caps for her teeth, a generous monthly allowance, and two abortions. The girls got along just fine and elected to share the same dressing room, where they could gossip, wisecrack, and compare notes on their men to their heart's content. They also shared Hattie Beavers, a black woman who was devoted to her "ladies." She dressed them, undressed them, ran their errands, and dispensed wisdom that some suspected she cribbed from fortune cookies.

Big Ike slammed an ugly fist on the mahogany table and shouted, "Don't you two gimme no arguments! I signed them for the show and they stay!"

"But niggers!" wailed the Weasel.

"Dan Parrish and Electra Howard are a class act! Don't yuh know? They played all over Europe before kings and queens and also royalty. Irving, you prejudiced against niggers?"

"But Ike, it's never been done before. Mixing niggers and whites in a club! For crying out loud, even the Cotton Club up in Harlem don't let no niggers into the place, and they're right in the heart of Harlem!"

12

"I ain't sayin' we'll let niggers in as paying customers, but we're sure as hell gonna hire them when they're great performers." His eyes shifted to Beethoven. "You wanna add your two cents?"

Beethoven took off his thick eyeglasses and placed them on the table. His voice was stronger than his eyes. "What I'm gonna add is worth more than two cents. We agreed when we decided to open the club that all decisions would be unanimous. So how come you go and sign them up without asking us first?"

Big Ike leaned forward, the movement threatening menace. "I signed them up because I had to move fast. Two other joints were after them and I wanted them for us. They're a class act and we're gonna be the classiest joint in town. If after they open you don't like them, I'll can them. Now listen, you two, what's more important is how do we get this here limey to headline?"

Bizet suggested, "You want me to send a few of the boys over to his place to convince him?"

"None of that stuff, Irving. Anyway, Diana tells me he's moving into her mother's joint. We don't want to mess it up. It's got antiques and more old stuff like that."

Fat Harry put his glasses back on, then waved away a cloud of smoke of his own making. "Has either of you two ever seen this guy perform?" They hadn't. "Then how do we know he's any good?"

Vivaldi spoke up. "Listen you two, he's a big name in show business. He's written a lot of good tunes. And he's real upper class, he's very cheek. The swells go for him big and we need him to bring the swells into our place."

Fat Harry snorted. "Swells! The only time they come to the West Side is when they need to catch a boat going to Europe."

"Oh yeah? They come here to the theater, right? And concerts, right? And they go to a lot of restaurants on this side of town. Wise up, you two, most of the money in this town is on the East Side and we gotta bring it west!"

The Weasel sighed. "I seen a picture of him in the *Daily News*. He looks awful lightweight."

Big Ike said, "I read someplace, looks are deceiving. I trust Diana's judgment. We gotta get Noel Coward."

* * *

13

Jacob Singer resisted pursing his lips and emitting a lowdown whistle when Abel Graham ushered Electra Howard and Dan Parrish into the office. He pushed his swivel chair back and got to his feet with his right hand extended. He shook hands with both of them and, when all were seated, expressed his condolences to Electra. Then he got down to cases.

"What was your sister doing in Shanghai?"

Electra crossed her shapely legs. Abel caught Singer's eye and subtly raised an eyebrow in approval. Electra said, "What do you think she was doing?"

"I could think all sorts of things, Miss Howard, and none of them very complimentary. My Shanghai associate's description of her makeup and costume could easily suggest she was working in a house."

"My sister wasn't a whore."

Singer shifted in his chair. "You filed the missing person's complaint several months ago."

"That's right."

"So she took off without letting you or anyone else know where she was headed."

"I was on tour when she left New York. I hadn't been in touch with her for some time. Maxine and I weren't exactly what you would call close. When I got back, she'd been gone a couple of months. My mother, who lives out in Queens, was very upset, of course, not having heard from her. I asked around town before I filed the complaint. Friends of hers, guys she'd been seeing, places she'd worked."

"I take it you're a performer, Miss Howard."

"I'm featured in Dan's dance troupe."

Parrish spoke. "Electra has been with me for oh . . . um . . . over five years."

Singer asked, "Did Maxine dance too?"

Electra said, "Mostly she sang."

Dan Parrish chuckled. To Singer's questioning look, he said, "She didn't sing too good, you know? I mean in a noisy joint where you couldn't hear her too well, she was passable. She got by on her looks. Great face, great body."

14

Singer was thinking that after submersion in the river, face and body were certainly no longer great.

Electra interrupted his thoughts. "How was she murdered? Shot? Knifed? Strangled?" She might have been reading a grocery list.

"You're close. She was garroted." Singer explained about the dacoits of the Chinese underworld. He elucidated further. "Detective Inspector Abraham Wang suspects she was shipped to Shanghai by an organization in the States that specializes in supplying Asian houses with girls."

"My sister was no whore," insisted Electra. "If she went anywhere, it would be with the promise of a singing job. Maxine was always the adventurous one. As a kid she was a tomboy."

"Aren't you wondering why she didn't let you or your mother know she was going to Asia?"

"I've been chewing it over all the way down here." She leaned forward, sending a wave of heady perfume to seduce Singer's nose. He sniffed and was momentarily hypnotized. "When she was a kid, Maxine always wanted to be a cop."

Abel Graham smiled; he saw in Maxine a soul mate. Too bad they'd never meet and discuss it.

Electra continued. "When I went into show business, Maxine got a taste of it, liked it, and decided she'd get into the business too. But along the way she had all sorts of odd jobs. Waitress, sales clerk, and occasionally she worked for a private detective."

Singer's eyes widened in astonishment. "Do you know his name?"

"I don't think I ever knew it. But she'd pose as a maid or a cleaning woman to get the goods on somebody's husband or somebody's wife. I think she was pretty good at it. She should have stuck to it." She shook her head sadly, suddenly wondering why she never tried to get to know her sister better, why she had disliked her for being loud, brassy, too forward.

Dan Parrish interjected a sober note. "Does this Detective Wang have any leads?"

"He's bringing the body back to New York." That didn't answer Dan's question; Singer had no intention of answering it yet.

Electra uncrossed her legs. "I was going to ask you about getting

15

her back. My mother wants to give her a proper burial. When do they get here?"

Singer said, "In a couple of weeks."

Dan asked, "Isn't it unusual for a detective to accompany a body home?"

"Abe Wang is a very unusual detective. He's a graduate of Columbia University. One of the few Orientals to crash the place. I met him then when he came around asking questions. Bright as a whip. Not of the Charlie Chan 'Confucius Say' school of Oriental detectives. He's coming here because he thinks the organization preying on these women is in the city."

Dan Parrish had a strange look on his face. "I wonder . . ."

"Yes?"

Parrish stared at Singer for a few moments. He liked his face, his gentle treatment of Electra, the way he obviously was taken with her sensuous sexuality, just as every man in the audience and a cross-section of women were mesmerized by her beauty. "What I'm thinking is, is it possible Maxine deliberately put herself in danger as part of a job of investigation?"

"It's a strong possibility," said Singer. He said to Electra, "Which is why I was hoping you knew the name of the private detective who once employed Maxine."

"I'll ask my mother. Maybe she knows."

"I'd appreciate that. Before I forget, have you any professional photos of your sister? We're going to break the story of her murder to the newspapers. It would help if you had some good shots of her. We don't want to use what the Shanghai police have."

Electra sighed. "Poor Maxine. Finally top of the bill and not around to appreciate it. My mother has pictures. I'll get one of my cousins to bring you some. You'll let me know when her body's arriving. I'll want to arrange a funeral parlor . . . you know . . ."

"We won't be releasing her body to you until we've done our own examination. Shanghai might have missed something."

"Shanghai," said Dan Parrish. "We never played Shanghai."

In Millicent Headman's apartment, Nicholas Benson had mixed and served the drinks and Mrs. Headman provided cheese and biscuits. Noel was his usual charming, urbane self and immediately cap-

16

tivated Diana Headman. Nicholas had seen the star onstage and realized with amusement that actor and person were interchangeable, and he said so.

Noel laughed. "How clever you are, Nicholas. I like to hear that I have a dashing, charismatic presence. There are so few of us who can interpret the upper classes of male society without offending the audience. Gerald du Maurier—a terribly good British actor of the boulevard school—and I seem to be among the very few who can bring it off."

Nicholas asked, "What about Ivor Novello?"

"Oh dear." Noel flicked an ash into a tray and said, "I wish I could master the fine art of blushing. Ivor, who's a dear boy, is a friend of mine, but mostly I find that as an actor he's perfectly dreadful. I wish he was dreadfully perfect. But Ivor's tragedy is he has a gorgeous profile, and you need more than that to be an actor, as John Barrymore has so exquisitely proved. What lovely drapes."

Millicent said, "I'm so glad you like them."

He didn't like them, he just wanted to change the subject. He said to Diana, "Your mother tells me you're going to be in the opening show of The Cascades thing."

"Yes, it's terribly exciting. I've been there to look it over and it's fabulously lavish."

"I loathe clichés, but don't judge a club by its decor."

"I'm not. My bosses have hired a marvelous team of experts to put on the show."

"Really? Anyone I've heard of?"

"Mickey DuVane is doing the dance numbers." Noel nodded sagaciously. He'd never heard of DuVane. "Nancy Adman is doing the costumes."

"Dear Nancy." He'd never heard of her either.

"And there's Chick Mason and his orchestra."

"Oh he is good, isn't he? And you're the chanteuse." He smiled a weak smile.

Diana continued eagerly while Nicholas studied Noel, wondering if the superficiality was a pose or a reality. "And there's going to be a very startling innovation."

"Oh really? I'm always so suspicious of innovations."

17

"They've booked Daniel Parrish and Electra Howard and their dancers."

"And why are they an innovation?"

"They're Negroes!"

"So? I've seen lots of wonderful Negro dancers."

"Never in a New York club with whites."

"Oh of course. That awful segregation thing. Well. How very brave of your employers to dare to break the color barrier. What are their names again?"

Diana laughed. "Vivaldi, Beethoven, and Bizet."

"How operatic. I'm sure they're all tone deaf. Are they gangsters?"

"Probably." She said it so matter of factly, Noel was amused.

"I suppose they pack 'gats' and have 'molls' and threaten to rub one out. I'm sure they rarely rub one in."

"They told me they've made you an offer to headline."

"Yes, and quite a generous one."

"Oh *please* accept."

Noel flicked more ash. "I don't much fancy doing cabaret. All that awful noise that accompanies it. Chattering patrons, obnoxious drunks, waiters clattering dishes and trays, really too dreadful to contemplate."

"Insist on a 'no serve' clause in your contract."

"No serve?"

"All service to cease while you're performing."

"Now that's very interesting! Do you suppose they'd agree to something like that?"

"I think they'd agree to anything to get your name on a contract. This is the height of the nightclub season in New York and there aren't many top-drawer names available."

Millicent chimed in. "Oh Noel. *Do* do it. I think it would be *so* exciting."

"I must admit it's all very tempting. The Cascades and the movie I'm doing in Astoria. Mr. Benson, why do you continue staring at me?"

"I was just wondering, what would happen if I scratched your surface, Mr. Coward?"

"You'd draw blood. I rarely share confidences too often, but I rather like you and I feel I should share this one with you. I have single-handedly elevated superficiality to a fine art. The way I flick cigarette ash, the way I sniff as though I'm in the center of a cloud of noxious odors, the way I cock my head like an anxious parakeet. It's all surface, dear boy, and it works for me. And what works for one is all that matters. Ladies, don't you agree? Diana, your mouth is hanging agape like a torn pocket."

She said with admiration, "You're a true perfectionist."

"Good God, I hope not. There's no one as imperfect as a perfectionist. Now Nicholas, let's learn something about you."

Benson was at the bar refreshing his drink. "There's not much to tell you. Family lost its fortune in the crash. I had some talent for writing. With the help of a friend, I was given an opportunity to write some articles for crime magazines."

"Oh you have so many of those here."

"True Detective, True Crime . . ."

"And I'm sure all too true to be good. And are you and Diana madly in love with each other?"

"Oh now Noel," cautioned Millicent.

"Oh now Noel what?" he said with a sniff. He asked Diana, "Do I embarrass you?"

"Hell no. You're a breath of fresh air . . ."

"Bringing with me a plethora of stale observations. Well, I do hope you're in love with one another because you look so good together. Tell me about Africa."

"What?" For a moment, she was a startled doe.

"Africa, dear. Rhodes. Your mother tells me you were married to a rancher. I've always been fascinated by Africa. I think in another life I must have been a slave trader."

"Now Diana," cautioned Millicent, "don't be upset. I happened to mention to Noel earlier today that you'd been married to a Rhodesian rancher."

"It was all very dull and very boring," said Diana while lighting a cigarette. "My husband was very provincial and very rich with no sense of humor."

"I see. Risibility zero."

"I'm sure Mother told you he was number three." Noel smiled.

19

"So I'm sure you can appreciate my caution in contemplating a husband number four."

"Three husbands and still so young. Amazing."

"You've never married, Noel?" asked Millicent.

"No. Never. I've had offers. I suppose I might submit if I could find the perfect combination of wealth and ignorance. In truth, I consider marriage about as valuable as an unsigned check. Now then, I hate to break up this charming soiree, but I do have plans for dinner and I must round up Jeffrey." He explained to Diana and Nicholas, "Jeffrey is my companion."

"Why didn't you bring him with you?" admonished Millicent.

"Because I wanted you all to myself, dear girl." He took her hand and kissed it.

A few minutes later he was strolling along the hall back to his apartment, all the while singing to himself, "Vivaldi, Beethoven, and Bizet . . . Vivaldi, Beethoven, and Bizet . . ."

Three
■ ⌐⌐⌐ ■

JACOB Singer was the envy of Abel Graham. Abel envied him his tough good looks, his friendships with a variety of celebrities, the stunning women Abel suspected he bedded frequently, his brilliant deductive reasoning even when he was all wrong, and his talent for listening. The way he handled Electra Howard and Dan Parrish was truly a lesson in manipulation. It was obvious from the moment they came into the office that within each of them smoldered a cauldron of hostility. But within a few minutes, by extending his condolences, by getting right down to the sordid tragedy of the victim's murder, by getting straight to the business of wanting to uncover the perpetrator, by astonishing them with the news Abraham Wang was personally conducting the body back to New York, Singer had them in the palm of his hand. Abel could tell Dan Parrish liked Singer. As for Electra, the jury was still out, but he was sure when it came back in the verdict would be "not guilty."

"You got a very dumb look on your face, Abel, what's eating you?" Singer had the closet door open. There were about a dozen neckties hanging from a bar and he was having a hard time selecting one.

"Jacob, I think you're one hell of a great cop."

Singer's shoulders sagged. The dullard he thought incapable of

21

being a dogcatcher admired him, and he had nothing to offer in return. He said with modesty, "I've had my foul-ups. What brought this on all of a sudden?"

"The way you handled the sister and her boyfriend. They came in spoiling for a fight and you never gave them the chance. Jacob, you're an artist where human nature is concerned."

Singer was embarrassed. If he didn't know better—or at least he hoped he knew better—he'd suspect a pass was being made. "Speak to your girlfriend at The Cascades today?"

"If she can get away, we're going to meet for a drink later tonight. Vivaldi's very jealous of Edna. It bothers him that she has a brain."

"Try to be sure he doesn't find a reason to bash it in." He was studying a tie that was blue and brown with yellow polka dots.

"Edna's smart and she's cautious. She's gotten very friendly with the other two bimbos, figuring they're also in a position to hear something that could be useful to us."

"Back in the twenties the Unholy Three made a fortune peddling flesh. There's no reason not to suspect they're still up to their old tricks, but on another level." Singer shook his head slowly. "Unbelievable, white slavery in this day and age."

"Maxine Howard was black."

"Look Abel, white slavery is just a general label, it covers a multitude of sins. But don't think about it too much, it's like wondering why does a bagel have a hole. I think I'll wear this one." He held up a Countess Mara original that had set him back twenty-five dollars. "Yeah, this one ought to make him sit up and take notice."

"You got a date with a guy?"

Singer grinned as he knotted the tie, delighting in the image reflected in the mirror that hung above the tie rack. "Actually, my date is a broad. Dorothy Parker. Ever heard of her?"

"Oh sure. She's in all the gossip columns. It's like everything she says is very witty. Is it?"

"Not when she's blind drunk. And half the things they claim she said, she didn't say. Actually, she's more bitchy than witty. Anyway, since you're dying to know, she's introducing me to a very famous English writer."

"George Bernard Shaw?"

"Oh they've been in jail, all right, but years back. Petty stuff. Thievery, housebreaking, pimping, beating up guys, you know, breaking a couple of knees here and there."

"Modest accomplishments," commented Mrs. Parker as she signaled the waiter for a fresh round of drinks.

Jacob continued. "When Prohibition was repealed, from what I was told, they tried to go legit, but they couldn't cut it. They disappeared from the local scene for a couple of years and now all of a sudden they're back. Fresh names, fresh bankroll, and we still suspect they're up to their old tricks again. Trafficking in flesh. Female flesh."

"Should we ask them over for dinner?" asked Mrs. Parker.

Noel tapped his fingers on the arm of his chair. "I could be walking into a hornet's nest, couldn't I? What do you think, Jeffrey?"

"Whatever I think, Noel, you know you'll do as you damn well please."

"How well you know me. I'm sure someday you'll be dangerous. Dottie?"

"I'm sure you could use the money."

"I could always use the money. Mother has a rapacious appetite."

"And there are all those sycophants of yours who come baying and howling when they hear you uncorking a bottle of champagne. All of course except Mr. Amherst here, who is independently wealthy and I suspect some kind of a subversive." She smiled winsomely in Amherst's direction. "I suppose you practice some rather quaint perversions?"

"Ever since he was knee-high to a pederast." Noel torched a cigarette, blew a series of smoke rings, one of which settled over Singer's head like a halo before expiring. "Well, Dottie, shall I do the club?"

"Get a percentage of the take."

"Why, Dottie, what a clever thought." Then, "What if I'm not the draw I think I ought to be?"

"You give newspaper and radio interviews in which you are blithely witty and coldly sardonic in condemning the bad taste of the great unwashed. I for one say fiddle-dee-dee and to hell with them, I think you'll be a smash hit."

27

"Why, Dottie, how rarely kind of you. Now then, what do I do for an act?"

"You have a large repertoire of songs you've written," suggested Mrs. Parker. "Surely you can do thirty to forty minutes of them?"

"Of course I could. And then what do I do for an encore?"

"You kill yourself."

"Dear Dottie, you are always such a comfort. Shall we dine here or someplace good?"

They decided to go to Sardi's, the theatrical restaurant just two blocks away; Noel declared a brisk walk would do them all a world of good. Jeffrey helped Mrs. Parker into her mink coat and she then took his arm while saying, "Having helped me with my coat, we're now old friends. We can leave Noel and Jacob to get to know each other while walking behind us. My but you're tall!"

"And my you're so tiny."

"Oh my God, nobody paid the tab!" exclaimed Mrs. Parker.

"Noel saw to it before you arrived."

"Oh dear. Now he'll positively have to do The Cascades."

They took their time about getting to Sardi's. Mrs. Parker liked to window-shop and Noel and Jacob were absorbed in conversation. Jacob told Noel most of what he knew about Vivaldi, Beethoven, and Bizet, who their girlfriends were, and how their wives had wisely chosen the anonymity of the suburbs, cushioned by large allowances of cash. He told Noel about his meeting with Electra Howard and Daniel Parrish and how Electra's mother had had a nephew deliver to him some excellent eight-by-tens of Maxine Howard.

"In the envelope was the name and address of the private eye she once worked for. His name's Casey Sterne."

"Ah! I believe that's what you would call a lead."

"I hope it is. He closed his office about eight months ago. He gave up private practice to join the Federal Bureau of Investigation. That's J. Edgar Hoover's gang of crime busters in Washington, D.C. I guess Casey Sterne studied law. You have to have a law degree to join the FBI."

"I suppose that leaves you out."

"It wouldn't even tempt me if I had one. I'm very happy where I am."

"It's so good to meet a contented man at last."

28

"I didn't say I was contented, Noel. I only said I'm happy where I am."

"How long have you been with the police?"

"A little over fifteen years."

"When do you plan to retire?"

"When they force me out. My turn, Noel. How long have you known Mrs. Headman and her daughter?"

"I met Mrs. Headman at a literary luncheon at the Ritz earlier this week. Charming woman, uses the correct silverware with a certain devil-may-care dash. That morning I'd agreed to star in the film but I didn't want to continue living at the Algonquin as it was getting too bloody expensive, room service and all those flunkies with their eager palms outstretched. Well, as luck would have it, she had two furnished flats available, one large one that she was occupying but perfectly willing to decamp from for the price, and one small one that had once been used as servants' quarters and that didn't interest me in the least. So before lunch today I inspected the larger accommodation, was enchanted by it, as it was big enough for Jeffrey and myself, and I made a deal. Then she told me about Diana, her daughter, who's also to appear at The Cascades. She sings. I haven't heard her. Have you?"

Singer laughed. "Actually, last year at some dump in the Village. She was the pioneer of society belles suddenly blossoming into nightclub singers. You must have heard of some. Adelaide Moffet, Eve Symington, et cetera et cetera. They're the big fad now. They won't last. What's that look on your face?"

"I was just thinking. You must have read Thornton Wilder's *The Bridge of San Luis Rey.*"

"Oh sure, Noel. It's one of my favorites. I had dinner a couple of times with Thornton." Noel's eyes were blinking like semaphores running amok. "I read the book four times."

"To build up an immunity? Anyway, somehow I feel this Cascades undertaking bears a rather similar resemblance to the plot of the book. A diversity of characters converging on a bridge that is doomed to collapse and kill them. Now here we are, myself, Diana Headman, Electra Howard, Daniel Parrish, the three creatures of questionable character, their women, and you. Tell me, Jacob, do you suppose we're all converging at The Cascades because fate has consigned us all to . . . oh dear . . . I shudder to think."

Jacob put his arm around Noel, a spontaneous gesture that made Noel feel warm all over. "Noel, let me quote from one of my favorite Shakespearean dramas, *Othello* . . ."

My God, thought Noel, he quotes Shakespeare.

"It's Desdemona's line. 'Kill me tomorrow . . . let me live tonight!'"

"And what the hell's *that* got to do with us and The Cascades?"

Mrs. Parker turned around and said, "Careful Jacob, someone might wash your mouth out with soap for quoting Shakespeare." She noticed his arm around Noel's shoulder. Then she saw the restaurant a few feet ahead. "Ah!" she said. "Sanctuary!"

Four
■ 〓〓 ■

A JAPANESE boat, the *Matso Maru*, was the fastest liner cruising the Pacific. Abraham Wang booked passage on it for himself and the solid lead coffin containing Maxine Howard's remains. He had quickly convinced his superiors that working in tandem with Jacob Singer, whose reputation they knew and respected, could expedite locating the white slavery ring and destroying it. They understood Wang's logic in going to the source of the problem. Shanghai was understandably just one of their many satellite operations. And Wang was anxious to see New York City after too long an absence. He was looking forward to seeing Jacob Singer again, though he found his constant name-dropping tiresome and monotonous. On the other hand, Singer's little red book was chock-full of names and phone numbers, a superb selection of available women of all sizes, colors, and denominations. But most of all he looked forward to a combo hot pastrami and corned beef sandwich at the Sixth Avenue Delicatessen.

Although the sea was rough and the fierce wind made the going difficult, Wang strolled on the top deck waiting for sleep to welcome him. His last conversation with Singer before setting sail provided him with a groaning board of food for thought. Electra Howard and Daniel Parrish. Vivaldi, Beethoven, and Bizet. Wang wondered briefly if he was becoming part of a scenario meant for the Marx Brothers. A showgirl informant with literary pretensions. Diana Headman. And for crying out loud, Noel Coward. *Noel Coward.* Noel Coward blithely entering a den of thieves to be a detective without portfolio in the service of Jacob Singer? Surely if Buddha was aware of this he'd wink an eye.

The liner rose and fell abruptly and sent Wang crashing against the ship's railing, momentarily knocking the breath out of him. A ship's officer, who had been sent to clear the deck of any passengers foolhardy enough to challenge the dangerous elements, struggled to his side and, with a firm grip on Wang's arms, propelled him to safety. Wang gasped his thanks and then made his way to the bar, where he ordered a large whiskey. While he waited for it to be poured, he sat on a stool and examined his fellow passengers through the large mirror built into the wall behind the bar. They were mostly Japanese men. The few women in the bar were probably American. The boat was to dock in Honolulu tomorrow and, after a few hours' stop to pick up cargo, would go on to San Francisco. From there it would be a four-day train ride to New York City by way of Chicago.

Wang thought for a moment and then sighed. He hoped Billy Minsky's burlesque shows were still playing on West Forty-second Street.

On stage at The Cascades club where there was a feverish frenzy of rehearsals, Noel Coward was examining an African blowgun. Daniel Parrish was using it in one of his routines with Electra and their six supporting dancers. A few feet away, Electra was watching Noel and said something to Daniel. Daniel moved away from her and joined Noel. "It's an authentic blowgun. It's from the Assegai tribe."

Noel hadn't heard his approach and gave a start on hearing his voice so unexpectedly. "Dear boy, you almost gave me a turn. Assegai did you say? Aren't they the ones famed for their spears?" Daniel nodded yes. "How very enterprising. Too bad they haven't been guided into the world market." Noel returned the weapon to Daniel. "You have a fascinating repertoire, Daniel. And I'm sure your dances are mostly authentic."

"Completely authentic," corrected Daniel. "I traveled for several years to study dance in its native habitat. Africa, Haiti, Cuba, Brazil."

"I find your voodoo number particularly fascinating. Electra's impersonation of a high priestess is absolutely spine-chilling. You don't by any chance shrink heads?"

Daniel tried to smile, but smiling did not come easily to him. "Nothing so drastic."

"The way Electra actually kills the chicken onstage. Dear boy, that sort of thing requires a cast-iron stomach. Doesn't it worry you that audiences might be nauseated by it, let alone offended?"

"We discussed it first with Mr. Vivaldi."

"And of course he saw no harm in it," adding with a sniff, "what with his background and training. I suppose the dead chicken is then whisked off to the kitchen to serve a useful purpose."

"Some night we might try killing a goat."

Noel's eyes widened. "What about virgins?"

"Those are not that easily available in this city."

"*Touché.* I haven't seen the number in which I presume you use the blowgun. Dear boy, you don't plan to use poison darts, do you?"

"Everything we do is simulation."

"Except killing the chicken."

"Mr. Coward, we were hired because there's nothing like us in the field of entertainment. We do the authentic, and if some of the authentic is outrageous then so be it. We are on the bill with you because, like you, we are original."

"How kind of you. Ah! There's my good friend Jacob Singer. Oh, you and Electra have already met him. How stupid of me." Electra was standing within earshot and Noel went to her and took her hand. "I completely forgot! What with all the rush of signing my contract and rehearsing here and preparations for my film, I haven't extended my condolences. What a dreadful tragedy. I am *so* sorry your sister is dead." Her expression was deadpan. Noel cocked an eyebrow. "Are you?"

She might now be smiling, thought Noel, or perhaps it was gas. The expression on her face might be considered whimsical or dangerous. "You're an astute judge of character, Mr. Coward. Yes, I'm sorry my sister's dead, mostly because I don't like the way she died.

33

You're right, I didn't like her very much. But she deserved a decent death. At least I can give her a decent burial."

"That's more than my last two plays received." He shouted, "Jacob! Up here! On stage! How nice of you to drop in on us. And who is this young pixie?"

Abel Graham blushed.

Singer explained, "This is my assistant, Abel Graham. He wanted to meet you." Abel smiled shyly.

Noel said, "Well, now that you've met me at last, what wonderful compliments do you wish to pay me?" Abel said nothing. Noel looked world-weary as usual. "Dear boy, you say nothing. I do understand. You're so overcome by my presence that you've gone mute." He winked at Singer. "Well, young Abel Graham, let me assure you I am a mere mortal like all the rest of you. More gifted than most, less gifted than many, and totally fraught with anxiety about this show we're preparing. Jacob, you haven't said hello to Electra and Mr. Parrish." Greetings were exchanged. "Good." Behind him, a tenor was rehearsing a song with the orchestra.

"Not a very strong voice," commented Singer in an aside to Noel.

"If he had a strong voice, it would break him. Why are so many American band vocalists so nasal? Do you suppose it's adenoids? I had mine removed years ago. Mother has them preserved in alcohol on a kitchen shelf. She's morbidly sentimental. Ah, here come the three sordid musketeers." Vivaldi, Beethoven, and Bizet had entered the room with another man in tow. "Dear God!" gasped Noel. "It can't be! But it is! Jimmy, what in heaven's name are you doing here?"

Jimmy Durante broke away from the three partners and hurried onto the stage, where he crushed Noel in a heartfelt bear hug. "Null!" he rasped hoarsely. "It's my old buddy Null from the mudder country. Hello Jake!" Singer smiled and was sure Abel Graham was now doubly impressed with Singer's connections. Durante scowled at the three partners. "D'ya three bums know how lucky you are to have Null opening your place? Yuh know he takes tea with kings and queens . . . I mean real ones . . . and remembers not to stick out his pinky when he lifts the cup. *Hotcha-cha-cha!*" He introduced himself to Electra and Daniel. "Didn't I catch your act in Paris last year?"

Daniel said, "We headlined at the Angry Pussy last spring."
"What a performance! What a showman!" He said to Electra, "If
I was in my right mind, I'd marry yuh. But if you're in yuh right
mind, I ain't got a chance. Null, wait till you see this bunch in
action! Yuh never saw so much blood onstage in all yuh life. They
kill goats, chickens . . ."

Noel refrained from adding, "And appetites."

Durante was steamrollering onward, ". . . and use blowguns and
machetes. I'm tellin' yuh, Null, what showmanship!" He stared
around the cavernous club and marveled at the decor, the architec-
ture, and the genuine cascades. "I'm givin' the jernt the once-over,
Null, because they want me to come in after your two weeks are up.
If I do decide to do it," with a wicked glance at the three partners,
"I might try and talk Kate Smith into sharin' the bill with me. I got
an idea she'd bring the house down floatin' down that there cataract
wearing a one-piece bathing suit. *Hotcha-cha-cha!*"

Vivaldi asked impatiently, "What do you think, Jimmy?"

Durante clapped both hands against his sides with feigned exasperation, a gesture familiar to audiences the world over. "Never ask
me what I think. I ain't got the necessary equipment." He crossed
to the stage apron and looked down at Vivaldi. "Whatever I do, I
trust to me instinct." He tapped his enormous nose. "This is me
instinct. It always tells me what to do." He returned to Noel and the
others and zeroed in on Jacob Singer. "What are you doin' here
anyway in broad daylight? Why ain't you home at your orifice givin'
some poor sap the third degree and beatin' him with a rubber hose?
How's your friend Mrs. Parker? Still slittin' her wrists when she
wants some attention?" He said to Noel, "Real flaky, that one. Tell
me, Null. Did these three bums strong-arm you into workin' for
them?"

"Certainly not!"

"Yuh can come clean with me. I know guys who are more dangerous than they are and indubitably still have their own teeth. Vivaldi,
Beethoven, and Bizet. Dey sure ain't the Boswell sisters! Why I
knew them way back then when way back then meant smugglin'
booze, and guns, and low blackmail in high society. Back when I had
me own club with my partners Clayton and Jackson, who I still got
woikin' fuh me because I'm true and lerl." He jerked a thumb over

35

his shoulder toward the partners. "D'you know them three useter traffic in white slavery? I'll bet they know what became of Judge Crater. He's still missin' these last five years." Vivaldi, Beethoven, and Bizet stood rigid, like Greek statues forever frozen in time.

Noel folded his arms, looking very stern, and asked, "If you so utterly disapprove of these people, why are you considering being employed by them?"

Jimmy did his familiar stiff-legged strut with his right hand upraised and waving the index finger with a wonderful air of *joie de vivre*. "Because I don't disapprove of the money they're offerin' me. Don't you remember me, Null? The old Schnozzola himself. The oldest whore woikin' the territory. Did I pronounce that correctly? I guess I did. Nobody's laughin'." He stood in front of Jacob Singer. "I saw that pitcher in the papers of that Maxine Howard."

"What about her?" asked Singer.

"She was a darn smart kid, maybe a little too smart."

"You knew her?" He saw Electra move closer to Daniel and clutch his arm.

"I met her down in Atlantic City a couple o' years ago when I was workin' one of the hotels. She was doin' a single at a crib called The Black Bottom. She wasn't too bad, y'know. She wasn't too good either, but then . . ." he laid a hand over his heart and smiled upward, ". . . there's good and bad in all of us."

Noel unfolded his hands to light a cigarette. "Thank *you*, Aimee Semple MacPherson."

"You spoken to her lately? I ain't heard from her in months. Not since she made that pass at me and I threw her Oliver Hardy to put her off my trail." He was back with Singer. "I see there's this Chinee detective bringin' her back dead . . . unlike Frank Buck, who brings 'em back alive. But we can't all be Frank Buck and who would want to? So tell me, Jake, does the investigation continue here? You and this Chinee Wong . . ."

"Wang," corrected Singer.

"Wang!" echoed Durante. "I'm glad there's only one of 'em, because I'm sure two Wangs don't make a Wong." The groan he heard came from Noel. "Anyway, Jake, she was a good joe an' I'm sorry she met such an ugly debt."

Jake indicated Electra. "Electra was Maxine's sister."

36

Durante spun in Electra's direction. "What a shame about your sister." Electra said nothing. "And despite the tragedy, here you are on stage rehearsin'." He slapped his hands against his side. "Well, like them assassins said after they sliced up Julius Caesar, On to the Forum, fellas, the show must go on!"

"How well did you know Maxine?" asked Singer.

Durante grinned and said, "Not as well as I tried to. Anyway, she had some john on the string, I think he was a private eye or sometin' like that."

"Could his name have been Casey Sterne?"

"What's in a name? How do I know? How do you expeck me to remember? I don't remember what I did ten minutes ago. Ah yes! But I do! I came here to give the jernt the once over. Well gennelmen, the once over is over. So long. So long, Jake. So long everybody. And a special so long to you, Null." He turned to the partners. "As to you three *gonifs*, you'll hear from my lawyer t'morra." He jumped off the stage and strutted his way out to the street, leaving in his wake three men who were seriously considering rescinding the offer they'd made to him.

Vivaldi, followed by Beethoven and Bizet, clambered up the stairs to the stage. Vivaldi said to his headliner, "Noel, I hear nothing but great things about your act."

"How nice. It's comforting to know that somewhere within your charmed inner circle there dwell a few creatures possessed of incredibly good taste. As long as you're here, perhaps you'd like to hear one of the two songs I've created especially for this engagement."

Vivaldi was beside both himself and his partners with joy. "You really wrote two new songs just for us?"

"Actually, I had a rather marvelous time writing them." He looked at the surrounding faces. "I recognize everyone except my accompanist. Jacob? Do you see Ivan Roth anywhere? After all, you recommended him to me and bloody good he is." He clapped his hands together loudly like a stern schoolmaster demanding order from his pupils. "Ivan Roth!" he shouted. The name echoed and reechoed as members of the company took up the cry. The heavy patter of hurrying feet was heard coming from the gangway that led from the dressing rooms to the stage and an owlish, bookish-looking young man of thirty appeared, slightly out of breath, hair disheveled, necktie askew, and a telltale lipstick mark on his left cheek.

"I'm here, Noel, I'm here!"

"So I see. Kindly wipe that bruise off your cheek. You should be careful about necking with chorus girls. You never know where they've been."

While taking a seat at the piano, Ivan wiped his cheek with a soiled handkerchief. Noel crossed to him and said something nobody else could hear. Diana Headman arrived at the club and took a seat near the orchestra. She asked one of the musicians, "What's going on?" He explained Noel was going to sing a number he'd written especially for his engagement at the club, and Diana's mouth formed an O. Noel crossed to center stage. The three partners were now seated and Noel had their undivided attention. He nodded to Ivan Roth. Ivan vamped the intro and Noel sang.

Vivaldi, Beethoven, and Bizet . . .

The partners exchanged uneasy glances.

Are clever operators in a very big way . . .

Diana was wondering who Jacob Singer and Abel Graham were. She had never seen them before.

They give you flash and splash—
In a dazzling display . . .

Edna Dore stood with Trixie Bates and Angie Murray in the wings at the opposite side of the stage from where the two detectives were standing. Abel Graham and Edna's eyes met briefly, but neither showed a sign of recognition. Behind them stood their dresser, Hattie Beavers, who might have posed for the logo of Aunt Jemima pancake flour. She tapped one foot in rhythm with Noel, while sneaking glances at Electra Howard and Daniel Parrish.

Noel was, as they say, wowing them. The partners, however, did not quite know yet what to make of the song. Obviously, they were meant to be flattered, but the obvious usually eluded them.

> Vivaldi, Beethoven, and Bizet . . .
> Are unique in every sort of way . . .

Abel Graham was unimpressed by Mr. Coward's delivery. His idea of a real great singer was Rudy Vallee, and Vallee was a college graduate. Jacob Singer was wondering who was the good-looking jane sitting next to the orchestra and grinning what seemed to him a grin that had been overrehearsed.

> They offer riches . . . and . . . er . . . witches . . .
> In a splendid array . . .

Diana Headman laughed. She didn't feel at all lonely.

Daniel Parrish whispered to Electra, "I think you're slashing the wrong throats." She bit her lip to keep from laughing.

> Relax and be willing . . .
> To accept what's eye filling . . .

Mickey DuVane, the dance director, who was sitting out front with Nancy Adman, the costume designer, wondered if he'd have to choreograph the girls to back up Coward. What the hell do you create for a song like this? A time step? A boogie? He settled on a gavotte.

> Face it . . . this gleesome threesome . . .

He paused and with a nonchalant look on his face sang,

> Are out for a killing . . .

Singer smiled. Good old Noel. Good old Noel was now prancing about as he gaily moved to the conclusion of the song.

> Hip Hip and hooray . . .

He pointed at Vivaldi.

Howard in Atlantic City, and of course the presence of the shadowy detective, Casey Sterne. Have you tracked him down yet?"

"As a matter of fact, he's due in from D.C. today for a meeting with the local FBI boys. He's phoning me at the precinct and I'm getting together with him before he goes back."

"He knows you want to question him about the dear departed?"

"Oh yes. Any suspicious-looking characters hanging around the rehearsals?"

"Dear Jacob. Dear dear Jacob. *Everybody* hanging around here looks suspicious. Let's go back to the others or they might begin to gossip."

"Am I wrong or do I get the feeling Diana Headman would like to dance attendance on you?"

"Oh no. You're not wrong at all. She means well. But Jacob, do let me advise you, people who dance attendance are usually badly choreographed."

Five

■ 呂 ■

BIZET was pacing about the conference room like a frightened hyena. Beethoven, a large cigar jutting obscenely out of the side of his mouth, was clipping his fingernails. Vivaldi was studying a sheet of paper on which were facts and figures to which only he and his partners were privy. He snapped at Bizet. "For crissakes will you sit down. You're making me nauseous."

"What's the matter with you two? Doesn't it make you nervous having Jake Singer visit the premises?"

"It don't bother me none. He's a friend of Coward's. So what?"

Bizet continued heatedly, "But Durante blurting out we were in the flesh business years ago . . ."

"That's history, what of it? They couldn't nail us then, they won't nail us now. We're clean." He slapped the sheet of paper on the table for Beethoven to see. "What the hell are these dumb figures for the booze? Don't we rate no discount?"

"We got the discount." He pointed to a line of figures. "There's the discount."

"For crying out loud, how are we going to show a profit?"

Beethoven said matter of factly, "We water the drinks."

"Okay," agreed Vivaldi. "But not the first drink. The first drink we tell the bartenders to give them a fair shot. The second drink gets watered."

43

Beethoven shifted the cigar to the other side of his mouth. "On the other hand, we could also divide the bottles in two and fill the rest with water."

Vivaldi chuckled. "You know something Harry, with your kind of mind, you could have become president of the United States."

"You nuts? It don't pay nothin'."

Bizet leaned on the table, propping himself up with his hands. "I don't like it! Goddammit I don't like it! It smells bad to me!"

Bizet's suspicions and insecurities were crosses the partners had learned to bear over the years. It was an effort that took great patience on their part, but they were genuinely fond of the Weasel, especially when he lost large sums of money to them in poker games. Vivaldi was back studying the sheet of paper. "Weasel, you're making a mountain out of a molehill. To all intents and purposes, we're running a clean operation here. In a couple of months when everything is running as smoothly as we're planning it to run, then we put the back end into operation. We put in the blackjack tables, the roulette, baccarat, the works. We move the 'B' girls in and those whores'll make us a very nice profit. Relax, Weasel, why don't you take Angie to a movie? It'll relax your nerves. Al Jolson and the missus, Ruby Keeler, are at the Strand in *Go Into Your Dance*. I took Edna to see it yesterday. We loved it. Helen Morgan's in it too. Sober. Go on, go see a movie. You're starting to make me nervous."

Bizet was wiping his sweaty palms with a handkerchief. "Aw hell. You know how I get when I think a copper is getting too close to me."

"They ain't never collared us, have they?" Vivaldi made a notation on the sheet of paper while Beethoven admired the clipped fingernails of his left hand.

"There's a first time for everything," offered Bizet in a small voice.

"I'll tell you something, Weasel." Vivaldi slammed the sheet back onto the table. "I've told it to you before and I'm going to tell it to you again. If you keep thinking about getting into trouble, then you'll get into trouble. So Weasel, do us and yourself a favor, *stop thinking.*" He said to Beethoven, "Harry, since when does a swank joint like ours order frankfurters?"

"The chef needs them for the lentil soup."

44

"What lentil soup? What happened to the onion soup and the vitchy swass?"

"They're still on the menu, but he thought there should be a couple of more soup dishes. So he added lentil, chicken, and split pea. I agree with him. It's good to have a varsity of things for people to choose from."

"You mean 'variety,' " corrected Vivaldi.

"You don't have to tell me what I mean. I know what I mean. So I ain't no genius." He thought for a moment. "I always say 'varsity.' It sounds good to me." He went to work on the fingernails of his right hand.

Bizet shouted, "Goddammit! I don't want to go to no movies!"

"More tea, Jeffrey?" asked Millicent Headman.

"Yes, thank you. It's delicious. This apartment is so cozy. If I were living alone, this is just the sort of apartment I would choose."

"Thank you. It serves its purpose." She refilled her own cup and leaned back in the comfortable Morris chair. "Of course when Linus was alive, there was our mansion in Oyster Bay. And," she trilled, "our Palm Beach estate. I do miss the yacht. She was truly yar. But," there was now a hard edge to her voice, "they had to go to cover the debts of Headman Pharmaceuticals."

"Your husband died two years ago?"

"Yes, poor dear. Heart attack. There were ugly rumors he'd committed suicide. But if he had, we'd have never collected on his insurance policies."

" 'We' includes Diana?"

"Oh yes. Linus bought the policies long before Diana chose marriage as her hobby. Actually, her first two husbands weren't wealthy, at least not wealthy in the way *we* would define wealth. It was James who was really rich." She laughed. "Filthy rich, as some might say."

"James was the Rhodesian, I gather."

"James Coleridge, a man of great wealth and many strange moods. Diana met him on a Caribbean cruise. She began her singing career doing cruises. My husband was on the board of one of the cruise companies, which of course helped. Anyway, it was a whirlwind courtship. They married in New York so that Linus and I could be in attendance. And then they were off to Rhodesia and the Coleridge ranch. Diana had no idea of the immensity of his wealth. She also had no idea her new husband was so thoroughly feared and disliked." Jeff was fascinated. Noel had warned him Millicent Headman was a nonstop talker, undoubtedly holding the world record for garrulousness in the Western Hemisphere, but Jeff found her fascinating. "He was monstrous to the people who worked for him and Diana suspected that he wasn't all that aboveboard in business. He died a frightful death."

"He's dead?"

"Very."

"I'm sure Noel told me Diana had divorced him."

"She instigated proceedings, but the divorce didn't become final. James died too soon." Again her smile. "Or perhaps not soon enough."

Jeff was intrigued. "What is a frightful death?"

Millicent stared into her teacup. Jeff wondered if the manner of Coleridge's death could be read in the sediment of tea leaves at the bottom of her cup. "James wasted away." Jeff had heard of heartbroken lovers wasting away, but a hale and hearty sadistic rancher? She might have been reading his mind. "It was astonishing and frightening, the way Diana described it. He complained of feeling ill one night and took to his bed. Diana summoned the doctor. He thought it was James's heart. But day by day he grew weaker and weaker. Diana's not a superstitious person, but she says the night the illness began, James found a dead chicken in his bedroom."

"Perhaps it had wandered in there by mistake."

Millicent smiled. "I know this sort of thing is hard to believe, but there were several voodoo practitioners among James's employees. They practiced a form known as the *obeah,* much the same as in Haiti and Cuba."

"I once did some reading up on voodoo, and I always thought it brought results only when the power of suggestion attacked a weak and superstitious mind." Jeff selected a chocolate biscuit as he spoke, and after biting into it, regretted the choice. It was stale. Being a gentleman and an Amherst, he devoured the remainder while managing a pleasant look on his face.

"I've had some experiences with voodoo," said Millicent, "and

I've seen some frightening results. Linus and I saw a man hack his wife to death with a machete on the dock in Haiti where our yacht was anchored. I can see it now and it's horrible. When the police came and overpowered him, he insisted it wasn't his wife he'd killed but an evil spirit impersonating her. He said the evil spirit had left dead birds nailed to his front door and caused his mule to sicken and die and his wife would no longer sleep with him. Well, since he'd known her to be exhaustingly oversexed, it was quite obvious there was an evil spirit in possession of the body that had once been exclusively his." She was looking out the window just past Jeff's head, and the sudden strangeness of her eyes disturbed him. "James just wasted away. Within weeks, his two-hundred-pound frame shrunk to a bit over one hundred. Diana doesn't talk about it and I shouldn't be talking about it either. But Diana tells me there's this black group doing a voodoo number in the show. I think it disturbs her, but like her father she's made of sterner stuff." Her father made of sterner stuff, thought Jeff, and yet old made-of-sterner-stuff perhaps committed suicide. "Have you and Noel been companions for a very long time?"

"No," replied Jeff, "it only seems like a very long time. We met some five years ago. He invited me on a trip through the Orient early in 1930 and it was a delightful experience, except for a period in Shanghai when he was taken seriously ill."

"How awful."

"Not really," said Jeff with an amused expression, while wondering if the stale biscuit would make him ill. "He spent the time in bed writing *Private Lives*. It took him all of three days."

"Not really! Three days to write a full-length play!"

"Noel never wastes time."

"What a unique man he is. Why do you suppose he's never married?"

The amused expression remained riveted to Jeff's face. He thought, surely madam, you jest. He said, "Noel once claimed to me that marriage is a premeditated crime."

"Oh surely he's not *that* cynical."

"Millicent, my dear, you don't know the half of it. And for your sake, I hope you never learn. Oh no, thank you. I have had enough biscuits."

* * *

Ten minutes after the rehearsals were ended for the day, Noel invited Diana Headman and Nicholas Benson to join him for drinks in the Hell's Bells bar across the street from The Cascades. It was located off the lobby of a seedy hotel, The Raven, a residence for retired gentleladies who drank too much and gossiped to excess, a haven for down-on-their-luck actors, a refuge for divorced men and women and a not too liberal sprinkling of perverts of exotic tastes and persuasions. The bar itself was a nightmare of red and purple walls decorated with photographs and paintings of past and present burlesque queens. Hell's Bells was an oasis for neighborhood prostitutes.

Noel overheard a man tell the bartender, "I'll have my usual."

"Sorry, your usual left with another gentleman."

Noel was lighting a cigarette. "I stumbled into this dreadful place the first day of rehearsal and felt at home immediately. There's something so wonderfully unique and special about New York sleaze. I mean in London, where women in bars like this . . . actually pubs . . . are rotten to the core but awfully good to the navy, and where the stench of stale beer, stale urine, simmering bubble and squeak, and unwashed bodies can stagger both the mind and one's olfactory senses, there's nothing quaint or original. They all smell and sound alike. But in New York, I find each bar has a personality all its own. Take this one. The drinks are cheap and generous. Herbie the bartender freely admits that he taps the till right under the owner's nose and for exercise beats his wife and children. He has a superb sense of humor. Herbie! A round of dry martinis please, as chilled as the gentleman who just asked for his usual."

"Y'got it, No-ell." Herbie grinned, showing very few teeth, as he set about filling the order.

"It's too bad Mr. Singer and his assistant couldn't join us," said Diana. "I find Singer fascinating. I've never met a detective before."

"Tut tut, my dear, you'll have Nicholas frothing at the mouth."

Nicholas demurred. "I never froth at the mouth. I sometimes pout or fall to the floor and kick my feet but I never froth at the mouth. As a man of the world, Noel, I should imagine you'd recognize that Diana and I are good friends and that's it."

"Well, that's a relief. There aren't enough good friends in this world. I mean, I can count on Gladys Calthrop, who designs my plays, Jack Wilson, who is my business associate, and his wife, Princess Natalie Paley . . ."

"A real honest-to-god princess?" asked Nicholas.

"Indeed. What's more, she's off to Hollywood to appear in a film with Katharine Hepburn and Cary Grant called *Sylvia Scarlett*. With those two I should imagine it will be a tremendous success." He added unenthusiastically, "It also has Brian Aherne. I saw his last film. I was hoping it would be his last film." He zeroed in on Diana. "What are you doing singing at The Cascades?" Herbie the bartender was serving the drinks.

"Doing just that. Singing."

"Isn't it a rather odd choice of venue for you? After all, you're supposed to be a café society singer. You should be singing in a café where you can rub shoulders with society, whatever that loosely defines as."

"I've always wanted to do a big club. When Ike Vivaldi made me his offer, I snapped it up."

"It sounds like you and Vivaldi are old friends."

She sipped her drink before answering. Noel suspected she needed the time to supply the wrong answer. "He caught me at the Statler last Christmas. The Philadelphia Statler."

"The Philadelphia Statler," repeated Noel, then asked archly, "are they as clannish as the Boston Statlers?"

"Oh go on!"

"Where to?"

Nicholas wondered aloud, "I wonder what Vivaldi has in the back of his mind."

"Anything but a brain," suggested Noel.

"Don't kid yourself about Vivaldi and his partners," said Diana. "They're very clever men."

"And also very dangerous," offered Nicholas before popping an olive into his mouth.

"I must say they're a motley crew," said Noel. He inquired of Diana, "I'm sure you're aware of their combined checkered past, and I think I'm making an understatement calling it 'checkered.' It's downright terrifying. Jacob Singer's told me all about them. I

49

say, it must have given those three a turn when Jacob appeared at the rehearsal."

"How'd you get so chummy with a New York detective, Noel?"

"Actually Diana, ours is a rather brief acquaintance. Dorothy Parker introduced us a few weeks ago. Singer's a bit of a celebrity hound. He takes great pleasure in dropping names in all directions. In fact, he tells a joke on himself. It seems during some Prohibition police raid he tripped and broke his leg. Mrs. Parker, when she heard his leg was broken, commented 'He must have dropped a pretty heavy name on it.' Dear Dottie." He sipped his martini. "Nice. Very nice. I wish our bartenders would learn to make these. Tell me, Diana, what do you think of the blacks?"

"In general, or just Electra and Daniel?"

"You know what I mean."

She said huffily, "I know many British are biased . . ."

"I'm only biased against bias. I'm rather pleased to be in a rare show that mixes whites and blacks, though I know there are strong currents out there that disapprove of it. I've seen most of what they're planning to do. It's pretty strong stuff, terribly violent, and I strongly abhor violence. I have never been capable of taking a stand against bullies. In the face of threatened violence, I display the virility of a dandelion in a strong wind. I'm just concerned that their act might be found offensive."

"Do you find it so?"

"I don't think amputating a chicken's head in full view of an audience is the candidate for a good taste award."

"You're probably right. But they're fanatics about authenticity and their voodoo is authentic. I know. I saw it myself in Africa."

"Rumor hath there was dissension among the bosses when Vivaldi hired them without consulting his partners." Noel flicked ash and sipped his drink.

"From what I know of Ike, he frequently runs roughshod over his associates."

"Dear Big Ike Vivaldi. A man of infinite charms. I'd drink to him except I rarely indulge in hypocrisy."

"If you dislike him so much, why are you working for him?" asked Nicholas.

"For the money, dear boy, for the money. Two flops on Broadway have left my bankroll severely decimated; in fact, it's dangerously anemic and desperately in need of a blood transfusion. Now tell me, you sly puss Nicholas, why have you been hanging around rehearsals so frequently? Surely it's not to offer moral support to Diana. The young lady strikes me as being quite capable of fending for herself, and then some. You suspect there's a good crime story lurking in the shadows, am I right?"

"You sure are. What it is, I don't know. But I've been doing a lot of digging around in the past of the musical trio and I find it hard to swallow that because of past adversity they've decided to go straight."

"Well then, dear boy, what could they be up to? Smuggling liquor is a thing of the past. Smuggling arms? Where and to whom and for what profit? There are only small wars taking place on this earth of ours these days, hardly worthy of anyone's notice but the participants, who are probably wondering why they're participating. Ah! The traffic in flesh. Jacob Singer tells me the spiriting of innocent young women out of the country and forcing them into the world of sin abroad is still a highly lucrative industry. Vee, Bee, and Bee once profited from that operation and perhaps you think they're doing it again?"

Nicholas shrugged and spread his hands wide. "Why not? I'll bet Singer suspects the same thing."

"Oh, Jacob has a terribly suspicious nature. He thinks Mae West is a man in drag. I think she's a terrific woman in Hollywood. Yes, he thinks the traffic is very heavy and getting heavier, he thinks Maxine Howard was a victim of these monsters, and I'm beginning to think that if Electra Howard starts analyzing some suspicions of her own, well . . . there's going to be an awful lot of decapitated chickens littering the neighborhood. Ironic, isn't it, the thought of Electra in the employ of a trio who might have been responsible for her sister's murder."

Diana sighed and said, "I think the three are straight. I really do."

"I shall tell that to Jacob when next I see him. Another round? Delightful. Herbie, encore! Will you two make small talk while I try to round up Jeff? He was taking tea with your mother, Diana, perhaps he's back in our flat by now. We're going to the theater

51

again tonight, Gladys George in *Personal Appearance*. The play we saw last night was so dreadful, the cast left during the intermission." Jauntily, he crossed to the hotel lobby, where there was a public telephone. Diana and Nicholas shared silence for a while. Diana was off on some obscure plane, lost in thought.

"A penny for them," offered Nicholas.

"What? Oh I'm sorry, I was thinking about Noel and chickens."

"A strange combination."

"Yes, that's what has me thinking. Nick, do you really suspect there's a dark side to The Cascades operation?"

"I think Noel knows more than he's letting on."

"Do you really? Why should he care what's going on behind the scenes, even if it's somewhat shady?"

"Maybe Jacob Singer's asked him to keep his eyes and his ears open."

"Oh don't be ridiculous. Noel is too debonair and other-worldly to spy for the police. He creates his own atmosphere and permits one to penetrate it just so far and no further. I was absolutely amazed that he asked us to have drinks with him."

"Exactly. He's been very amusing and very subtle about it, but I think our Mr. Coward has been looking for information."

"Oh nonsense. What would either one of us know about anything going on at The Cascades?"

"Not either one. I know as little as Noel knows. You're his target."

She paled. "Me? What could he possibly expect to learn from me? I don't know anything."

"Nuts." Herbie smiled his semi-toothless smile as he placed a dish of salted peanuts on the table and then distributed the fresh martinis. He hurried back to the bar, which was filling up with its usual denizens.

"Relax, darling, you're not in the hot seat. I just made an obvious observation. If Noel's digging for information about The Cascades, you're the one he's trying to get it from, not me. You're an on-the-scene observer. I'm an outsider trying to get a look in. And I do think something smells in Denmark, if I may be permitted a paraphrase, and I do think Jacob Singer is housing a very impressive stack of suspicions of his own . . ."

"Well, of all the ridiculous . . ."

"All the ridiculous what?" asked Noel as he rubbed his hands together, warming to the prospect of a fresh ice-cold martini.

"Nothing important," said Diana, and Nicholas popped some nuts in his mouth. "Did you find Jeff?"

"Yes, he had a marvelous time with your mother."

"Oh I'm so glad."

"She was apparently in great form. I'm sure it's no secret among us that when Millicent gets wound up, she's off to the races, never to stop until she crosses the finishing line. Jeff and I are dining at Frankie and Johnny's. Care to join us? We're meeting in fifteen minutes. I do adore their thick, juicy steaks."

Nicholas said he needed to work on an outline and Diana had plans to dine with her mother.

"Too bad. Jeff was looking forward to seeing you both. Diana, do tell your mother Jeff had a delightful time at tea. I'm sure she'll be glad to hear it. Actually Diana, in some strange way they got onto the subject of your late husband . . . Coleridge, I believe, as in Samuel and *The Rime of the Ancient Mariner* . . ."

"Yes, James Coleridge." Her voice was strangely husky.

"Is it really true, what your mother told Jeff?"

"I don't know. What did Mother tell Jeff?"

"That Coleridge died of a strange wasting illness. That it was suspected he was killed by a voodoo spell."

This was apparently news to Nicholas. "Really?" he asked. "Is that so, Diana?"

"There are times," said Diana, "when I think Mother's tongue should be cut in half."

"Oh, my dear," said Noel as he reached for a peanut, "if it was, she'd have plenty left."

Six

CASEY Sterne, the former private detective turned government agent, was an attractive, husky man in his late thirties. He admired the warmth of Singer's greeting when he entered the office and then remembered they had met before. Singer didn't remember. "When was it? What was the occasion?"

"About five years ago. A missing wife case. A New Jersey bookie whose wife ran off with a jockey."

Jacob smiled. He remembered. "Sure, the bookie who wanted his wife back for sentimental reasons. Did you find her?"

"Oh sure. She went back to her husband. He slit her throat. So what can I do for you, Jacob?"

"You can tell me about Maxine Howard."

"Poor Maxie. I read about it in the papers. Garroted." He mimicked a shudder. "Not a nice way to die."

Singer told him what he knew about the murder and what he and Abraham Wang suspected. In conclusion, he said, "We think she was an undercover agent sent to Shanghai by you people." Casey said nothing. "Correct me if I'm wrong, and if possible, fill in the blank spaces when I'm right. Maxine had worked for you when you were a private eye."

"That's right."

"And she was good."

"She was better than good. She was aces. She never lost a tail and thought nothing of treading where angels fear. She near broke my heart when she turned in her stripes to try for a career in show business."

"Jealous of her sister?"

"No, not really. They didn't like each other. I think Maxine had a quickie with Electra's boyfriend . . ." He snapped his fingers to jog his memory.

"Daniel Parrish?"

"That's it. Dan Parrish. Electra went after Maxine with a machete, but although Electra was the dancer, Maxine was quicker on her feet. Electra cooled down eventually, but after that the girls kept their distance from each other. You know, Electra's a voodoo priestess."

"I suspected something like that. She and Parrish are opening at the new Cascades club in a couple of weeks. My old buddy Noel Coward is starring. Saw some of the rehearsal this afternoon. Electra and Dan have this number where they decapitate a chicken." He paused. "When I said Cascades, you didn't flick an eyelid."

"Why should I have?"

"Vivaldi, Beethoven, and Bizet."

Casey smiled. "Nobody ever said you were a dumb cop."

"So Maxine was working for your company."

"She was doing too good a job. She was close to nailing those three bastards for me when their boys in Shanghai caught up with her. I was arranging to get her out of there. God, I'll never stop blaming myself."

"Her body arrives tomorrow. You know Abe Wang?"

"Not personally, but I've heard nothing but good things about him."

"He's bringing Maxine home. Believe it or not, Electra's been making a big fuss about giving her a bang-up funeral."

"Oh, our Electra's quite a showman. She makes Barnum and Bailey look like extras in the background."

"Actually, I dropped in on the rehearsal to give the Unholy Three something to worry about. I plan to spend a lot of time there."

Casey said archly, "Now don't go making a pest of yourself. I

55

know those three. Not well, but well enough. Vivaldi and Beethoven have iron constitutions. Nothing fazes them. Knock them to the floor and they pick themselves up, dust themselves off, and start all over again. But Bizet, he's something else. I think he's going to be their ruination. A very nervous type. The other two are very protective of him. Vivaldi nicknamed him 'The Weasel,' which is right on the nose. Amazingly enough, they're very loyal to each other, very protective. Nobody knows how they survived those years recently when they were broke. I suspect they met somebody very simpatico who bankrolled them and probably continues to bankroll them. We suspect that once the club clicks, and there's every likelihood it will, they'll move in a gambling operation."

"I won't sit still for it if they do," cautioned Singer.

"Oh yes you will," overrode Casey. "If we don't get the goods on them by then, then they bring in the gambling and we move in and smash the operation."

"Okay, then. Now tell me, how do they get away with the flesh racket? I don't know why I can't bring myself to say 'white slavery,' it's so old hat. I mean this is 1935, not the turn of the century. How do they lure girls into their net?"

"Jacob, you still sound like you're wet behind the ears and shame on you. They get these girls in a dozen different ways. They advertise in theatrical newspapers for singers and dancers to work clubs overseas. That's how we got Maxine in. There are dozens of sleazy theatrical agents across the world who entice girls with promises of good money and lots of glamour and a chance to get the hell away from their humdrum existence and into a world of exotic foreign places. There's a world-wide depression on. You got Okies escaping the dust bowls. You got sharecroppers down South struggling against decimated cotton crops. Farmers are going broke all over the country, so what's to become of all those farmers' daughters? There aren't enough traveling salesmen on the road to pick up the slack. So the girls go looking for opportunities elsewhere. These vultures run ads in romance magazines, women's magazines and movie magazines, and dangle the kind of bait these poor fish can't resist. How often do you check the Missing Persons files?"

"Fairly often."

"Then you're aware missing females outnumber missing males on

56

a ratio of three to four to one. Most of them never turn up again, right?" Singer nodded agreement. "I'll tell you something funny. No, it's not funny, it's positively tragic. A lot of these girls, once they're entrapped, are too ashamed to try to escape and come back. They come from rural, religious, bigoted backgrounds. They're afraid of their parents. They have no occupations, they haven't been trained to be anything but domesticated ninnies, wives and mothers, cooks and house cleaners. So they stay away and fuck for a living, although they get to keep precious little of the money they make. Most of them never make it to forty unless they're lucky enough to meet an Oriental protector who buys their freedom and then enslaves them in another kind of life."

"Don't a few of them at least get to write their memoirs?"

"Well, actually, you've got one of them in Hollywood now, a Eurasian. She's there by way of London and a nut case Hungarian producer, but what the hell, good luck to her. She'll never have to look back again anymore. No Jacob, it's a living hell for these women." He sighed and then said, "The really funny thing about all this is, Maxine sent us information about a lot of girls who are making the best of it. And why? Because they're eating good and eating steady, they wear fancy dresses, and they get lots of coke and opium to keep them adrift in happy happy land. They don't think about that time when they're too old, too worn out, and too sick to be of any more use to their masters. If they're not murdered, then they commit suicide, or suffer the slow death of working a cathouse in the slums where nobody gives a damn how old you are or what you look like, as long as important organs still function. And let me tell you, my friend, when they reach thirty, they're already on their way out."

"Don't any of them ever come back?" Singer was depressed.

"Some of them do. Lucky for us, some of them do. We've gotten good information from some of these derelicts, and that's what they are—derelicts. The Salvation Army takes care of some of them, the church and religious orders absorb some of them, and the rest are absorbed by their local rivers."

"You have cheered me up immeasurably. How's for some coffee?"

Casey glanced at his wristwatch. "No time. I've got to go soon.

Lots to do and a lot of guys to meet with before I catch a train back to D.C. You got any plants at The Cascades?"

Singer told him about Edna Dore being a willing recruit for Abel Graham.

"Can she be trusted? How did this Graham land her?"

"She can be trusted because when the shit hits the fan she's been promised immunity. She's a smart girl. She reads a lot. Fannie Hurst, Edna Ferber, Maxwell Bodenheim, *War And Peace*. She had one year of college until the Depression did her in. She wants to go back and finish, get a degree in literature, and maybe teach. A very smart young lady."

"I hope she gets to be a very smart old lady. I suppose you can't do better then Vivaldi's mistress."

Singer told him about Noel Coward. Casey guffawed. "Him? Noel Coward an undercover agent? You got to be kidding."

"I swear on my mother's grave even though she isn't dead yet. I tell you you haven't seen such enthusiasm. He's traveling with this swell, Jeffrey Amherst, and he's his backup. They've certainly uncovered a lot of information on what goes on with the voodoo set." He told Casey about Jeff's conversation with Millicent Headman.

"Dear old Millicent," said Casey.

"You've met?"

"Oh yeah. She had me on her husband's tail for a while."

"Old Linus cheated on Millicent?"

"Old Linus was up to a lot of things."

"Suicide, wasn't he?"

"That was the rumor. But Millicent denies it ferociously. And when Millicent denies something ferociously, put up the storm windows. She's a nonstop talker with an impressive vocabulary. Then there's the three-times-married daughter Diana. She's another peach."

"I kind of like her. I go for the type."

"Tread carefully and carry a big stick. She's already a three-time loser."

"Loser? Noel says she's loaded."

"I wouldn't doubt it. She was always after big game. She practiced on her father."

"Oh my, is incest raising its ugly head?"

58

His question was answered with a Gallic shrug. "You know, Jacob, I used to pity the old lady. She was absolutely nuts about her husband. I've seen pictures of her when she was a youngster. One hell of a looker, especially in those Gibson girl outfits. And rich beyond belief."

"No kidding."

"It was old money."

"Money is ageless, my drunken daddy always reminded me."

"Ageless indeed. I gather Linus worked hard to get his share of it."

"The old Horatio Alger story. Poor but steadfast and the rich girl chose him above all her wealthy suitors."

"On the nose. She was sought after by an Astor, a Vanderbilt, let me think . . . oh yeah . . . old man Rockefeller himself, and in England she turned down Winston Churchill."

"So did Ethel Barrymore. I'm sure neither one of them has any regrets."

"So it was Millicent who had the money, and Linus finally got his hands on her fortune. He was a chemist and in time created Headman Pharmaceuticals."

"All by his lonesome?"

"I doubt it. Millicent said he had no head for business, but she suspects there was at least one silent partner who helped make it a billion-dollar industry. I have a suspicion there was foreign money involved. Money smart enough to pull out before the crash when they saw the handwriting on the wall . . ."

"Or got a smart tip from a Wall Street insider."

"Who knows? And we'll probably never know. Well, Jacob, I feel we've had a very fruitful session. We know where to reach each other, so as Helen Keller said to her teacher, let's keep in constant touch."

"I won't quote you."

Casey chuckled, waved good-bye, and left. Singer pulled open the bottom drawer on the right side of his desk, where he had a hidden recording machine. The disk was still rotating. Singer flipped a switch to stop the rotation. The disk rewound and Singer flipped a switch to hear the playback. He settled back comfortably in his swivel chair, feet crisscrossed on the desk,

59

hands behind his neck, and watched two flies fornicating on the ceiling. He listened to the playback, loving the sound of his own voice. He also wondered how much Casey hadn't told him.

A New Jersey bookie whose wife had run off with a jockey?

Singer hadn't really remembered any of it. But he didn't want to be impolite. He wondered what Abel Graham was getting from Edna Dore.

The Turkey Bar on West Thirty-ninth Street off Eighth Avenue was in the heart of the garment district. Edna Dore and Abel Graham sat in a secluded booth at the rear, fairly positive that in the dim lighting they wouldn't be recognized in case anyone was there who might know either one of them.

"The Weasel's a nervous wreck. Angie says four times last night he woke up screaming. It's very unnerving. He also talks in his sleep, but he slurs his words so half the time she don't know what he's talking about. And half the time she thinks *he* don't know what he's talking about."

They were both drinking rye on ice. There was nothing unusual about Edna's good looks. But she had a way of carrying herself that made her sexy and alluring. She wore very little makeup and her long eyelashes had been bequeathed by nature, not Woolworth's. Singer had warned Abel against making a pass. But the pass was long past, weeks before she'd admitted to being Big Ike Vivaldi's special girlfriend. They'd met at a rent party in Greenwich Village, where guests were charged a few dollars' admission that went toward paying the apartment occupant's rent. Edna was brought by Trixie Bates, Beethoven's beloved. It was a night when the Unholy Three were tied up in a business meeting. In short order, Trixie was making time with a self-proclaimed poet who was possessed of neither rhyme nor reason, and Edna let herself be wooed by Abel, because he was polite, spoke well, and seemed fairly intelligent. And yes he'd read Ernest Hemingway's *Men Without Women* and F. Scott Fitzgerald's *Tender Is the Night*, but no, he could not discuss Kafka's *Metamorphosis*, let alone spell it. They spent a lovely night together in Abel's furnished room uptown on Seventy-eighth Street and Columbus Avenue and the clandestine affair lasted until shortly before the announcement of the opening of The Cascades.

"You and Singer are the reason the Weasel's suffering palpitations."

"That's good."

"He can't stand the sight of cops."

"I hear there's a lot of that going around in their set."

"Vivaldi and Fat Harry don't give a crap. They're the fearless twosome."

"Aren't they worried the Weasel's bad case of nerves could pose a threat?"

"Nah! They love the little bastard and they're all the friends he's got."

"He's got Angie, doesn't he? Can't she give him some help?"

"Listen Abel, she's a whore, not a guidance counselor."

"I hope you're there when the Weasel cracks."

"I hope I'm not. Time bombs are dangerous. Anyway, to continue. There's some tension between Electra and Daniel."

"You know why?"

"I think it's got to do with her sister getting back to town tomorrow."

"For crying out loud, Maxine's dead."

"Listen, Abel, even though they're dead, the dead can do a lot of damage." She tapped her head with an index finger. "It's all up here. I know. I been reading this here Sigmund Freud." (She pronounced it "fraud.") "Electra's got guilts," she said knowledgeably. "She didn't like her sister and now it's too late to kiss and make up. Well, maybe if there's an afterlife."

"If there's an afterlife, they might be going in opposite directions."

"Huh," said Edna, "wouldn't that be ironic? And by the way, *what* is with this Noel Coward for crying out loud?" Abel grinned. "I mean is he for real? It's 'Dear girl' this and 'Dear boy' that. I mean I know he flies, but does he have a license? The girls think he's cute. He sure has a mouth on him, though. He told the dance director Mickey DuVane he has all the charm and grace of a bull moose in heat, and then I heard him ask Fat Harry if obesity ran in his family, or did it crawl at a snail's pace. Ha!" She slammed a hand down on the table. "He's a riot and I think some day he's going to cause one. I mean Fat Harry took it without his lower lip trembling,

61

which it does when he's angry. Then he tells Trixie and Angie they're two of his favorite houris, and of course they're ready to punch him out till I explain houris are Egyptian dancing girls. It helps to read a lot."

"What about Diana Headman?"

"She sucks up to Coward a lot but nobody's kidding him. Her friend Nicholas is all over the place. I kind of like him. I have a feeling he's finding out things that are a little dangerous for him to know."

Abel was lifting his glass, but his hand now remained suspended in midair. "Such as?"

Edna shrugged. "I don't know. He writes these crime stories and crime writers are suspicious of the toilet paper they use."

"Try to find out."

She said with exasperation, "I'm trying, I'm trying. God, I can't wait until I get a big enough bundle to take myself away from all this!" She knocked back her rye. "I'll tell you something that *I* suspect." She poked her chest with a thumb. "That there Diana piece bought her way onto the bill."

"It's possible. It's been done before."

"Well, I'm pretty suspicious."

"You've heard nothing maybe about girls being sent abroad to work?"

"You're so delicate all of a sudden. But I'll tell you this, when the Weasel gets mad at Angie, he says to her something like 'How'd you like to end up on a slow boat to Mandalay?' I always thought you took a road to Mandalay, but I don't know everything, do I?"

"You're doing okay, kiddo. You're doing real okay."

"Thanks for the pat on the head. It's almost as nice as when you used to pat me on my tush. I got to get back. I'll leave first." She blew him a kiss, followed by a wink, and then she left. Abel was hypnotized by the movements of her hips and wondered if he'd ever get lucky in the hay again the way he had scored with the delectable Edna.

Nancy Adman was fitting Noel for the Harlequin costume he was to wear in one of the production numbers. "Please don't fidget so, Mr. Coward, I'm trying to get a measurement."

"I can't help it, my dear woman, I suddenly feel your fingers in the strangest places. Now what was I saying? Damn, I can't remember. The point has been killed and now I am in mourning for it. I think I look a fool in this thing."

"That's how you're supposed to look. You're Harlequin. A lovesick idiot."

"You get along with the powers that be?"

"I don't think they remember I'm here."

"Strange that the unwholesome threesome never brook interference. Very strange."

"Why's that Bizet always so irritable?"

"He's teething."

"What do you think of the voodoo number?"

"I'll never eat chicken again."

Noel surveyed himself in the full-length mirror in Nancy's workroom. He hated the costume and said so. "I don't know whether to wring my hands or wring your neck. Still, it is a bit soigné, I must admit."

"What?"

"Soigné, as in 'Climb upon my knee, soigné boy.' Now why in the hell did I let Mickey DuVane con me into doing this Harlequin number?"

"I for one am glad he did. At least it's something he made his mind up over. He's so damned indecisive. Every time I try to talk to him his mind wanders."

"He should be careful about that. It might get lost. Dull boy. He should thank his lucky stars he doesn't have to live by his wits. If he did, he'd starve to death. Ouch! Be careful with those pins!"

She backed away from Noel to get a better perspective on the costume. "I think it's pretty damned good if I must say so myself."

"You might as well. I doubt if anyone else will. I think I look like Edna May Oliver in drag."

"Take heart, the show's overlong as it is and I heard Mickey discussing tentative cuts with Chick Mason. This number may be one of them. They've already decided to drop 'I'll Be Glad When You're Dead, You Rascal You'."

"I should think so, if only in deference to Electra and her loss. Help me get out of this bloody costume. If Gertie Lawrence is out

63

front opening night and catches me in this getup, I'll never hear the end of it. Dear Gertie. Such a poseur."

Edna, Trixie, and Angie were very good to Hattie Beavers. They tipped her well, Edna hired her to clean her apartment, and they made no excessive demands of her. When she was younger and much thinner, Hattie had danced in Harlem nightclubs. Married briefly, her husband ran out on her and he wasn't missed. Old friends from the bad old days helped her find work backstage.

Hattie liked her three ladies, and she always referred to them as "My girls," but she didn't like working at The Cascades, and shared her misgivings with Edna Dore.

"What kind of curse do you think is on this club?" Edna was buffing her nails while Hattie was ironing Edna's underwear.

"I know you're laughing at me, Miss Edna . . ."

"I'm not laughing, Hattie. You made a serious statement and I asked a serious question. If you say there's a curse on the joint and I'm spending a lot of time in it, I'd like to know what I'm up against and what to do about it. You know how superstitious I am."

"I know, I know honey, I know. I told my Grandma Sadie I'm getting bad vibrations here and right away she says, 'It's the hand of Satan rockin' that evil boat.' It's that Electra Howard and Daniel Parrish for starters. They's voodoo!"

"They dance voodoo, so what's wrong with that?"

Hattie thrust her head forward. "They's *real* voodoo. He's a priest and she's his priestess. They carry on something fierce in their studio in Harlem. Everybody in the neighborhood knows about it. There's a lot of starvation in Harlem, honey, but they gettin' mighty fed up eatin' chicken. Although a couple of weeks ago they got a dead goat, and the Lord only knows what they'll be sacrificing next. Maybe young virgins!"

"You got nothing to worry about."

"I got three daughters!"

"Heavens, I forgot about them." She chuckled. "How are the girls?"

"Virginal. And I aim for them to stay that way."

"Well, they're only booked in here for two weeks. We open soon and those two weeks will fly by faster than you can say Bill Robinson."

"They ain't the only bad vibrations around here."

Edna was now setting up her left foot to polish the toenails. "Go on, Hattie, tell me the rest."

"Diana Headman."

"What about her?"

"I plain don't like her."

"Well, that's not a good reason for bad vibrations."

"I heard her having a spat with that boyfriend of hers."

Edna was amused. "Was it a hot and heavy or the polite society kind where they talk through clenched teeth?"

"It was polite but she say to him, 'You be careful. It's not good to know too much in this place.'" Edna was making mental notes. She never dreamed she'd strike oil with Hattie Beavers. Hattie asked sharply, "You listening to me?"

"I hear every word." She was Mary Cassatt painting a toenail.

"And he say, 'Then you be careful too. You working for gangsters,' if you'll pardon the expression . . ."

"I've heard it before."

"And he say, 'And you're playing with fire. And your mother isn't too happy either.'"

"Oh boy. The plot thickens."

"And Miss Diana, she say, 'And I'm not too happy with Mother. She's got to watch that damn mouth of hers,' only she didn't say damn, she used a word a good God-fearing church-going woman like myself don't dast repeat."

"I'll bet it was a humdinger."

"I heard you say that word about Mr. Vivaldi."

"Oh *that* word. You got more to tell me? It's getting very interesting."

"And then he say something about her sucking around Mr. Noel Coward too much and she say again he should go sell his tomatoes someplace else and maybe stop hanging around here so much and he say he's here on assignment, whatever that means, and then I heard someone coming up the steps from the stage so I stopped listening and I went to the drugstore across the street to call my Grandma Sadie and I tell her everything and she say, 'Granddaughter you be careful. Don't you go messin' with them ofays. I looked in my crystal ball . . .' "

"Her crystal ball! Are you kidding?"

"No, Miss Edna, I am not. Grandma Sadie tells fortunes for a living. Crystal ball, tarot cards, tea leaves, and bumps on the head. She one of the best. She reads a lot of celebrities. Ethel Waters, Cab Calloway, Duke Ellington, Nina Mae McKinney . . ."

"And a large supporting cast. Say, you're not thinking of quitting us, are you?"

"No Miss Edna. No way. You're my babies too and I'll look after you until my ship comes in."

"You know what, Hattie. You can always confide in me. When you hear something that bothers you, you come and tell me. I'll make sure no harm comes to you, vibrations or no vibrations. Okay?"

"Miss Edna, now I know why you're my favorite."

"Hattie, I love you too." She raised her leg for Hattie to get a good look at the freshly painted toenails. "What about them, Hattie. Ain't they something?"

Hattie said gravely, "Miss Edna, you look like you've been wading in a pool of blood."

Seven

JACOB Singer and Abel Graham were at Grand Central Station early the next morning to greet Abraham Wang and his grim cargo. Wang was one of the first to alight, followed by a porter carrying his luggage. He and Singer fell into each other's arms. "You haven't changed a bit!" said Wang exuberantly.

"Well, you've certainly filled out since leaving the States," commented Jacob.

Wang was patting his stomach. "It's the trip that did it. I did nothing but eat."

"No cute tootsies to tempt you?"

"Seems cute tootsies are out of season." Jacob introduced him to Abel.

A train conductor said to Wang, "We're ready to unload the coffin."

Singer signaled three men from the coroner's office who had arrived with a meat wagon and they took over the transfer of Maxine's coffin from train to wagon.

Abel relieved the porter of Wang's luggage, Wang tipped the man, and Singer took Wang by the arm, leading him out of the noisy, crowded station to the police car parked on the Vanderbilt Avenue side. As they pushed their way through the crowd with Abel behind them struggling with the luggage, Jacob gave Wang a quick replay of his investigation at The Cascades and what he had learned from Casey Sterne.

Wang told him, "We've managed to get some undercover agents into some of the cathouses. It was easier managing the ones that have gambling, a lot of our boys are excellent dealers. We've even got a piano player doing honky-tonk in one of the joints. The coast guard is stepping up its patrol since we got a tip a lot of girls were being brought in on chartered yachts and freighters."

The police driver's eyes were glued to the Chinese detective's face in the rear-view mirror. A chink detective, he was thinking to himself, and all the way from Shanghai. So much for the ads imploring consumers to "Buy American!" Abel shouted a warning and the driver swerved to avoid hitting a trolley car.

Singer told Wang, "I booked you into the Algonquin. I figured you'd want to be where the action is. I was going to put you into the Royalton across the street, but there's no bar."

"The Algonquin suits me fine. You still friendly with Dorothy Parker and the Round Table?"

"The Round Table is now strictly for squares. Most of the originals have scattered. Benchley's in Hollywood, from which Mrs. Parker and her husband, Alan Campbell, commute. Woollcott's about to make his film debut and he still has his 'Town Crier' radio program. Them days are gone forever. Heywood Broun is fat and sick and Edna Ferber mostly travels these days, researching her novels. I go there for a drink every so often because the lobby is still quiet and pleasant. Had drinks there a couple of weeks ago with Mrs. Parker and my new best friend, Noel Coward."

"I can't wait to meet him."

"After we check you in and get you unpacked, we'll drop in on the rehearsal. Abel and I make the Unholy Three uncomfortable. One of them, Bizet, goes near berserk when we're around. But wait until they get a load of you and I tell them you're a Shanghai flatfoot, they just might have kittens." He told the driver he could report back to the precinct after dropping them at the hotel. The driver considered stopping off first for some Chinese food. Wang was making him hungry.

* * *

At the club, Hattie Beavers stood in the wings next to Noel, who was holding a steaming cup of India tea. Hattie wore a huge silver crucifix and Noel commented to himself it was fortunate her ample bosom could comfortably bear the weight of it. He also thought to himself, she might be at peace with her Lord, but from the way her eyes shifted about as though they had special ballbearings, he did not think she was at peace with the club.

"Hattie, you look disturbed. What's bothering you?" Electra and Daniel were doing a very suggestive high-strutting routine to a wild arrangement of "The Darktown Strutter's Ball." He indicated the dancers. "Is it them?"

"They's bad news." She clutched the crucifix. "My Grandma Sadie read me in her crystal ball last night." Noel was intrigued. Grandma Sadie and her crystal ball. There wasn't much of that in London's West End. "She says heavy heavy hangs over this place."

"That could mean a rainstorm," said Noel with a twinkle in his eye.

"They's going to be a storm all right, but it ain't going to be no rain. You got to take my Grandma Sadie serious, real serious. She looked into that crystal ball last night and she see dead bodies, lots of dead bodies."

"And where were these ill-fated creatures? In a mortuary?"

"No, sir. Right here in this club."

"Really? Are you wearing the crucifix to ward off evil spirits?"

"I wear this because I'm a faithful Catholic. I believe in God and God will protect me. The lord God Jesus Christ."

"Jesus Christ," echoed Noel softly. "Local boy makes God."

"You have to believe in something, Mr. Coward. Otherwise you are without a soul and you are a sinner."

"Hattie, I trust you implicitly. Will you keep an eye on me? Will you warn me if Grandma gives you a hot tip I'm in imminent danger?"

"Don't fool with me, Mr. Coward."

"Oh I'm not fooling at all. I'm dead serious . . . no pun intended. I've been feeling a little uneasy myself this morning."

"Too many martinis last night, maybe."

"Good heavens, you're also a mind reader."

A tornado of laughter came twisting out of her mouth. Noel

considered hugging her but decided not to, there was so much of her to embrace and he might spill some tea. He saw Jacob Singer and Abel Graham coming in from the street entrance with Abraham Wang in their wake.

"Ah! Here comes the metropolitan police with their guest star from Shanghai."

Electra saw them too and left Dan to finish the strut by himself. Dan started to yell, when he too saw the Oriental detective and followed Electra. Singer introduced them to Wang. Wang took Electra's hand and offered his condolences. She asked Singer, "When can we have her body?"

"As soon as they do the autopsy. Probably by tomorrow afternoon."

"So I can plan the funeral for Friday?"

"There should be no problem. If there's a delay, I'll let you know right away."

"Thank you." She asked Wang if he had any good leads as to her sister's murderer and he told her they were swamped with information from their usual informants, most of it useless.

He added, "That's why I decided to come here. I think the solution is right here, right here in the city." Singer feared he was going to say "right here in the club," which might not have been a bad idea when he realized Irving Bizet was standing within earshot.

"Hey Bizet," Singer beckoned him, "Come say hello to Shanghai's great detective, Abraham Wang."

Upon hearing the word "detective," Bizet's eyelids began fluttering. He almost lost his balance crossing the few steps to join the group. Singer said, "Irving Bizet meet Abraham Wang." He said to Wang, "Irving is one of the three partners in the club."

Wang said affably, "I wish you the best of luck." It pleased him that Bizet was perspiring. He decided the Weasel suffered from high blood pressure.

"Ah! The touring company has arrived at last!" Wang recognized Noel immediately. They shook hands and Noel's eyes traveled to Singer's tie. "Jacob." His voice had dropped an octave. "That tie."

Jacob grinned. "It's a Butilicci original."

Said Noel with a sniff, "Butilicci should be arrested for instigating a riot." Then he awarded Wang his attention and the detective's

70

eyes widened in astonishment as Noel let flow a stream of impeccably accented Cantonese Chinese. "I see you're astonished. Well,
don't be. It's a speech I was taught phonetically when I toured the
Orient five years ago. In fact I was taken terribly ill in Shanghai."

"Never drink the water," cautioned Wang, locking the barn door
after the cow escaped.

"Never drink the gin," countered Noel as Dan and Electra returned to the rehearsal. No one had noticed Abel had left them to
wander about backstage. He had caught a high sign from Edna
Dore, who was chatting with Hattie. Diana Headman, talking to
Nancy Adman on the opposite side of the stage, was studying the
group in which Wang was the center of attraction. Irving Bizet
looked as if he was about to have a heart attack. He left the group
and hurried away, presumably to tell his partners the Shanghai
detective had arrived. Then Diana saw Abel, Edna, and Hattie deep
in conversation. She commented to Nancy, "I wonder what the
detective wants with Hattie?"

"Maybe her recipe for barbecued spareribs New Orleans style.
Edna tells me she's a hell of a cook. Hattie did a dinner for Edna
a few weeks back and I salivate every time I think of Edna's description of the superb cuisine."

"I think Hattie's frightened, the way she's clutching that crucifix."

"I don't suppose you've heard of Hattie's Grandma Sadie?"

"No I haven't. What about her?"

Nancy told Diana all about Grandma Sadie and her doomsday
predictions, related first to Hattie and passed on to Edna, who had
then related them to Nancy during a costume fitting. "Hattie's
terrified of Electra and Daniel, you know."

"Why?"

"Don't you know? I thought everybody did. They're voodoo
priests." Diana's sudden intake of breath didn't escape Nancy.
Then came the dawn as an invisible sun rose and settled over
Nancy's head. "Oh of course. You lived in Africa. Then you must
have had experiences with the voodoo there."

"Some," said Diana. She saw Nicholas Benson advancing on
them.

"I see Mr. Wang has arrived. Have you met?" asked Nicholas.

71

"Not yet," said Diana. She asked Nancy, "Is it cold in here? I feel chilly."

"I feel perfectly fine. Maybe you're catching a cold?"

"I hope not. All I need is a sore throat with the opening a week away." Nicholas excused himself and went to join Noel, Singer, and Wang. Bizet returned to the room with Beethoven and Vivaldi in tow. Vivaldi said after spotting Wang, "He don't look like much to me. What are you afraid of, Weasel?"

"The way he said he thought the solution to the Howard girl's murder was right here. I overheard him."

Beethoven's eyes had narrowed. "Right here in the club?"

"Right here in the city. He didn't mention the club." He was mopping his brow again. He hadn't stopped mopping it since Wang's arrival. Beethoven found himself wondering how Bizet would behave at a policemen's ball.

Vivaldi growled, "We got nothing to worry about."

"That's what you keep telling us," said Bizet, "but that still don't stop me from worrying."

Beethoven growled, "Hey Ike, what's Edna doing talking to the cop? They look kind of cozy."

Hattie saw the Unholy Three staring at them and nudged Edna. Edna saw the three from the corner of her eye and bid a hasty good-bye to the two and then strolled nonchalantly toward Vivaldi.

"Hi hon'," she said airily, "you meet the cop from Shanghai?"

"What you doing talking to the flatfoot?"

"It was Hattie doing all the talking. She was telling him about her grandma. You know, what I told you last night. Her seeing all them bodies in her crystal ball."

"What the hell is with crystal balls all of a sudden?" asked Beethoven. Edna told him Grandma Sadie's predictions. "Balls," said Beethoven.

"Only one," said Edna, "Grandma Sadie's." She turned impatiently to look at the stage. "Say, what the hell is with that Mickey DuVane? Why ain't we rehearsing 'The Shadow Waltz' number? Busby Berkeley he ain't and we need a lot of work." With a sigh of exasperation, she asked Vivaldi, "Are we or ain't we eating tonight?"

"I don't know. I'll let you know later."

" 'Cause otherwise I'm going to see a show. I don't like sitting around the apartment with only the radio for company."

"You run out of books all of a sudden?"

"Listen, my eyes also get tired."

Nicholas Benson was questioning a cooperative Wang at great length and jotting his responses in a pocket notebook. Graham and Singer sat at a table with Noel and told them about Grandma Sadie's predictions, which were news to Singer but not to Noel, who'd already heard them from Hattie herself. Then Graham told them about the tension between Diana and Nicholas, overheard by Hattie. Electra and Daniel, in the meantime, surrendered the stage to Mickey DuVane, who was beginning to work with the chorus girls and the showgirls.

Noel asked Singer, "I wonder, Jacob, just how much Diana Headman had to do with voodoo when she was living in Rhodesia. You know, what Millicent told my Jeff of how Diana's husband died of a 'wasting' illness."

"That could have been symptomatic of some form of cancer," said Singer.

"Oh, let's not bring cancer into this. It's so commonplace. I prefer to play with the voodoo theory. I really love all this. Voodoo. White slavery. Everything but Boris Karloff with electric plugs protruding from the sides of his neck. Now back to Diana and her late husband. Apparently he was a rather nasty lot, and he just might have mistreated a black employee with very heavy voodoo connections." He mused aloud for a moment, "I wonder if there might be a song in this." He ad-libbed, "I think it's hoodoo, When you do that Voodoo . . . What can that boiling brew do . . ." He paused and then said irritably, "Oh the hell with it. It's more Cole Porter's sort of thing than mine. Now where was I? Oh yes. A maltreated black employee with voodoo connections."

"And maybe this employee cast a spell over the husband."

"Why not?" Noel looked from Singer to Abel. Abel had his frequent blank expression.

"You believe in that sort of thing?" Singer asked. "You think it could be effective?"

"I've never had that kind of spell cast over me. At least not to my knowledge. There's Daniel Parrish. Perhaps he can enlighten us.

73

He's not terribly talkative, I'd better warn you, but maybe we'll have better luck with him this time." He hailed Dan and the dancer joined them. Noel wondered silently if the four of them—touching fingers—could possibly reach Jack the Ripper, and then posed the question as tactfully as possible. He wasn't *au courant* on voodoo priests and couldn't be sure if they became a bit testy when asked if one of their unique incantations could raise the mortality rate.

"Voodoo is a very serious business," said Dan in a sepulchral voice. Noel expected a clash of cymbals but none was forthcoming. "It is a form of religion handed down from generation to generation in Africa, and it traveled the world with the slaves captured there. I am a fifth-generation voodoo priest."

"What about Electra?"

"I taught her everything. Who is this person who was cursed with the wasting sickness?" They were joined by Wang and Nicholas, who took notes, much to Noel's annoyance. He could see they were being watched by Diana Headman and Electra and Vivaldi.

"Diana Headman's most recent husband, the dead one. James Coleridge. He was a rancher in Rhodesia. Not very well liked albeit veddy veddy rich. In many areas, I'm sure you know, wealth does compensate for other shortcomings. I get the feeling if I tweaked Diana's nose, there'd be a rush of coins gushing from her mouth. What's the matter with you Nicholas? You look as though you've eaten a bad clam."

"Nothing. Nothing at all." Nicholas looked toward Diana, but she returned no sign of recognition.

Dan asked, "Diana was there when he died?"

"Presumably," said Noel. "They were married, though divorce had been discussed. There *is* voodoo in Rhodesia, isn't there?"

"There is voodoo everywhere except in Russia and Tibet." He said to Wang, "There is voodoo in the Orient. But you have to look hard to find it. Voodoo can have many disguises. Voodoo can not only create death, it can create the living death. The zombies. But it can also give life. I myself have seen a dead man come back to life after a very strenuous voodoo ceremony. His wife wasn't too happy, but that's another story."

"I'd love to hear it sometime," said Noel with genuine curiosity.

74

He wondered if an international ledger of voodoo victims had ever been published.

"I did not know Diana had knowledge of voodoo," said Dan.

"I don't know if she's ever dabbled herself. You know her well, Nicholas, has she?"

Nicholas was barely audible. "This is the first I've heard of how Jim Coleridge died."

"Oh really?" Noel was truly astonished. "Have you never taken tea alone with her mother? Why, my Jeff heard it all from her over a cup of tea. She gushes away like a wildcat oil well."

Dan's voice smothered Noel's. "The wasting sickness is the cruelest of punishments. It takes great patience and much preparation to cast this spell effectively. Only once in my lifetime have I been a witness to it. I was a small boy and my mother was angry with one of her many lovers. My mother was a high priestess. Also two of my fathers."

"Good lord!" exclaimed Noel. "How many fathers did you have?"

Dan shrugged. "My mother was a very versatile woman. She was also a great entertainer. Perhaps you've heard of her? Cassandra Parrish?"

"Heard of her!" Noel was impressed. "I saw her at the Folies Bergère. Good God, the fantastic things she did with a boa constrictor—but I'll leave all that to a more favorable time."

"She was supplanted by Josephine Baker. Mother took her revenge. She made her sterile."

"Let's get back to the wasting disease," said Singer impatiently.

"It is irreversible," Dan said, his voice making Wang think of graveyards and tombstones and mausoleums.

Singer asked, "Dan, do these spells really work?"

"Would you like me to cast one on you?"

"Not today, thanks."

Dan continued. "Believe me, gentlemen. A voodoo spell is terribly powerful and can be very dangerous. I have seen the results of spells that maim and cripple. That cause the loss of a limb. That cause blindness and deafness."

"Dear God!" said Noel. "Is voodoo never charitable?"

75

"Sometimes, Noel, voodoo can bring about a charitable death to those who are suffering miserably with a terminal illness."

"Dear Dan, is it possible to use it on a few drama critics?"

Wang suddenly spoke up. "Can it cause hypnosis?"

"Yes. It is the first stage to turning someone into a zombie."

Wang continued, "I mean the kind of hypnosis in which people do and say things against their will."

"Yes."

"It could wrest a confession of murder?" persisted Wang.

"It could. Show me your suspect and I will do the rest." He stood up to go. "You will excuse me now. I feel Electra wants me." He left them and a brief silence overcame them. Noel had rammed a cigarette into his holder and Nicholas whipped out a lighter and torched it.

Noel thanked Nicholas and said, "I find that rather fascinating. I must have some further discussions with Daniel." He turned to Nicholas. "Fancy your not knowing how James Coleridge died."

"Diana rarely discusses her past. Not even with close friends. I think she's annoyed with her mother for telling your friend Jeffrey the story."

"Ah but Nicholas, most people find Jeffrey irresistible. I'm sure if he went out into the Eygptian desert, he'd have the Sphinx chattering away in a matter of minutes. He has this unique quality of extracting confidences, even from perfect strangers. Diana's mother was a lead-pipe cinch. She's so deliciously shallow. I wonder, was Diana's mother with her in Rhodesia during Coleridge's wasting-away period?"

"Yes. She and Linus were both there. They stayed until after Jim's death while Diana settled the estate. The three sailed back to America together. Shortly after they returned, Linus had his fatal heart attack."

"And it wasn't a suicide," persisted Noel.

"I don't know. I wasn't with him when he went. He didn't die right away. He hung on for about three days."

"And then took a turn for the hearse," said Noel blithely.

Singer laughed, Abel Graham chuckled, Nicholas seemed not to have heard Noel's crack, and Wang looked inscrutable. He turned to the others and asked no one in particular, "Do you suppose voodoo could bring Maxine Howard back to life?"

Noel responded swiftly. "I hope not. I should think by now she looks a positive sight. Ah! The chorus is about to do 'The Shadow Waltz.' "

Wang positively sparkled. Girls! He felt better. The sight of beautiful women was more satisfying than murder, voodoo, or resurrection. The orchestra was loud and jazzy. The chorus girls wore black costumes trimmed in purple bugle beads. The showgirls posed on multileveled platforms wearing as little as possible. Angie Murray chewed gum and looked bored. Trixie Bates fidgeted because she had a suspicious itch in her crotch and if the cause of it was what she suspected, she'd give Beethoven holy hell. Her dour thoughts were interrupted by a gasp from Edna Dore.

"What's the matter, honey?" asked Trixie. "Indigestion?"

Edna was flailing her arms wildly and Mickey DuVane shouted up at her, "What the hell do you think you're doing, Edna!"

Singer and Wang leapt from their seats.

Abel Graham tore past them yelling "Catch her! Somebody catch her!"

Ike Vivaldi sped up the stairs to the level that held Edna, and caught her as she plummeted down. "Jesus!" he gasped. "Jesus!"

The feathers that gave the dart its balance were colorful and graceful. They were yellow and orange and blue and green and brown, all drenched in blood from the wound in Edna's neck.

Abel Graham's mouth was dry but he managed to gasp, "A dart!" He turned to Singer and Noel, who huffed and puffed their way up to the level. "A dart! She's dead! She was killed with a dart!"

Noel said to Singer, "They use a blowgun in their act."

Singer didn't have to ask him who "they" were. It was obviously Daniel and Electra.

Eight

Don'T touch the dart!" said Singer sharply, staying Abel's hand. "There might be prints, probably not, but there might be." He waved two stagehands into action and they reluctantly carried Edna's body to the dressing room she shared with Trixie and Angie. The two women were in shock and grief-stricken, but they were no match for Hattie's spine-chilling caterwauling. Wang had phoned Jacob's precinct to report the murder, and the coroner and his assistants were on their way. Nicholas and Diana stood to one side as the stagehands and the corpse moved slowly past them. Diana's arms were folded and she held them tightly against her chest. Nicholas darted away in search of a phone. Edna's murder was worth some dollars to him from the city desk of one of the tabloids. Vivaldi fled to his office to phone the club's press agent, and Beethoven put one arm around his beloved Trixie and the other around Angie. "She didn't suffer," he said softly, "I can tell from the peaceful look on her face."

"Bullshit!" raged Angie. "She's dead. Killed in cold blood. Why would anybody want to kill Edna? What the hell's going on around here anyway?"

Electra and Dan hurried to Singer, who said, "You're just the people I want to see. Where's that blowgun you use in your act?"

Dan said, "It's gone. It's not in our dressing room. I searched the prop room and it's not there either."

Only Noel Coward was calm, cool, and collected. He was carefully organizing in his mind the scene being played in the club before Edna was struck down. He had everybody placed in position, except something was wrong. Someone who should have been in the scene was not there. His thoughts were interrupted by the sight of Jeffrey Amherst hurrying onstage. "Why Jeff! Dear boy! Wherever did you find that blowgun?"

Jeff was in the spotlight, a location he usually preferred to avoid. "I found it in your dressing room, Noel. It was lying across your dressing table. What were you doing with this thing? Doesn't it belong to the dancers?"

"I was doing not a damned thing with that cursed instrument, and yes I do believe it belongs to the dancers."

"That's our blowgun," said Dan, sounding like a teenage boy who'd just broken a neighbor's window with a baseball and was now demanding the baseball's return.

"I'll take it." Jeff handed the blowgun to Jacob Singer. Singer knew testing it for fingerprints would be futile—Jeff had handled it and it had served as a prop for several dancers. He heard someone chuckle. It was Noel.

"What's the expression the police use? 'Planting incriminating evidence to cast suspicion on an innocent party.' The very idea of placing that obscenity on my dressing table. I have barely enough breath to inhale a cigarette let alone blow a dart at a moving target."

"Edna wasn't moving," said Abel, "she was standing perfectly still."

"Dear boy," said Noel with his Cheshire cat's grin, "I do believe I was sitting out front with you and Jacob when the poor thing met with her unfortunate end." Hattie's pathetic wails were horrifying enough to frighten a banshee. "Poor Hattie. Her Grandma Sadie was damned right. There will be bodies strewn about, probably like rose petals in the path of a dewy-eyed bride." Diana Headman was lavishing her lips with rouge. "Aren't you the cool one?" commented Noel. "Applying war paint after the battle's been fought."

"I may look cool," she said while blotting her lips with a tissue

79

she found in her handbag, "but I'm a mass of shattered nerves inside."

"Have you never seen a blowgun before?"

"Yes. In museums. Artifacts were, or should I say are, very common in Africa. They're always on display."

"This one's an Assegai," said Noel with a brazen display of his second-hand knowledge.

"How do you know?" asked Singer.

"Because Dan Parrish told me. The Assegais are a ferocious African tribe. They specialize in spears and surprise attacks. They sound like a very humorless bunch to me. Not the sort you'd invite to a Sunday brunch." He casually sauntered to Electra's side. "Tell me, darling, have you ever used a blowgun?"

"It's solely a man's weapon. Only Dan uses it in the act. It is traditional. African women do not use weapons other than their femininity. African women are docile and domesticated. Child-bearing machines. I have no respect for them."

"You didn't by any chance wander into my dressing room and place it on my table?"

"No, Mr. Coward. I have no reason to do that just as I had no reason to kill Edna Dore. I don't think she and I exchanged half a dozen words since we began rehearsing."

Singer said, "Noel, I'm the investigating officer around here."

"Dear Jacob, do forgive me. It's my director's instinct. I do tend to take over, usually where I'm least appreciated. But actually Jacob, trying to incriminate me was terribly stupid of the murderer. Tell them, Jeff, I couldn't murder a soul."

"He has wanted to," said Jeff, "but so far he hasn't."

"A rather backhanded testimonial, but it'll have to do."

The coroner arrived with his pall bearer's mien followed by two assistants, one carrying a rolled-up stretcher. "Hi Jake," he said in a deceptive basso profundo, "where's the body?"

"In her dressing room," said Noel, "resting."

Abel said, "I'll show you where it is."

"There's a dart in her neck?" the coroner asked Singer.

"You can't miss it."

"And obviously it didn't miss her," said the coroner. "A dart, and probably poisoned too."

Wang finally spoke up. "I'd look for potassium chloride."

"You would?" asked the coroner, wondering where the Oriental came from. Still, this was a nightclub in New York City, where you can expect anything to show up.

Wang explained to Singer and Noel, "It's a rare poison, Africa is its origin. It kills instantly, simulating a heart attack and not easy to detect."

"Like cyanide."

"Oh, vastly different," said the coroner. "Cyanide's a bitch. You can't smell it. You can't find it unless you're sure that's what you're looking for. That's what you want to use when you want to poison somebody." He addressed that piece of advice to everyone in general. Noel was imagining an imminent outbreak of cyanide poisonings.

"Doc," said Singer, "I'd like to have the dart when you remove it, carefully wrapped so we can test for prints."

The coroner nodded and he and his entourage followed Abel to Edna's dressing room. Jacob confronted Dan and Electra. "I'd like the rest of your stash of darts."

"We don't have any," said Dan.

"I could order your dressing room searched," threatened Singer.

"Go right ahead. We don't use any darts in the act. When I lift the blowgun to my lips, I simulate the act of blowing a dart. The dancer I'm aiming at times it perfectly and falls writhing to the floor."

"He's telling you the truth," said Electra. "We frown on the use of darts and deadly weapons in our act."

"Oh dear." Mr. Coward again.

"What?" asked Singer, amused by Noel's expression of disbelief.

"Well, my dears," he said to Electra and Dan, "you don't enchant those heads from the chickens. You lop them off with a machete, or whatever you call those deadly things. And if that isn't a deadly weapon, then I'm the son of Alice B. Toklas." Having said the name, he realized there were probably few people present who had ever heard of Alice B. Toklas. He crossed to Jacob and asked as he took the blowgun from the detective's hand, "May I? Just for a moment?" He examined the mouthpiece, murmured "Hmmm," and then handed the weapon back to Singer.

Singer was curious. "What's on your mind, Noel?"

"So many things, dear Jacob, so many many things, it may take me hours, perhaps days to sort them out." He saw Bizet sitting on the stairs down which the showgirls were meant to parade, holding his head in his hands. "My dear Mr. Weasel, what's troubling you besides the prospect of the police's investigation?"

"I don't feel so hot, Noel. I really mean it. I think I've got a fever."

Noel felt Bizet's forehead with the palm of his hand. "Good heavens! You most certainly have a fever or a reasonable facsimile. We'd better summon the coroner."

Bizet's head shot up with an incredible look of fear on his face. "I ain't dead, for crying out loud, all I got is a fever!"

"Doctor Livingstone's very last words before he expired." Noel asked Jeffrey sotto voce, "That is what got Livingstone, wasn't it?"

"That or a lack of donations." Jeff was wondering how some day in the future Noel would profit from this experience. A play? A film? An operetta? *Murder in Three-Quarter Time* perhaps.

Noel had Singer's attention. "Jacob, this dapper little thing here has a fever. He needs looking after." As an afterthought, "He does dress tastefully. I must get the address of his tailor. If he survives."

Still sobbing, Hattie arrived followed by Trixie, Angie, and Beethoven. The girls' eyes were red-rimmed and Beethoven was patting Trixie on the back with sympathy and affection. Trixie said between hiccups, "Cut it out, Harry. I feel like burping."

Noel took one of Hattie's hands and said, "Grandma Sadie sure knows her onions."

Hattie sniffled and said in a cracked voice, "This is only the beginning." Vivaldi was now onstage and sitting with an arm around the Weasel. "You mark my Grandma Sadie's words. There's gonna be an awful lot of them."

To a perplexed Jeff he explained, "She means she expects there to be an impressive body count in the near future. A proliferation of corpses. Undoubtedly dropping about like ripe fruit from a tree. In the dear sweet words of King Lear, 'Ripeness is all.' "

They heard Diana Headman say, "Oh my God." The coroner arrived followed by his assistants carrying between them the stretcher on which lay Edna Dore's body covered with a blanket.

Some of her hair was visible and Diana's hand flew to her mouth. Nicholas Benson, having phoned in his scoop to the *Daily News*, was making notes of the tragic event. He had already cursed himself for not owning a candid camera and was sure the newspaper's photographer wouldn't arrive in time to get some shots of the body being removed. He didn't know the club's press agent had swiftly notified all the local papers and news services and right now there was a small army of reporters and photographers laying siege to the stage door, being held back by several patrolmen sent to accompany the coroner.

The coroner was saying to Singer, "I'll get to her right away."

"I appreciate that."

"Now why would anyone want to murder a beauty like this? What a rotten shame."

Trixie Bates overheard him while delicately moving to one side to scratch her crotch. "They don't make them like Edna no more." Then she turned on Beethoven. "Listen you, we got something to discuss in private. Let's go to your office."

Jacob stopped them. "I want everybody to hear this. A murder has been committed and I intend to conduct a very thorough investigation."

"Listen," interrupted Vivaldi, "I got a big show opening here next week. We're all sorry Edna's dead, but you know the old saying, 'The show must go on.' "

"Why must it go on, dear boy?" asked Noel, blowing a smoke ring past Singer's ear.

"Well, if it don't go on, Mr. Coward, you don't get paid. Nobody gets paid."

A murmur arose from the company that sounded to Jeffrey Amherst like an attack of killer locusts.

Singer was waving his arms and shouting, "Hold it! Hold it! Listen to me! People, listen to me." He had their attention. "There's no reason for a postponement or a cancellation. We'll conduct our investigation while you're rehearsing. You'll have to learn to live with us. And don't anybody make any plans to take a sudden trip out of town."

Ivan Roth, Noel's accompanist, had surfaced from his headquarters in the chorus girls' dressing room. "Mr. Singer, in case you haven't heard, there's a depression on. There's a lot of jobless. I think a lot of us are grateful to be working. I think I'm speaking for everyone when I say we'll all be sticking around."

"Dear Jacob," said Noel, "from what Dottie Parker's told me about you, I'm sure you'll conduct an exemplary investigation. Precise, swift, bloodless, and then in for the kill. And I shall give you all the assistance at my command. I deplore murderers, they have very bad manners."

Said Singer, "I wish I'd said that."

"You will." Noel concentrated on Bizet and a frightening thought struck him. He confronted Dan Parrish. "Daniel, do me a favor and have a look at Bizet the Weasel. Unless my intuition's failing me, is it possible he has the symptoms of the . . . dare I say it . . . wasting sickness?" Parrish crossed the stage to Bizet. Staring at the sick man, his eyes were like lasers. Angie Murray had brought Bizet some brandy and he was taking dainty sips. Dan returned to Noel.

"Well, Doctor Parrish, what's the prognostication?"

"Too soon to tell. He's sweating, but he always sweats. His eyelids are fluttering, but they always flutter. His skin is sallow and sickly, but it's always sallow and sickly."

"Quite a depressing inventory. Well, we're certain of one thing, whatever he's got, it's not good. Let's hope it's not contagious."

Dan Parrish joined Electra, who was leaning against the proscenium wondering why someone hadn't thought of asking the coroner for a sedative for Hattie Beavers. She also didn't like the way Hattie kept flashing her ominous looks. As though by some strange beckoning brought on by the forces of the supernatural, Hattie crossed quickly to Electra. "Woman, you tell me, you tell me now. Did you hex my Edna?"

"Oh go away." Electra's right hand moved to push Hattie aside, but the older woman caught the younger one's wrist in a viselike grip.

"I know you a voodoo priestess. I know you practice black magic in his studio." She indicated Dan with a quick toss of her head. "I warn you, woman. There's a power stronger than yours. Stronger than your black magic. Stronger than your spells and hexes."

"Let go of my wrist!"

"You know what that power is? It is the power of my great Lord

Jesus Christ working arm in arm with the power of my Grandma Sadie!" She released Electra's hand. "I'm going to church now. I'm going to pray something fierce for the deliverance of my poor Edna baby's soul." They heard Trixie screaming at Beethoven, her voice exploding from his basement office and making its way with hurricane force to the stage.

"What the hell's going on down there?" shouted Singer.

Hattie gave him her undivided attention. "It's one of my ladies. It's Miss Trixie. She has got crabs. She is cursing out the perpetrator." With one last threatening look at Electra, Hattie started for the stage door.

"Just a minute!" Singer's voice caused Hattie to freeze. "Where do you think you're going?"

Hattie thawed and confronted authority bravely. "I am going to church to say a prayer for my Miss Edna."

"You'll go when I tell you to go. Abel! Get everybody on stage. I want everybody standing where they were when Edna Dore yelled." Uneasy glances were exchanged, there was nervous coughing, then a murmur of voices followed by the shuffling of feet. The musicians took their places, the showgirls moved to their levels, but hardly with alacrity. Abel had rounded up Trixie and Beethoven and Trixie was heard to say to Beethoven, "This is worth chinchilla!" Wang went to the table he'd been sharing with Noel and Singer. Jeff started to leave the stage with Noel's accompanist, Ivan Roth.

"Hey you two! Where do you think you're going?" shouted Singer. The duo stopped in their tracks, turned and faced Singer.

Jeff said very matter-of-factly, "I arrived shortly after the murder took place. In fact, I went first to Mr. Coward's dressing room thinking that perhaps he might be resting. That's when I found the blowgun. Surely you haven't forgotten I found the blowgun."

"I haven't forgotten," replied Jacob evenly. "And *you?*"

"I was downstairs in the chorus dressing room," said Ivan.

"And what were you doing down there?"

"Waiting for the girls to come back."

Wang guffawed while wondering how he might get a piece of that action.

"You two go out front with Noel and Mr. Wang. I want everybody where I can see them."

Finally, after much hemming and hawing and shifting and reshifting everyone was seemingly in place. Noel's eyes were suspicious slits. Something was wrong. True, he hadn't been paying all that much attention to the rehearsal because he was trading Shanghai stories with Detective Wang. But when Edna screamed and began flailing her arms in the agony of her death throes, he was positive he had turned to see where the scream had originated, and in doing so, had in a few seconds caught with his eyes the entire cast of characters onstage. Something was definitely wrong, but he wasn't going to say anything about it to Singer until he was positive he had figured out what was bothering him. Singer sent Abel for the police photographer, who was waiting with the other officers at the stage door. The reporters and press photographers were clamoring for admittance but Singer was adamant about keeping them out until he was finished with the company, his suspects. While Abel went in search of the photographer, Singer asked Wang and Noel, "Does it look kosher to you?"

Wang spoke first. "Jacob, I can't be of too much help to you because I was chatting with Noel, and quite honestly I only sought out the source of the scream. When I saw Vivaldi catch the poor girl as she fell to the floor, only then did I think of looking around. And by that time, just about everyone had moved."

"Okay. Noel?"

"I'm sorry to say I'm more or less of the same, old boy." He hoped God would forgive him, but in truth, he did not yet trust his suspicions. Listening to Wang's recital, he realized that he too might have deluded himself with a wrong conclusion. When he turned to see who had screamed, he now realized that people had moved or begun to move. For instance, he wasn't too sure where Bizet had been. Or for that matter, Vivaldi and Beethoven. Then he caught himself and snapped his fingers in annoyance.

"What's bothering you, Noel?" asked Singer.

"I'm just terribly annoyed with myself. I couldn't remember where Vivaldi had been and of course it was he who was running up the stairs to see to Edna. The memory certainly does play tricks, Jacob."

"Yeah. So do murderers." Abel returned with the photographer, a chubby little man whose shoes were desperately in need of oiling.

He grinned with delight at the sight of the chorus girls and the showgirls.

"Now this is an assignment I like," the photographer said to Abel.

Singer instructed the photographer to get a wide shot of the stage to include the entire company. "Don't anybody move! Keep your positions!"

Diana said to Nicholas, "Have you any idea what this is going to accomplish?"

"I think I do. He's going to study the group photo until his eyes pop out. Then he's going to have everybody else study this photo until they spot something that's all wrong, all out of place."

"Such as?"

Nicholas shrugged, but he said nothing.

Noel said to Wang, "I'm sure when you left Shanghai you didn't expect to land in a mare's nest of intrigue and murder."

"Noel, a good cop learns never to expect anything. I did know I was coming into a plot involving white slavery and Maxine Howard's murder. And I did have a feeling that maybe one or two people might bite the dust in the line of action. And I only just got here and I haven't had enough time to size up the situation other than for the three partners and Maxine's sister and her boyfriend. They were the obvious ones and easy to pinpoint. I didn't know Edna Dore. I didn't talk to her. All I know is that she was Vivaldi's girl, and probably not his exclusive property."

"Knowing Edna, I'm sure she was into diversification. But I think that finished when she met Vivaldi. Big Ike was very good to her. I admire him for handling his grief stoically. But from the occasional way I saw him look at her, especially when she was talking to another man—and he was certainly prone to jealousy—I think he adored the girl. I'm sure Jacob told you, but if he hasn't, let me tell you. Edna Dore was working undercover for the police. Abel Graham recruited her. They'd had a fling, albeit a brief one, a fling looked back upon by both as a tender memory. It's quite simple and quite obvious why poor Edna was dispatched to the great Ziegfeld Follies in the sky. To shut her up. I think Edna knew more than she realized. She may have read Sigmund Freud, as she told me she did, but I doubt if she absorbed enough of that great scientist's writings to practice what he preached. *Très domage.* She might have had hidden literary talent. She might have written a best-seller. She might have been another Louisa May Alcott, God forbid. We'll never know. But what we do know is she's dead, very very dead. And I have the uneasy feeling that she's the first in a line of marked victims. Care for a cigarette?"

"Tell me, Noel. Are you familiar with the plays of Frederick Lonsdale?"

"Of course. He's a contemporary. We have a sort of scribbling rivalry. Why do you ask?"

"I think he really writes great dialogue."

"Oh, do you really? He hasn't had a hit since *The Last of Mrs. Cheyney.*" He applied a lighter to both their cigarettes. As he exhaled a puff of smoke, Noel said, "I think Lonsdale has a great future behind him."

Nine

A WORKTABLE was brought on stage at Singer's request and four chairs were set in place: for Singer, for Abel, who would be taking notes, for Wang, and for the suspects one by one. Noel was busy talking to Vivaldi, who was worried about Bizet's worsening condition. Noel found it strange that Vivaldi's grief over Edna's death was so short-lived and said so. Vivaldi screwed up his face.

"Grief? What's grief? You mean I ain't wailing and tearing at my hair? Noel, my kind of person is conditioned to keep their emotions in check, under lock and key, squelched."

"Like a volcano." Vivaldi made a small gesture with his shoulders signifying nothing. He reminded Noel of the innumerable small part players in films who were relied on to shore up the background of crime films because of their resemblance to gangsters of ethnic origins. "But in time volcanoes erupt. You left Edna's side quickly enough to rush down to the basement, presumably to your office."

"I'm running a club. The show must go on. I phoned our press agent. We need the publicity, and we'll get plenty of it."

"You should consider erecting a monument to Edna Dore."

"For what? For getting herself murdered? Let me tell you something, Noel, since you're so chummy with Singer. My partners and me, we ain't dummies. We wasn't born yesterday. We're pretty sure of what's been going on around here and will keep going on around here. We know why Wang is here from Shanghai. I suspected Edna was finking on us, but what the hell, there wasn't all that much for her to learn and pass on to her lover boy, Abel."

Noel arched an eyebrow. "So you knew about that, too."

Vivaldi said wearily, "I know about everything. How the hell do you think I survive? My partners and I, we were out of commission for a couple of years. Repeal almost finished us, that along with a lot of bad investments and some sweet old pals who couldn't wait to shaft us. But that time out was really a godsend. It gave us time to do some fresh thinking," he tapped his head, "for the reservoir to refill. And to look for some new connections. Well, here we are, we're back, stronger and healthier than ever."

"With a refilled reservoir and a fresh bankroll."

"Yeah. Now as to Wang, I'm sure he's one smart fortune cookie. He's got Maxine's murder to solve. It's obvious she was working under cover, and those Shanghai boys don't believe in second chances. They don't forget and they don't forgive. I know. I worked with them years ago and I never accepted an offer to visit them." He ran a finger across his throat. "I knew better and I know better now. The old days are behind me. Me and my friends, we've got new ambitions. You see this club of ours? That's only the beginning. From here we move into the Broadway thee-yater, and from there we go into the movies. There's a whole world out there for us to conquer, and by God we mean to conquer it."

"From the look of Mr. Bizet, you're going to be a bit lonely while conquering unless you get him to a doctor."

Vivaldi looked at Bizet. "Shit!" He looked around for Beethoven and saw him still dodging flak from Trixie. "Hey Harry! Over here! Quick!" Harry covered the distance from Trixie to Vivaldi like a dirigible gliding in for a landing. "We got to get the Weasel to a doctor. He looks like he's gonna croak."

Fat Harry went to Singer and said, "Listen you, the Weasel needs a doctor. He needs one fast." Singer looked to where the Weasel sat on the stairs, his head hanging forward, looking like a rag doll, Noel dabbing at the Weasel's damp forehead with a handkerchief he'd taken from the Weasel's breast pocket. "Come on, Singer, stop stalling. None of us killed Edna and you know it. We were standing

90

together on the other side of the stage. And you know we ain't leaving town. We've got to get Irving to a doctor."

Singer said, "Go ahead. But alibis or no alibis, I want to talk to the three of you, and at great length." Fat Harry hurried back to Vivaldi and the Weasel. He and Vivaldi propped the sick man up between them, one of his arms around each of their shoulders, and they half-dragged him across the stage to the stage-door exit.

Singer was finished talking to the chorus girls. They knew nothing, saw nothing, and were frightened. Likewise the musicians. Of the showgirls, he saved Trixie and Angie for the last. Wang wished he would get to Electra and Dan. Electra was Maxine's sister and Maxine was his case. He watched the Unholy Three making an exit with difficulty, Bizet having fainted and been rescued from slumping to the floor by the powerful Vivaldi. Then Wang saw Diana Headman and Nicholas Benson. He wished he could hear what they were saying to each other. It didn't look like too friendly a conversation.

What Diana was saying was, "Don't pry too closely, Nick. Stick to the story you were looking for when you first began snooping around here."

"I'm not snooping, I'm investigating. It's what I'm being paid to do. Your bosses don't seem to mind my presence, why do you all of a sudden?"

"Oh damn it, Nick, can't you see my nerve edges are exposed? This room is too big for me. I know that now. Noel's been a dear, he's been helping, he's been wonderfully supportive. He's given me every tip he knows to help me cover my flaws."

His voice softened and grew tender. "Why don't you give it up, Diana? You don't need this. You know there's no future in singing, you're very rich . . ."

She interrupted brusquely. "Very rich very rich very rich. That's all I seem to hear from anyone. Mother harps on my wealth like a broken record and now you. I'm young, I'm beautiful. I've flopped at everything I've tried. I'm an unsuccessful bride and wife, a three-time loser, and I have no intention of going for a fourth. I've tried to write. Yes I have, in Africa I tried to write. I tried a lot of things in Africa because there I had nothing but time. Time and boredom and Jim Coleridge, who made Jekyll and Hyde look like

91

Laurel and Hardy. And now this! Murder! In a few hours there'll be
newsboys shouting lurid headlines and I'll have to face my friends
and their nasty gibes." She aped the voices of members of her set
viciously. " 'Why Di darling, did you really see her killed? How too
too morbid.' 'Oh Diana, was there much blood? Did you know the
girl?' 'You certainly aren't going to continue working there, are you?
But it's all so sordid, dear.' "

"To hell with your friends," counseled Nicholas.

"I said to hell with them a long time ago. Why do you think I
married Jim and went to live in Rhodesia? You don't really think I
loved the brute, do you? But after the dismal failures of my first
marriages . . ."

"They were dismal failures because you married dismal failures."

"Oh none of your hindsight, Nick. It's unbecoming. I was only
sixteen when I married Reggie Carewe. I thought he was fun. I
thought marriage would be fun. So I learned to my despair that
marriage isn't a continuous house party. And Reggie didn't have a
bean. His father kept a tight fist on the family finances. Reggie had
to go to him with hat in hand. Poor Reggie. He was so young even
for nineteen. And then shooting himself with the hunting rifle." She
sighed. "It was his best one. My father gave it to him for a birthday
present. Dear dear Reggie. How he messed up the library.

"And then a few weeks later when I married Carter Quince. I
wasn't in love with him either."

"Nobody thought you were."

"Poor Carter. Poor dear Carter. So handsome. So vain. So stupid.
And I was still so naive. Why didn't you *tell* me he preferred men?"

"I couldn't. I thought of it, but I couldn't. I told your father."

"So *you're* the one."

"Well, I tried. I assume Linus didn't tell you."

"He told me at the funeral. He thought the knowledge would ease
my conscience. I thought it was all *my* fault Carter couldn't get it
up for me. The awful way I raged and nagged at him. The way he
flew out the bedroom window with arms outflung and that last shout
of 'Tally ho.' What an awful life I've had. Reggie . . . Carter . . . and
then Jim wasting away." Abel Graham joined them.

Nicholas asked, "Does Singer want me?"

"No," said Abel, "he wants Miss Headman."

Diana followed Abel, looking much the way Mary of Scotland might have looked when climbing the steps to the scaffold where she was to be decapitated. Noel was watching Diana and the brisk way she crossed the stage. Handsome girl, he thought, a minimum of talent and a maximum of wealth and *chutzpah*. What was so enigmatic about her? Which led him to thinking about her mother. Sweet, sad, silly Millicent. Was the true substance of the woman hidden behind a false facade? If so, what did she have to hide? What do we all have to hide, come to think of it? With me it's the love "that dare not speak its name," or risk incarceration in a British jail, much like poor dear Oscar Wilde decades ago. There are so many of us who don't dare admit to our true sexual orientation as it's against the law in dear old blighty, where fair play is presumably all.

Diana hoped she look relaxed as she crossed her legs. Singer asked the routine questions. Where were you when Edna screamed? Did you notice anything suspicious? Had you seen anyone leaving the stage during the number being rehearsed? Diana proved to be all three monkeys rolled into one—see no evil, speak no evil, hear no evil. She fascinated Wang. He was lighting a cigarette while watching her, and as she answered Singer's questions he was impressed by her clear, concise replies. She provided no information of value, unless Wang was remiss in not listening between the lines. She was not like the others, who were mostly indifferent or nervous or on at least three occasions (musicians) belligerent. As his mother would have said, she was a cool drink of water. He tried to remind himself of an old Chinese proverb, but he couldn't remember any so he concentrated on Diana's beauty.

Noel now hovered within earshot, all the while casually eyeing Nicholas Benson, who was standing with his hands in his pockets, rocking back and forth on his heels, waiting his turn to be interrogated. Just beyond him, Angie Murray sat on a chair, tightly clutching her handbag, worrying about the Weasel's illness. She wished she had paid more attention to Edna's advice and husbanded her money instead of hoping for a husband. "These bums never leave their wives for bimbos like us," Edna had advised her wisely, "so take a tip from me, Angie, open a savings account. Put the rocks he gives you into a safety deposit box, because good jewelry never depreciates. And what Anita Loos wrote in *Gentlemen Prefer Blondes* is absolutely gospel, to wit, 'Diamonds are a girl's best friend.' " Angie felt a tear rolling down her cheek.

Trixie, who'd brought a chair with her and sat next to Angie, asked with concern, "What's the matter, sweetie?"

"Aw hell. It's beginning to hit me. Edna dying like that. Gee, kid, it might have been one of us. We were standing on each side of her."

"Yeah, I already thought about that. It gave me a chill. Lucky the killer took such good aim."

"Oh, for crying out loud, Trixie." She was dabbing at her eyes with a dainty handkerchief. "I'm worried about Irving."

"Yeah, the Weasel didn't look too good when they hauled his ass out of here. I wonder what he's got." Then she winced. She certainly knew what she had and she wished Singer would get a move on so she could get back to her apartment and doctor herself.

"I hope it's nothing serious. I lose him, I lose everything."

Trixie's eyes widened. "Ain't you got no nest egg?"

"Not much of a one. And if Irving goes, it ain't gonna be easy finding another john like him. There's a depression on."

"Yeah, well, that's true, but there's an awful lot of hungry hoods in this town with plenty of moola. You're still in your twenties . . ."

"And how long will that last?"

"For as long as you learn to lie gracefully. My mother was twenty-eight until I was nineteen years old. And she'd still be twenty-eight if that cement mixer hadn't crushed her. Poor Mom. What a mess."

"That Headman broad's one cool customer," observed Angie.

"I wonder if she's really all that rich, Anj, whaddya think?"

"I asked the Weasel a couple of times, but he said he didn't know for sure so I let it go at that. But she sure dresses rich. Anj?"

"What?"

"Um, you know, every so often, from the way he sometimes looks at me, I think Big Ike has a thing for me. What do you think?"

Angie said magnanimously, "Why not? You got more meat on you than Edna and in all the right places. Why not? And what's more, though it hurts to say it, you ain't layin' on no slab in the morgue."

"Oh please, don't. It's like a sacrilege. She was our best friend."

94

Trixie watched Diana Headman leave Singer's station and stop to talk to Noel Coward.

"Well, that looked rather painless," said Noel.

"I don't think I was of much help." Diana was searching in her handbag for a cigarette. Noel smartly produced his case, a gift from the Prince of Wales, and then lit the cigarette for Diana.

"Jacob isn't looking for help. He's looking for information." He selected a cigarette for himself. "Perhaps you inadvertently supplied him with some information, possibly something useful." She looked bemused. "That's what interrogations are all about, my dear Diana." He took her arm and walked her slowly to the other side of the stage where Nicholas now paced impatiently, anxious to get to his typewriter to write his bird's-eye view of the murder. Noel continued, speaking suavely and enunciating clearly and impeccably, the trademarks he had slavishly developed to make him unique among the actors of his generation. "That's what a detective's job is all about. He asks question after question after question, all the while sifting the replies carefully to winnow one small fact, one hidden gem that would turn out to be of immeasurable value. My dear, many a murderer has been trapped by an outpouring of nouns, verbs, and adverbs without realizing he or she has released a scintilla of a hint that here indeed sitting before the inquisitor is the guilty party. Have I said anything to annoy you?"

"Do I look annoyed?" Diana looked actually as though she'd been caught with her hand in the cookie jar.

"Perhaps 'annoyed' is much too strong. Surely you've been interrogated by the police before?"

Now she was truly annoyed. "Why should I have been?"

"Forgive me if I disinter painful memories, but your mother did tell me husbands one and two were suicides. Surely that meant police inquiries."

"Yes, it did. But on both occasions I was the grieving widow, so things went easier with me."

"Why are they always grieving widows? Aren't there any widows who jump with joy, pour themselves a stiff whiskey, and fling open the windows to cry to the world 'Good riddance!' Why, I repeat, why?"

Diana laughed. "You're a cold-hearted brute."

"No I'm not. Underneath this studied sophisticated pose of mine there lies a very warm and very loving gentleman. Why, my dear Diana, just thinking of Mr. Dickens' Little Nell mushing her way to heaven can drive me to tears. I sobbed my heart out when King Kong fell from the top of the Empire State Building and crashed to his death, unloved, lonely, unmourned. Well, I loved him and mourned him. He was a hell of a lot sexier than Bruce Cabot, the improbable hero of the film."

Nicholas couldn't hear them and wondered what they were talking about. Diana caught his eye and the look on his face made her feel uncomfortable. Noel continued, "Asking questions is an art, you must believe that. That's the difference between a master journalist and your everyday journeyman reporters who have about as much imagination as a camel, one of the world's stupider animals. I know a theatrical reporter who just misses being an artist at his craft. True, he made a small name for himself, but it stays small. But ah," he clapped his hands together, "when an interrogator has done his or her homework, and asks you things about yourself that are so cleverly worded and so magically put to you, why, the most amazing things come flying out of your mouth. At least they did from mine. Jacob Singer, I am told by people whose opinions I value and respect, is a master at the art of interrogation. And I'll bet you might find that inadvertently you said something you wish you hadn't."

"I hope not." The voice was small and tired.

"Cheer up, my dear. Electra Howard insists that women are just no good at handling blowguns."

"I'll bet *she* could." She dropped her cigarette to the floor and crushed it under her shoe.

"Oh dear. You say that with such damning authority."

"To my way of thinking it stands to reason, considering her background and her training. Good heavens, Noel, I'm not insinuating that it was she who murdered Edna Dore."

"Of course not, because I don't think she has a motive. Unless she ran into her at a party and they were both wearing the same dress." He stared at the chandelier overhead, the very design of which he considered an abomination, and then said to Diana, "You know, I wonder, as in so many murder mysteries one reads or sees on stage and screen, if the murderer isn't the least likely suspect."

96

"Oh, now really, Noel."

"I'm dead serious. There was a case of espionage in England a few years ago and there were several suspects. One was the headmaster of a boy's vocational school. Poor chap happened to be a midget. Well, after much huffing and puffing it was proven that this midget was indeed a master spy. He was accused of low treason, found guilty, and stretched. Hung, that is."

"You're pulling my leg."

"Not ever, dear girl, not ever."

Trixie was now sitting across from Jacob Singer and made the most of the silent attention being paid her by Abraham Wang and Abel Graham. She crossed one very shapely leg over the other and leaned forward, presumably the better to hear Singer's questions, but actually to afford her admirers a closer view of her delectable cleavage.

"You were a close friend of Edna's."

"Close enough to be her twin. Edna, Angie, and me. The Three Musketeers."

"Do you know anyone who might want Edna dead?"

"Only Mrs. Vivaldi, but she never comes around to the club. Anyway, Mr. Singer, let's not play games. Angie and me, we suspected Edna was slipping this one . . ." she jerked a thumb in Abel's direction ". . . stuff about the boys. It didn't bother us none. We ain't got stars in our eyes about the three of them, we know what they were, we know what they are, but they've been real good to us."

Singer couldn't resist. "Well you've been real good to them."

"And how. Above and beyond the call of duty. Still," she said with a diffident flip of a wrist, "I got no real training in anything useful, and when you look the way I do," Wang ran his tongue around his lips, "it's easy standing around on stage half naked and all bored, and it's even easier letting a generous john pay the bills, buy you clothes and jewelry, and take you dining and dancing at the fanciest places you never dreamed you'd ever get to visit. I got no complaints."

"Something wrong? You're fidgeting."

"I got one complaint, and if you'd finish with me, I can get home and get rid of it."

"Just a few more questions."

"Shoot."

"Did Edna ever express a fear for her life?"

"Only once, when she was afraid Big Ike might know she was kadoodling around with this one," again another eloquent jerking of her thumb toward Abel, who blushed charmingly.

"Do you think Vivaldi suspected Edna was feeding us information on him and his partners?"

"Big Ike suspects everything. He trusts very few people. Not even Fat Harry and the Weasel. Well, maybe the Weasel a little bit. Ah, why not? They really love each other. I hope the Weasel's okay."

Behind them, Mickey DuVane, the dance director, was pacing nervously. He'd been phoning around looking for a replacement for Edna Dore, but the word was already around town that there was a murderer on the loose at The Cascades. Nancy Adman was hoping the replacement would be able to fit into Edna's costumes, except of course the blood-spattered one, and that was barely a costume. She watched as Angie Murray replaced Trixie Bates at Singer's table. Those poor bitches, she thought. Such a short career span. They're fine until their behinds sink and their tits sag and then it's off to some department store to sell lingerie or perfumes if they're lucky enough to snare the jobs, especially in these Depression days. Thank God her mother had taught her how to design a dress, cut the pattern, and then stitch it together. Her mother continually reminded her, you'll always make a living if you keep people in stitches.

"What's with that sigh?" asked Mickey DuVane.

"What sigh?" asked Nancy.

"The sigh you just sighed. Like you just thought of something sad."

"Well, actually, I was thinking of my mother. And how grateful I am to her for teaching me how to be a costumer. We don't have to worry about aging, like the showgirls do. That's what I was thinking."

"Crazy," said Mickey, shaking his head and walking away, "real crazy."

Angie was being about as much help to Singer as Trixie was, but he kept firing questions at her, hoping that something of value might come popping out of her mouth. But she did nothing but express concern and worry over Bizet's health. Wang wasn't completely happy with Singer's line of questioning. Although he realized unveiling Edna Dore's murderer was his chief concern, he wished here and there he might have slipped in a subtle inference of the three partners' involvement in the white slavery operation. Singer soon knew he was getting nowhere with her and there would be no improvement so he dismissed her. He said to Wang and Abel, "Who've we got left?"

"Nicholas Benton, Electra Howard, Dan Parrish, and the three big shots."

A familiar voice said, "And Noel Coward."

Ten

■▐⚏⚏▌■

NOEL looked prepared to joust with the ever-present cigarette holder. The cigarette was freshly lit. "I have some significant
observations to make about the murder and scene of the crime, in
the center of which we are holding our discussion." He sat opposite
Singer and looked at his wristwatch. "Four o'clock. Time for tea.
Well really, Jacob, the least you could do is provide tiffin or else
sherry and biscuits."

"Noel, this isn't a garden party. It's a police investigation."

"Have you gotten any results? I'm sure you got nothing from
Mickey DuVane and Nancy Adman. Likewise little from Diana
Headman. Trixie and Angie? *Quién sabe?*" He said with a smile to
Wang, "That's Spanish for 'who knows.'"

"I know," said Wang. "I graduated Columbia University. I speak
seven languages fluently."

"So much for my arrogance," said Noel. "Forgive me. I consider
my wrist slapped. Now then, Jacob, still you're not asking me any
questions . . ."

"You're not a suspect."

"Even though Jeff found the blowgun in my dressing room?"

"We don't know that for sure, do we? Did anyone see him find
it in your dressing room? He just came carrying it onstage and
claiming he found it there."

"Now really, Jacob. On the rare occasion Jeff lies, his ears wiggle, and when he brought us the blowgun his ears were on their most perfect behavior."

"You didn't kill Edna Dore because you were sitting right here with us."

"Indeed? All the time?"

"Sure, all the time."

"Jacob, after Nicholas Benson finished interviewing me, and I'm being polite calling it that, I sat with you and Abraham. But my chair was actually behind yours because with Abel also at the table and the three of you hogging the space with your chairs placed so you could watch the 'Shadow Waltz' number on stage, there was no room for me except behind the three of you. So frankly, Jacob, I could have crept off as quiet as a mouse and made my way backstage through a side door, and I assure you there were no witnesses who could have seen me because that side of the room is always inadequately lighted and I have two bruised shins to prove it."

"Noel? Are you confessing to the crime?"

"No, Jacob, I am not. But I'm trying to enlighten you as to something I'm sure you know all about, and that is, things ain't what they seem to be, especially in retrospect. Isn't that the reason why you had the photographer take a panoramic shot of everyone who was onstage at the time of the murder so you could have a reference as to who was where when the murder happened? But how accurate is it, Jacob?"

"Accurate enough."

"I challenge that and I'll tell you why. All involved stood where they thought they stood. But in all the confusion of the murder with people running about and flying this way and that, who could accurately remember where they were when the dart hit Edna? I can vouch for the four of us because I was right behind you. But quite frankly, had I been onstage rather than here with you, I'd be hard put to remember exactly where I was standing. And I'm going to tell you something else that I want you to mull over in that most excellent mind of yours. I remember my eyes sweeping the stage when Edna screamed and I was looking for the source of the scream. Well, my eyes darted all over the place until they zoomed in on Edna

101

keeling over. I saw Abel arriving in time to see Vivaldi catch her. Then I remember Vivaldi dashing off stage right, to his office to phone his press agent, he later told me. I remember seeing members of the company crowding around Edna. Jacob, when you had the entire company restage that moment, I knew at once that the placement of someone in that photo was all wrong. There was something terribly wrong with that tableau. I know someone put themselves where they shouldn't have been." A thought struck him and he snapped his fingers. "Or possibly someone put themselves there, *when they hadn't been there at all in the first place!*" He sat back, folded his arms, and crossed his legs with a triumphant look.

"Bravo," said Wang.

"All kudos gratefully accepted," acknowledged Noel. "Well, Jacob, what do you think?"

"I'm not saying you couldn't be right and I'm not saying you couldn't be wrong. But you're an awful lot of fun to listen to."

Noel unfolded his arms, uncrossed his legs, leaned forward, and said, "I'm looking forward to seeing that photograph. I hope it won't be out of focus."

"My boy shoots a very good picture. When it's developed and printed, we'll take a look at it together. By the way, what were you looking for when you examined the mouth of the blowgun?"

"I was looking for a trace of lipstick. There wasn't any."

"Good thinking. Despite Electra telling us women don't use a blowgun."

"Electra may be an authority, but she's hardly the last word. There are those who claim women are inferior archers, which causes me to jog their memories by reminding them of the tribe of women warriors known as the Amazons. According to legend, they were brilliant markswomen."

Nicholas Benson interrupted them. "Could you possibly quiz me next so I could get back to my typewriter?"

"Sure. I'm very fond of volunteers. Noel, anything else on your mind?"

"Give me time, dear boy, give me time." He surrendered his chair to Nicholas and strolled to the piano, where he sat and softly played some of his own compositions. As Singer questioned Nicholas, Wang was delighted by the melodic accompaniment. There'd been nothing like that in Shanghai.

With "I'll See You Again" dominating the background, Singer asked, "How well did you know Edna Dore?"

"Well enough to flirt a bit. She had an active libido, or so I assumed."

"Did you score?"

"No. I wasn't really trying to. I wasn't interested in provoking Big Ike."

"You're an old friend of the Headman family, right?"

"Very old friend. Our parents were close friends. It was assumed that Diana and I would marry. But we didn't."

"Weren't you in love with each other?"

"We were in love with the idea of being in love with each other. It was F. Scott Fitzgerald time and most of us wanted to emulate Scott and Zelda. It didn't work for Diana and me because Diana gave us no time. She wanted free of her mother and father and so got married at sixteen. That was a sad mistake ending in her husband's suicide. Same with the second husband."

Noel was beautifully interpreting "Zeguener." Abel Graham was thinking that it was hardly a fitting accompaniment to a murder investigation, but what the hell, it was original. Standing at the piano, Electra and Dan Parrish were inspired to start improvising a dance. Noel was delighted. Singer was ready to call a halt to the impromptu exhibition but could see Wang and Abel were entranced by it. Christ, he thought, interrogation by Singer, musical interlude by Noel Coward, terpsichorean embellishment by Electra Howard and Daniel Parrish.

Singer asked Nicholas, "And husband number three wasted away in Rhodesia?" He added somewhat pompously, "How so like Hemingway."

"Which Hemingway?"

"Any Hemingway."

"Something seems to be escaping me," said Nicholas while lighting a cigarette. "Why all this interest in Diana? It's Edna who was murdered."

"I wasn't happy with her when I cross-examined her. I thought

103

I was interviewing flesh and blood, but what I ended up with was the Snow Queen. She's way out of place in a joint like this."

Nicholas advised staunchly, "Diana isn't the murdering type."

"What's a murdering type?"

Nicholas was patently uncomfortable. "You know. Someone who could kill."

"Everybody could kill," said Singer flatly. "And still waters run deep."

Nancy Adman, passing by, heard him and added, "And a stitch in time saves nine." She was carrying an armload of costumes to the dressing rooms.

Singer reminded himself aloud for Abel to hear, "We didn't question her or the dance director. Although I'm sure they've got nothing to tell us."

"You never can tell," cautioned Wang. He had some questions of his own to ask people and was plotting how to find the opportunity to get them alone. Singer had returned his attention to Nicholas.

"You were with Miss Headman when the dart struck Edna Dore, right?"

"No, I was out front interviewing Noel."

"Oh no," countered Singer. "I remember you were finished and headed back to the stage just before Edna screamed."

Noel had segued into the romanticism of "Someday I'll Find You," possibly, thought Abel, as a subtle reminder to Singer that he had a murderer to catch. Daniel and Electra were doing a series of exquisite lifts while Noel was entertaining the possibility of creating a musical about Cleopatra for Electra to star in. He wondered if she sang. What nonsense, of course she sang, all black women seemed to be blessed with lovely voices.

Nicholas looked perplexed. "Now you have me baffled. When we grouped for the photograph . . ."

"You placed yourself next to Diana Headman."

"I did?"

"You did." Singer had a trace of a smile on his face. Here it was, Noel's theory being proven. Who really remembers where they were and what they were doing at a given moment when asked to re-create the scene?

"Was Edna feeding you tips?"

Nicholas rubbed his chin. "I suppose you could say that."

"I didn't say it. I asked."

Vivaldi and Beethoven had returned and Vivaldi, observing Noel playing the piano and the two black performers executing a perfect arabesque, asked Beethoven, "Ain't that classy? It's new. I ain't seen it before. Hey Noel!"

The performance ceased. Electra left Dan and walked away. Noel said, in a voice that was appropriately chilled, "Yes, Mr. Vivaldi."

"I like the routine, I like it, I like it. Let's keep it in."

Noel arose from the piano. "We were improvising out of boredom and for our own amusement. And what's more, I am not an accompanist, I am a star. You're certainly well aware of this by now."

"Sure, Noel, sure. But it looked real good."

Beethoven was watching Singer and Nicholas. He said to Nancy Adman, who was on her way back from the dressing room, "The detective learning anything?"

"Don't ask me, ask him." She continued on her way without breaking step.

Noel asked Vivaldi, "Where's Bizet? Where did you leave him?"

"He's in a private suite at Roosevelt Hospital. I got my doctor looking after him. He's going to do tests. Frankly, he's baffled. He's seen nothing like it before. The high fever, the sweats, the dehydration."

"Dehydration?"

"That's right. It's like maybe he didn't drink any water for days."

Noel caught Dan Parrish's eye and he suspected that Parrish now recognized the symptoms of the wasting disease.

Beethoven asked of Noel and Dan, "Where's the girls? Where'd they disappear to?"

Noel said, "After being questioned, I gather they repaired somewhere for repairs. Probably Trixie's place as Trixie was desperately in need of repairs." Beethoven glowered and started to cross the stage.

Singer said to Abel, "Tell those two to stand by for questioning." Abel caught up with Beethoven, who continued glowering, and then buttonholed Vivaldi. Vivaldi reached into a pocket for a cigar, bit off one end, and placed it in his mouth. Noel offered his lighter but Vivaldi preferred a kitchen match, a number of which he carried on

105

his person. Noel admired the way Vivaldi lifted his right leg and ignited the match by drawing it quickly across the seat of his trousers.

"What a marvelous trick," said Noel in genuine admiration. "I wonder if I'd dare do a thing like that onstage." He thought about it. "Actually, I suppose not. Noel Coward uses a cigarette lighter, otherwise he's Edward G. Robinson and that will never do."

Nicholas had told Singer that what might have passed for tips from Edna were useless to him. Singer summed it up, "So you had no cause to want to kill Edna."

"You mean she might have given me a bum steer and so I decided to kill her?" Nicholas found that funny. "I think the only one who might kill for a bum steer is a rancher. Anyway, I couldn't have killed Edna. There was no time. I was on the floor interviewing Noel and then . . ."

"I know, I know," said Singer, cutting Nicholas dead and wondering if he was any nearer to a clue as to the killer's identity. He announced to Wang and Abel, "Let's re-create the murder. Let's figure out where the killer had to stand in order to get a proper bead on Edna."

"What's happening?" asked Noel, in lieu of stifling a yawn.

"I'm re-creating the crime. I want to figure out where the killer stood and why he wasn't seen."

"Or why *she* wasn't seen."

"You still think one of our ladies might have done it, eh Hawkshaw?"

"Not really, but I'm a feminist. My mother, in her time, fought for women's rights and, knowing Mother, probably still does. Poor Father."

Singer couldn't resist asking, "Noel, how'd you like to stand in for Edna?"

Noel looked like a clever lizard. "I'd be delighted." Very precisely and expertly mimicking a showgirl's strut, arms outstretched, hands making little circles, Noel made his way to what had been Edna's level. Singer, Wang, and Abel went behind the masking curtain that hung behind the orchestra. The area contained a stepladder, some chairs, and a worktable and left little room for much physical action. Abel was examining the floor. "No footprints."

106

"No kidding," said Singer. "This ain't a flower bed."

They heard Wang say, "The killer struck from here." Singer and Abel hadn't noticed a hidden flight of stairs that led to a platform above them on which were placed several spotlights. They joined Wang and the three of them had a perfect view of Noel. "Why didn't the killer leave the blowgun here instead of risking carrying it to Noel's dressing room?"

"Just plain mean, that's why. Noel's dressing room is only a few feet beyond the bottom of the stairs. It must have seemed like a fun idea." He shouted, "Okay Noel, you did just fine!"

Noel lowered his arms and raised his voice. "Do I get the job?"

Jeffrey Amherst arrived followed by Herbie the bartender from the Hell's Bells bar across the street. Herbie carried a tray that held a large pot of tea, a big thermos of hot water, a saucer of sliced lemons, a gravy boat filled with milk, a cup of sugar, and a plate of biscuits. Jeff carried a tray that supported cups and saucers and silverware, plus a plate covered with thinly sliced buttered bread and a jar of strawberry jam. At the sight of them, Noel made an elaborate fuss usually reserved for a returning hero. "Oh Jeffrey, dear boy, you *are* a treasure. And Herbie, how kind of you to assist him."

"It's a pleasure No-ell. How about this spread?" Noel ordered Abel and Wang to push two tables together and then supervised the transfers from the tray to the tabletops. He fussed about like an old maid aunt presiding at a family reunion and was clearly in his element. "Now Jacob," he cautioned with a wicked glint in his eye, "no slurping tea from the saucer."

Vivaldi said to Beethoven, "Welcome to the nut house. I'll get the brandy. It'll give me a chance to phone the hospital."

In the Weasel's private suite at Roosevelt Hospital, Angie Murray, whom the Weasel had had a nurse summon to his bedside, was spraying an atomizer. "This'll cool you, Irving, it's essence of lemon." The nurse, a thirty-year veteran of the hospital wars, wrinkled her nose in distaste. "I hope it's making you feel better, Irving."

He said weakly, "I don't smell nothing. I can't smell. I can't taste.

My eyes hurt and my ears tingle. Oh mother of God, is this the end of Irving?"

Angie placed the atomizer on a night table and sat on the edge of the bed, holding one of the Weasel's feverish hands. "Don't talk like that, Weasel."

Weasel! The nurse's eyebrows shot up and might have hit the ceiling were they not firmly attached to her anatomy.

"I asked the doctor and he says these kinds of weird fevers could break unexpectedly and you'll be fine again." Angie looked to the nurse for confirmation.

"Of course you will, Mr. Bizet." There was nothing but doom in her tone of voice. She knew a croaker when she saw one and this one was a croaker.

"Angie," asked the Weasel, "they find Edna's killer?"

This case is a lulu, thought the nurse. A weasel and a murder and heaven knows what else to titillate an angel of mercy who was thoroughly merciless.

"Not yet. They been questioning everybody in the company." She noticed the nurse through the corner of her eye and she looked like a bird dog on the verge of pointing. "I can't think of who would want to kill poor Edna. She never did nobody no harm."

"She had a big mouth," wheezed the Weasel.

"Irving," pleaded Angie, "Irving, you didn't kill her with the blowgun, did you?"

Blowgun! The nurse was enthralled. She had seen Johnny Weissmuller and Maureen O'Sullivan attacked by a tribe of pygmies with blowguns in *Tarzan, the Apeman* a couple of years back and hadn't been able to sleep for days.

"You silly twat, I was on the verge of collapse. Oh dear God, have mercy on me, I feel like I'm drowning. Like I'm floating away someplace. Like I ain't got no legs anymore. Angie, look under the blanket. See if my legs are still there."

Angie took a good look under the blanket. "Everything's just where it should be. Everything."

"Nurse . . . nurse . . ."

"I'm right here, Wea . . . Mr. Bizet."

"Where's the doctor? I want the doctor."

"He said he'd be back at six. It's almost that now." She said to

Angie, "I think you'd better leave. I've given him a sedative and it sounds like it's beginning to take effect."

Weakly, the Weasel protested, "Don't leave me, Angie. Stay with me, baby."

"Your wife is on her way, Mr. Bizet."

"Beat it, Angie!"

Eleven

MEANWHILE, back at The Cascades, the tea party was over and the remnants cleared away, and Vivaldi was in the hot seat at Singer's table protesting hotly. "Get this straight! I loved Edna but I wasn't in love with her, there's a big difference. Right, Noel?"

Noel said with a haughty sniff, "I wasn't in love with her either. But you're absolutely dead on, there's an absolute difference between loving a person and being in love with them. I should know. I'm an authority. I have the scars to prove it."

"Why would I want to kill my girl? There ain't many Ednas out there available to a guy like me. Anyway, I was with Fat Harry and the Weasel when she got it in the neck."

"You could have arranged for someone else to kill her."

"That's a fucking lie!" Vivaldi leapt to his feet, his face blazing red, fists clenched and ready to strike.

Beethoven said, "Cool it, Ike. He's only needling you."

"Make some distance between us and you, Harry. I'll be getting to you soon." When Singer loathed, he loathed with a vengeance. And he loathed these men. He didn't think they were the witless clowns as portrayed in certain gangster comedy films. There was nothing funny about professional gunmen. He'd been after the Unholy Three for years, patiently waiting for the break he needed to finger them. He knew they hated him. Jacob also knew that they had instigated and engineered several of the past attempts on his life. He wished Bizet was here, because Bizet was truly terrified of him and he loved watching Bizet suffer in his presence. On the other hand, thought Singer, if he's dying, that's better yet.

Vivaldi sat down slowly, his eyes no longer masking his hatred of Singer. He said in a hoarse voice, "I don't need no hired killers."

"That's good to know," said Singer. Wang relaxed. He thought Vivaldi was going to attack Singer. Wang had a black belt, he was a champion, and he would have made short work of Big Ike. Abel relaxed the hand that had flown to the gun in his holster under his jacket. He was a crack shot and it would have pleased him no end to have maintained killing Big Ike was in the line of duty.

Singer continued his usual line of questioning. "Do you know if Edna had any enemies? We know you know she was a police informant. It didn't bother you?"

"There was nothing to inform," said Vivaldi, lighting a cigar.

The questioning continued for another few minutes, Wang growing more impatient with Singer's apparent reluctance to touch on the white slave trade.

Fat Harry Beethoven wasn't much help either. Singer dismissed him after only a few minutes. Electra was next. It had been a long and tiring day for her, but she looked as fresh and vibrant as she had when arriving eight hours earlier. When he returned to Shanghai, Wang would wax poetic about her. "She has a haunting, sultry voice that promises to legalize the forbidden." Now, studying her magnificent face, Wang thought of Maxine after she'd been fished out of the river and suppressed a shudder.

Again the routine questions and again the routine answers. Noel had been content to remain in the background since partaking of the highly satisfying and refreshing tea, but now he was itching to stick his oar in. Singer saw that Noel was fraught with anxiety and said, "Noel, stop hopping around like a Mexican jumping bean. What's on your mind?"

"The blowgun!" he exploded. "Electra, why can't women use a blowgun?"

"I didn't say they couldn't. I said that by custom they don't."

Noel wasn't satisfied. "Have you tried to use a blowgun?"

111

Her eyes were slits. "There isn't anything I haven't tried, Mr. Coward. But in the case of blowguns, I'm very choosy about what I put in my mouth. And in the case of Edna Dore, I didn't kill her because I had no reason to kill her." She said to Singer and Wang, "Unless the two of you think she was in some way connected to my sister's murder. If she knew what was going on with this white slaving, then I'd want her alive where I could ask her a lot of important questions. Like who are the operators? Where are they operating from? Who bankrolls them? Who gave the orders to snuff her? A lot of questions and I mean to get a lot of answers. Any more questions, Mr. Singer?"

"Did you see anyone leave the stage a few minutes before Edna was killed?"

"I didn't notice anything. I was busy talking to my partner. That's right, isn't it, Dan?"

"That's right, sweetheart."

Singer said, "So the two of you cancel each other out."

Noel was mesmerised by Electra. Her eyes were two flashing danger signals. Her ten fingers as she opened and closed her fists looked like a lethal set of miniature daggers. At any moment he expected deadly flames to shoot from her mouth and render all adversaries into smoking piles of ashes.

"Anything else?" Electra asked Singer.

"Oh, an awful lot, but not right now. I'm too tired."

Noel said blithely, "You might try casting a spell that would cause the killer to come forward and confess."

Electra awarded him one of her rare smiles. "Mr. Coward, you're cute."

"My dear Electra, I am but a simple traveling player with a talent to amuse. You, my dear girl, are rather magnificent." He espied Mickey DuVane. "Mickey! Rehearsals tomorrow at ten, as usual?"

"Ten on the nose, Noel. I finally found a tootsie to replace Edna and she'll have to learn all the routines."

"How tiresome."

Five minutes later, at a table in the Hell's Bells bar, Singer asked Noel, while Wang and Abel gave Harry the bartender their orders, "Noel, have you ever been threatened?"

Noel said, while lighting the ever-needed cigarette, "I've never

112

known anyone with the vocabulary for a threat." He added smugly, "I am loved by everyone, including people to whom I haven't been properly introduced. I truly have a great gift for friendship and I treasure it. A man without friends is like a city without suburbs. Now then, Mr. Singer and associates, when do you begin to bear down on the Unholy Three?"

"From the bulletins from Roosevelt Hospital, they may soon be the Unholy Two."

"I assume you get your information directly."

"We have informants everywhere." Harry was placing the drinks on the table. "Don't we, Harry?"

Harry said to Noel, "They even got them in private terlets."

"That presents an odious picture." He sipped his dry martini. He said to Singer, "Jacob, do you really believe a spell could be cast over a person?" He looked at the others. "Gentlemen? And I call you that advisedly."

"Like Coleridge?" asked Singer.

"And the Weasel," reminded Noel.

Singer said, "I once read an article on voodoo. This article claimed voodoo wasn't black magic, but a religion. Like Santeria, which is practiced mostly in the Caribbean and Latin America. And there's *obeah*, another cousin to voodoo. There are several varieties. When I was in Haiti a couple of years ago, I was taken to see a zombie. He lived with his mother and wife in a shack near a swamp. At first I thought it was a put-up job, something to amuse the tourists. The guy sat on a chair, stripped to the waist, his hands held stiffly at his sides. His eyes were lifeless. He responded to nothing.

"My guide told me he'd died over a year ago. The mother wanted him buried at a crossroads, right in the center where two roads crisscross, to prevent him from rising from the dead."

"Really?" Noel was fascinated. "Does Haiti have enough crossroads?"

"It hasn't got that many zombies. The way the story goes, the wife was a Catholic and insisted he be buried in the church graveyard. The mother fretted, the son having died of what could have been a wasting sickness. The mother insisted a spell had been cast on her son by a voodoo priest who wanted to possess her daughter-in-law. You know, he had the hots for her."

113

"How quaint." Noel blew a smoke ring.

"So the wife overruled her mother-in-law, the husband was given a proper Christian burial, and a couple of days later, during a driving tropical storm with all the right sound effects made by thunder and lightning, the husband came walking stiffly down the dirt road to his mother's house."

"And didn't this frighten the hell out of them?"

"Oh sure, Noel. But then they settled down and accepted him back."

"I see. It's so nice to have a man around the house, no matter what condition he's in. I wonder where this left the priest who was hot for the wife, as you so daintily put it. Tell me, Jacob, when a person is dead, and I assume the zombies are the walking dead, don't the bodies rot?"

"I guess not," said Jacob, taking a swig of his bourbon neat.

Noel sniffed the air, a habit of his when harboring a doubt or a suspicion. "I should think he presents a rather annoying hygienic problem."

"His grave was investigated by the police, brought in by the neighbors who didn't take too kindly to a stiff parading around the neighborhood. He had pushed up the coffin cover and dug his way up to the ground. Or so it looked."

"I'm certainly not going to ask if you've heard if that zombie is still alive, because if he's a zombie then he should be dead and somehow I find myself thinking that he wasn't properly dead when he was buried. He might have been in a catatonic state or something like that. What do they feed a zombie? Is there some special diet like pineapple and lamb chops? I gather it's the latest fad of half the women in this country trying to lose weight."

"Zombies don't eat." The information came from Wang. "I'll tell you something interesting, Noel. It's a true story. It's been documented. In the jungles of Sumatra, the authorities learned of a plantation that was suspected of employing slave labor."

Noel's eyebrows had shot up. "In this day and age?"

Abel said, "Noel, they've found slave labor camps in our own South and Midwest."

"Unbelievable. You certainly won't find any in the Cotswolds. Go on, Wang, we're in the jungles of Sumatra."

"It took them weeks to locate this camp, but when they did, they wished they hadn't. All the slaves were zombies."

"Isn't it more likely they had been drugged? There are so many strange narcotics available in the Far East."

"The zombies were sent to attack the invaders. When the police used their guns, the bullets struck a number of the zombies and they reported none of them bled and none of them fell. Nothing affected them."

"They sound like chorus boys." He drained his glass of the martini and considered another one, but he had sent Jeff back to the apartment and had promised to join him there shortly. Herbie the bartender replaced the empty glass with a fresh martini and Noel blessed him. "So what it boils down to is, there is every possibility that voodoo spells do exist and are terribly effective."

"There's a theory that people who are susceptible to the powers of suggestion are the most likely victims of voodoo spells."

"Diana Headman's husband, Mr. Coleridge, doesn't sound as though he was noticeably weak-minded. From what I've heard about him, he strikes me as having been a man possessed of a very strong mind. On the other hand, I always thought the Weasel needed his head examined, along with other rarely used parts." His face lit up. "I say, chaps. Wouldn't it be a splendid idea to have Electra or Dan or both cast a spell over someone?"

"Who'd you have in mind?"

"No one in particular, possibly Alfred Lunt." He smiled at Wang and asked somewhat pompously, "You have heard of Alfred and his wife, Lynn Fontanne? Dear friends of mine, wonderful actors when they remember my lines."

Wang shifted in his seat. "Yes. And I've heard of Shirley Temple and Mickey Mouse and Flash Gordon in the twenty-fifth century."

"Dear Wang, I didn't mean to sound so patronizing."

"It's quite all right. Who else would you like to see spellbound?"

"Actually, Millicent Headman, Diana's mother."

"Why her?" asked Singer.

"When I first met her, I found her very anxious to be helpful, also loquaciously tiresome, and diabetically sweet. But lately, I've been dwelling on her a bit more than perhaps she deserves. It's something Maxine Howard's former employer, the private detective . . ."

"Casey Sterne," elucidated Singer.

"Yes, yes . . . that's him. Something he said. Something he dropped during your interview with him and you seem to have tossed it away in the background like an ex-lover." Singer waited while Noel stubbed out one cigarette and lit another. "Sterne told you there was a time when Maxine was assigned by him to tail Linus Headman, Millicent's husband. Weren't you curious to find out what that was all about?"

"I was very curious. But when we met, and it was a very brief meeting, I concentrated on finding out what I could about Maxine Howard and why she was in Shanghai. I subsequently phoned him in Washington to ask him what the deal was with Linus Headman." He signaled Herbie the bartender for refills for himself and Wang and Abel. Herbie acknowledged with an O formed by thumb and index finger.

"Well?" asked Noel impatiently. "Or is it privileged information?"

"Noel, you must learn to appreciate that people must be respected when they move at their own tempo. I'm not quick like you. I take my time. I'm a slow eater, as I'm sure you've noticed. I go slow because I don't want to miss anything. I pity the poor woman you may some day marry."

"Me? Marry? The one and only time I ever proposed marriage, and that was to my dear friend Gladys Calthrop, I immediately threw up my hands and pleaded temporary insanity. Now then," he snapped, "let's stop derailing our thoughts and get back to Linus. What did Millicent suspect he was up to? Another woman?"

"She suspected him of conniving to bring about his own financial downfall."

"Really?" Noel was truly amazed, as were the other two men. "But why?"

"To get the money out of the country to a safe place, out of reach of his stockholders and the creditors. This was shortly before Headman Pharmaceuticals took its final tumble."

"So the old boy was a criminal!"

"We've got a lot of them with fancy addresses."

"Did Linus succeed?"

"Casey Sterne thinks he did. Maxine thought she was onto some-

116

thing. Maxine thought Linus might have been planning to divert his funds to someplace other than the usual, the usual being Switzerland or Liechtenstein or Nassau."

"It's comforting to know the old boy harbored an occasional original thought. From what I learned about him from his wife and daughter, precious little though that was, Linus was beginning to sound like a bit of a dry stick. Anyway, don't prolong the suspense, Jacob. If he succeeded in getting the money out, where did he get it to?"

"Rhodesia." He enjoyed the look of surprise on the three faces in front of him, especially Noel's. "But don't all slap hands and play pat-a-cake right away, Casey's only surmising. When you think about it and mull it over, it makes a lot of sense, even though it can't be proved." Herbie was serving the drinks and wondering what the four conspirators, and they certainly looked like conspirators, were plotting. After years of bartending where he traded gossip and confidences, Herbie was a certifiably incurable *yenta*. But Noel was having none of him at the moment and waved him off with his stock smile of gratitude, the one where he bared his teeth and looked about to leap forward and bite.

"I'm sure you're interested in the scenario." Singer had their undivided attention. "It goes something like this and you're free to rewrite anytime you like, Noel."

"You're too generous. Get on with it, Jacob."

"Here's Linus Headman." Linus was the index finger of Jacob's right hand. Noel admired the well-manicured nail. "He knows the world is in for a financial shake-up. Don't ask me how, a lot of them rich ones had the inside information, the Vanderbilts, the Astors, the Rockefellers. They didn't jump off roofs or end up on street corners selling apples. Linus knows his company can't weather a storm. So while there's still money there and the Headman name still carries enough clout to borrow from the banks, he devises a scheme to put together a small fortune that he can shrewdly siphon off and transfer elsewhere. Then when the dust settles, and his company has gone bust and he's presumably a broken man, he can go claim all the jack he's swindled."

"I feel I really missed something by not knowing Linus," com-

117

mented Noel while flicking ash, "he sounds such a delightful scoundrel."

"So fate smiles on Linus in the person of a Rhodesian rancher, James Coleridge. James is in New York, we assume on business concerning his ranch. It's a good-sized spread, producing whatever it is Rhodesian ranches produce."

"Mostly headaches, from what I've heard." Noel crossed a leg and hoped Jeff wasn't too cross with him for being late.

"As luck would have it, daughter Diana has met Coleridge and has set her cloche for him. She brings him home for momma and poppa's approval, and from the look of James and his situation, Linus approves wholeheartedly. James, we must assume, while wooing Diana, presents the pleasant Dr. Jekyll side of his personality. Mr. Hyde only surfaces in Rhodesia, God knows why."

"It's the weather, Jacob. Beastly."

"So before long, Linus and James have agreed to become partners in the swindle. Remember, this is all supposition. I don't say I know positively this is how it happened."

"I think you're doing superbly, Jacob. Wait till Sam Goldwyn gets wind of you." He could see Abel and Wang were also impressed by Singer's well-thought-out narrative.

Singer continued. "The swindle is on and so is the romance between Coleridge and Diana. Linus more than approves; with Diana in Rhodesia, he's got someone in the family to keep an eye on Coleridge, just in case James is planning a sting of his own."

Noel apologized for interrupting. "All this despite Diana's animosity toward her father?"

"Animosities have been known to fade and wither away when the prospect of considerable financial improvements await on the horizon."

"Don't get too flowery, Jacob, I might be tempted to star you in a revival of *Merely Mary Ann*."

"Now we're in Rhodesia. They're married. And Jim turns out to be a groom of a different color. He's a mean rotten sadistic shit."

"Just like the Shubert brothers."

"Diana hates him and lets the folks back home know it. Linus gets edgy when he hears this. Now I've got some blank spaces in my scenario, which any of you boys can feel free to fill in. We jump to

118

Coleridge getting sick, the illness mysterious and quite possibly fatal. Diana cables the folks, who come running."

"Excuse me a moment, Jacob." Noel's face was a mask of confusion. "Do you think Millicent and Diana were in on the impropriety, if I may put it so delicately?"

"That's a couple of my blank spaces. I'm not sure. But I do know that Diana stood to inherit everything when Coleridge died."

"And what about her thinking of divorce?"

"I think she tabled that when he came down with the fever. Coleridge had no other survivors, I had that checked out."

"Clever boy." Singer appreciated Noel's verbal pat on the head.

"Now remember," Singer reminded them, "back in the U.S., Linus's business is in the hands of the receivers. I assume they were living on whatever Coleridge sent back to Linus whenever the old man requested it. I do think Coleridge kept the deal aboveboard. He stood to earn plenty, I'm sure. Linus must have promised him a healthy share."

"And there must have been plenty. That is, if Diana is as wealthy as we've heard she is. Do you think she's all *that* wealthy, Jacob?"

"I don't think she'll ever have to burst into tears. So now we have Linus and the wife journeying to Rhodesia to comfort their daughter in her hour of need. Coleridge is wasting away. Diana is supervising the running of the ranch. Maybe she's got her husband's power of attorney. She was playing around, I assume."

"Any proof?"

"The Rhodesian police, local small-time stuff but pretty damned astute, hint she had a dingdong with Coleridge's attorney. Also the foreman of the ranch, or one of them. If it was that big a spread there had to be more than one foreman. Keep in mind, boys, all this is hearsay and would never stand up in a court of law."

"I had no idea anyone was on trial," offered Noel smoothly.

"That's right. No one's on trial. This is just a scenario by an amateur writer. In the couple of years Diana bit the bullet and stuck it out with Coleridge, she became rapidly acclimated to life in Africa. She made friends with a lot of important ladies and they showed her the ropes of colonial life."

"Ropes Diana could easily have twisted into nooses," said Wang.

"Don't be naughty," said Noel, wagging an index finger. "Our

119

Diana is indeed a caution who has made a bit of progress in show business with a minimum of talent and a maximum of money. But as a murderer, she's not exactly the best bit of casting."

"Let me continue," pleaded Singer, "I'm almost finished. Coleridge is wasting away. The doctors are up against it. They can't deal with it. Someone tells Diana that one of the many disgruntled employees has cast a spell over Coleridge. He's doomed. Linus is going bats. Coleridge is non compos. Linus doesn't know where the money is."

"Very stupid of Linus in the first place."

"Not from Linus's point of view. He's got a paper signed by Coleridge saying he's got the money for safekeeping or for African investments, who the hell knows how he worked it out to protect himself. I suspect he steered some of the money into a private account for Millicent before he went into liquidation."

"That was decent of him, I must say." Noel brushed ash from his shirt front.

"Oh, Linus was a pretty good guy until he came up against it. So we're still in Rhodesia. And Coleridge dies. Diana now gets all the money. And Linus is yelling his head off. The money's his, but Diana doesn't give a damn what he claims. She inherited fair and square and Linus doesn't dare reveal his written agreement with Coleridge because it'll get him a vacation up the river. So, defeated, he goes home, maybe now tells Millicent the whole story if she didn't already know it, and then either conveniently dies of a heart attack or else commits suicide, you takes your choice, one from column A or one from column B. And the word is out that it was a voodoo spell what did Coleridge in.

"But that's not the end of it. A lot of people lost a lot of money when Headman Pharmaceuticals collapsed. People who put their trust in Linus because he was a close and trusted friend. Among them was a certain Ira Benson, whose son Nicholas he thought would someday marry Diana Headman and so bring together two big financial families and they'd spend happily ever after. Except Ira was wiped out and took a header off the roof of the apartment house where he lived after his wife's death."

"Good heavens!" exclaimed Noel. "All this lacks is a score by Richard Wagner." He tapped some fingers on the table. "So Nicholas might stand to profit at last if his childhood sweetheart would finally marry him."

"I don't think that's in the cards," said Singer.

Noel suggested, "Perhaps we should consult Grandma Sadie and her crystal ball."

"Noel, we know all about Grandma Sadie. She's got a record as long as a ballplayer's arm."

"How disappointing! It doesn't appear to disillusion Hattie Beavers!" Noel was preparing to leave.

But Wang spoke and riveted his attention. "When Casey Sterne assigned Maxine Howard to tail Linus Headman, what was she supposed to be looking for? Certainly not a possible sting operation by Linus. Millicent Headman had to want some other kind of information."

"You're good, Abraham, you're real good," said Singer. "Millicent sure did want some other information. Linus was fooling around behind her back, she suspected it and she wanted proof, maybe because she too had divorce on her mind and wanted to squeeze every last nickel out of the bum."

Noel clapped a hand to his forehead. "Of course! Jacob, tell me I'm right. When old fools like Linus Headman decide to fool around, they go to the most obvious display case. Broadway. The theater. Nightclubs. He found himself a showgirl. By God, he did, didn't he? And it was Edna Dore!"

"Noel," said Singer, "you go to the head of the class."

Twelve

NOEL phoned Jeff to apologize and explain why he'd be late, and Jeff was his usual agreeable self and said to take his time as he was finally catching up on *The Well of Loneliness* and finding it hilarious. The idea of a heroine with a scar running from her ear to the edge of her mouth. British lesbians, all gusto and no imagination; no wonder so many of them bred dogs and horses.

Peanuts and potato chips had now been added to the table at Hell's Bells and drinks had been freshened and conjecture reigned. Noel wondered if Millicent had told Diana about Linus's affair with Edna Dore or was too circumspect to involve her daughter.

"After all, Diana had enough black marks against her father."

"I don't think Diana would give a damn one way or another, from what I know about her," said Wang. "After all, to us Chinese, for a husband to take on any number of mistresses or a second or third wife while still married to the first is quite commonplace. Having concubines is a way of life for wealthy Chinese people. The wives teach the concubines how to sew and clean and cook and minister to the husband's every wish."

"And quite civilized too," condoned Noel. "It teaches these young ladies to be useful and it keeps them off the streets." He paused to pop a peanut in his mouth and while munching contentedly said, "Actually, it's poor Nicholas Benson who's been gnawing at my benevolent brain. Quite a nice young chap, don't you agree? Not much substance, but he's eager enough. Do you suppose he holds a grudge against the Headman survivors for what Linus did to his father?"

Said Singer, "I doubt if he's aware there was a swindle. I'm sure if Diana and her mother suspect or know there was one, their lips are sealed. A scandal is the last thing they want brought down upon their heads."

Noel wondered aloud, "Do you suppose Nicholas has ever had the occasion to use a blowgun?"

"Why would he want to kill Edna Dore?" asked Wang.

"For practice."

"Noel," Singer pronounced the name with an undertone of exaggerated patience, "nice young chaps don't go around murdering showgirls for the hell of it."

"Oh, I don't know," said Noel airily, "supposing he did know there'd been a sting and suspected some of his own father's hard-earned cash had gone into feathering Edna's love nest and that made his blood boil, causing a storm in his brain. Maybe Linus was a blabbermouth and when he formed his unholy liaison with Edna couldn't resist crowing to Benson *père*, and Benson *père*, presumably finding it either too funny for words or thoroughly disapproving, shared the dirt with his son."

After a very long silence, Abel finally spoke. "I think Edna and Nicholas liked each other. He said she'd been giving him information for his article."

"True," agreed Noel, "but surfaces can be deceiving. A frozen pond can look perfectly safe to skate across and then it suddenly collapses under you and you're floundering around on the verge of either freezing to death or drowning. Abraham Wang! You look positively fed up with the three of us."

"I'm not fed up," said Wang, "I'm wondering if I'm the only one here who suspects there might be some link between Linus Headman, James Coleridge, and the white slave operation."

"What a splendid thought," approved Noel. "Jacob? Any thoughts on the subject?"

"Lots of thoughts on the subject, but nothing concrete. Abe, I

123

know you're anxious to get down to it, but Edna Dore's murder was an unseen complication. The Weasel's fever likewise. We're positive he and his partners are in on the operation, but we need absolute ironclad proof and I admit I'm stumped."

Noel said, "I still think it would be marvelous if either Electra or Daniel could hypnotize them into confessions." Again a pause. Then, "I say, oh my, has anyone else among us considered this? If Electra suspects Vivaldi, Beethoven, and Bizet were somehow party to her sister's murder, could she have been the one who cast the spell over the Weasel?"

"I think the Weasel is suffering from a bad case of shattered nerves. He's not in the best of health to begin with. Angie told me he'd told her he'd been a small sickly child."

"Now he's a small sickly adult," said Noel. "But he certainly dresses well." He reached for another peanut and said, "I'll tell you what really puzzles me. Several things about The Cascades, other than the three partners. Why did Beethoven hire the black dancers without consulting his partners? I learned from Edna, may she rest in peace, there was a bit of kerfuffle over that. And what is Diana Headman with her thin little voice doing singing, if you can call it that, at The Cascades?"

"They've got microphones, don't they?"

"Of course they do, Jacob, but she really is not in any way a professional singer. I mean I have one of the thinnest voices in show business, and come to think of it, who wants a fat voice, which is neither here nor there, but I've learned to turn it to my advantage. I make the audience listen *harder* and I have impeccable enunciation. I don't strain for a note that's out of reach, in fact I make damn sure I don't compose them as I sing only my own songs and, when necessary, 'God Save the King.' Diana can't do it now and she never will. I know. I've been working with her. What the club needs is a belter. An Ethel Merman, a Lillian Roth, or a Sophie Tucker, may God forgive me for such an obscene thought."

"She bought the job," Singer told them.

Noel was satisfied. "Just as I suspected. Then it stands to reason she just might be a heavy investor in the club."

"I can't get the exact figures, but she's in for sure."

"Jacob." Noel had Singer's attention. "There's something else terribly strange about The Cascades. There's a kitchen staff all training under the chef and his *sous-chef*. There's the maître d' instructing the waiters and the bartenders. There's the hatcheck girls and the very competent backstage crew, in fact I'm terribly impressed by them, but there's no secretaries."

"What?" Singer was amused.

"No secretaries. No office staff. The Big Three operate from the basement conference room. I gather they're too lonely to separate into their own offices and yet they answer their own phones, do their own office chores, and I happen to find that most peculiar."

Wang nodded his head in agreement. "Very strange indeed."

"It's not so strange," said Singer. "That struck me when I first started coming around to the club. Then I reasoned it out. Less business staff, fewer people nosing around and maybe finding out things they shouldn't be finding out. It's like a lot of Broadway sharpies whose offices are in their hats and who use telephone booths. You ever notice something else about the Big Three? They sometimes use the phones in the lobby. Guess why? They're afraid of taps on their office phones."

"And are there taps on their phones?" asked Noel.

"Of course. But we haven't learned much." He looked at his wristwatch. "Well, my friends, I'm calling it a day. Abel, we've got to get back to the precinct. Wang, you staying with us?"

"I certainly am. Noel?"

"Jeffrey awaits at home. I could use an evening in. I'm terribly tired. We will-o'-the-wisps exhaust easily." Jacob had signaled Herbie the bartender to total their tab. "Dear Jacob, are the drinks on you? How kind. I feel much too exhausted to reach for my wallet."

Wang and Abel went out to the street while Singer settled the bill. "Jacob, I'm sure you understand the pecking order of crime much better then I do." He had taken Singer's arm and was walking him out of the room. "There's a likelihood of additional fatalities, isn't there?"

"Unfortunately yes."

"Who else do you think is in danger?"

"Whoever murdered Edna has got to feel there are others who pose a threat."

They paused at the exit. "I'll tell you what I think, Jacob. Everyone thinks Edna was killed because she talked too much. I think Edna was killed because of something she knew and was keeping to herself until the time or the price was right. Do I make sense?"

"I hope you do, because that's exactly my theory."

Noel brightened. "Aren't we both clever! So there's the strong probability there are others among us who share Edna's clandestine knowledge. Hmm. Marvelous name for a Scottish dynasty."

"What is?" asked Singer, ever on the alert for Noel's non-sequiturs.

"The Clan Destine. And don't groan. I rather like it."

"Noel, as Mrs. Parker said, no matter how banal you are, you never cease to delight me."

"Thank you. Tell me, Jacob, have you ever thought of writing your memoirs?"

"It's crossed my mind from time to time. Alec Woollcott has been after me for years to tell all. He's offered to work with me."

"For a healthy share of the profits, I'm sure."

"Why not? He's aces when it comes to writing about true crimes."

"Yes, I'll give him that, but little else. Who's that other highly respected local detective . . . ?"

"Johnny Broderick?"

"That's the one, yes. I'm told he's working on his book. Do you suppose he'll tell all?"

Singer's face hardened. "I wouldn't lay a bet on it. Broderick's a sadist. He uses his fists and then thinks later. He's the terror of the neighborhood."

"You thoroughly disapprove of him, I gather."

"Thoroughly."

They were now outside. Above them was a star-spangled sky and a full moon. "Oh dear," said Noel forlornly.

"What's wrong?" asked Singer.

"Up above the world so high. A full moon. That bodes ill. It's the witch's moon. There'll be mischief abroad tonight. But ah!" He pointed to the neon-lighted exterior of The Cascades across the street. "Doesn't my name look lovely in lights? I never cease to thrill at the sight of it. Some day my star will dim so you have to under-

126

stand, Jacob, I make the most of it while the most is here to be made." They joined Wang and Abel at the curb.

Wang asked, "What's it like to see your name in lights, Noel?"

"Ask Jacob. I just told him."

Jacob told him and then asked Wang, "Anything special you'd like to do tonight, Abraham?"

"I'd like to be unfaithful to my wife."

In Beethoven's office, he and Vivaldi were holding a council of war. Among other pressing matters, the state of the Weasel's health was of prime concern. "I know the Weasel's got a safe-deposit box, but where? Do you know, Harry?"

"The Dime Savings, downtown branch. What's worrying you?"

"What's in that box could be damaging to us."

"I know what's in the box, mostly. His insurance policies, his own and the wife's. His will. Jewelry, a lot of very good pieces. Some are heirlooms, handed down from his great-great-grandmother, who was the mistress of some Russian czar. And let me think, oh yeah, his diaries."

Vivaldi was about to light a cigar, but the hand holding the match froze in midair. "He keeps diaries?"

"Very meticulous."

"You ever read any of them?"

"He once read me some of it. Very childish." He laughed. "Poor Irving. If he hadn't gotten into the rackets, I don't know how he would have survived. The little punk. Don't ask me why I love him, maybe it's because when we was kids he did crazy things that none of us other kids would think of doing. Y'know, like setting fire to stray dogs and alley cats. Trapping cockroaches and then letting them loose in the bakery. Sitting on the roof with his air rifle and shooting BBs through open windows where he thought couples were screwing. And oh yeah, catching mice and then setting them loose in a crowded movie house on Saturday nights." He shook his head in awe of the memory of the Weasel's youthful peccadilloes. "Weasel was a real fun kid. I still can't figure out how he grew up to be a nervous wreck." He thought of Bizet hovering near death in the hospital. "I hope his number ain't up."

"Me too. At least not until we get our hands on his diaries."

127

"Why? You got nothing else to read?" Vivaldi's reading tastes ran to comic books, Zane Grey westerns, and *Black Mask* magazine.

"He could have written down a lot of stuff that could be incriminating to us."

"I don't know if he has or hasn't." He gave this some serious thought. "I can get the key from him."

"That's a good idea. We don't want to take any chances. Especially if that crazy wife gets her hands on that box."

Harry defended Bizet's wife. "Clara's okay. And she's not all that crazy. I mean just because she likes to dance flamingo around the house half-naked. Weasel should never have given her those castanets he got from that Spanish dancer he was screwing in Havana. Boy, she was some piece!"

"Go get the key from him."

"Now? It's after visiting hours."

"Harry. Go get the key."

"Okay, okay. I'm going, I'm going. I gotta eat something first." He reached into the bottom left hand drawer of his desk and brought out a two-pound box of chocolates.

Vivaldi exhaled cigar smoke. "Since when you been buying chocolates for yourself?"

"I don't. This box was on my desk the first day of rehearsals." He opened the box.

"Who sent them?"

Beethoven selected a sweet and consigned it to his mouth. "All the note said was something like 'This is for good luck,' something like that. Damn it! Weasel's been into the box. He's eaten most of the soft centers."

"The note wasn't signed?"

"It was signed but it was kind of squiggly. I couldn't make heads or tails of it. Shit. Caramel. Oh god, there goes my bridge."

Vivaldi reached over and replaced the lid on the box. "Someone you don't know sends you chocolates, and you eat them?"

"Why not? Weasel ate more then I did. He was with me when I found the box. You know what a mean sweet tooth he's got. And he snuck back in here and ate some more behind my back. Why' put the lid back on? I want a couple more pieces."

Vivaldi arose, picked up the box of chocolates, and said, "Come on."

"Where we going all of a sudden?"

"To the cops."

"*What?* Are you nuts?"

"I'm the only one of us three who ain't."

Noel strolled home after leaving Singer and the others. It was a brisk evening and Noel dwelt heavily on Edna Dore's murder and the cast of suspects. He ignored the possibility of danger lurking in the doorways of the dilapidated tenements and the once proud and beautiful brownstones, now fallen from grace. Boardinghouses, whorehouses, some in such dangerous states of disrepair they'd been boarded up with official signs nailed in front warning off trespassers with threats of arrest and prosecution. Noel recognized one of them as the one in which Dorothy Parker and the artist Neysa McMein lived across from each other on the second floor. How warmly they had welcomed him back to New York seven years earlier when he had returned in his revue, *This Year of Grace.* The wonderful parties they gave where love affairs were either kindled or destroyed, where friendships blossomed or withered on the vine, where promises were made solely to be broken, and where bright ambition rubbed elbows with shattered illusions.

Nineteen twenty-eight, with Mrs. Parker's wit at its sharpest. Her acid comment about German actor Conrad Veidt's wife: "She was the driving force behind his success. He got to the top by the sweat of his frau." And when told of the notorious Ivy Brandt of Teaneck, New Jersey, who'd slain her husband with poisoned mushrooms: "Poisoned mushrooms. Tsk tsk. The fickle fungus of fate." And when an unusually striking looking young woman entered with a homosexual scion of the Donahue millions, she asked "Who's the lass with the delicate heir?" Ah, those were the good old days.

Nineteen twenty-eight. His thoughts darkened. Probably when Linus Headman's sleight of underhand went into action. When the seeds of iniquity were sown that would lead to the deaths of James Coleridge, Maxine Howard, and Edna Dore. Of the three, he had known Edna Dore and rather liked her. There were no pretensions about her, and where once there had been vulgarities, she had over a period of time refined them into personable attitudes. She was the only person he'd ever known who, when she advised you to "Go screw yourself," left you with the immediate desire to get on with the suggestion. Poor Edna. A poisoned dart. How melodramatic. He wondered what her autopsy would reveal. He must phone Jacob at his precinct and ask him if the results were in, as on an election night. Jacob. The dear boy. The dear name-dropper. A solid friend. A dangerous enemy. God knows, there was no police officer resembling him back in Old Blighty.

"My dear Noel. You're talking to yourself."

He realized he had reached his apartment house on West Fifty-eighth Street, where Millicent had just paid her fare to the taxi driver now clattering off toward Fifth Avenue muttering about a chintzy five-cent tip.

Noel said affably as he led her into the lobby, "I frequently talk to myself, Millicent. It's the rare occasion when I participate in an intelligent conversation."

He pressed the elevator button. Millicent searched in her handbag for her door key. "I've just seen a dreadful film. British, I'm sorry to say."

"Why? So many of them are. So few are imported into this country. The one you saw must have escaped and found passage by stowing away."

"It had such a lovely title too. *Waltzes From Vienna*. I adore waltzing and I adore Vienna, but there was very little of either. *So* disappointing."

"Ah yes. The film was shot last year. Unfortunately, it survived." The elevator arrived. Noel followed Millicent in, both greeting the elevator operator by name. Andy. At Andy's feet there was a small stack of afternoon newspapers. Noel bought one. The headline was Edna Dore's murder. Noel stuck the newspaper under Millicent's nose. "Have you seen this?"

Millicent was fumbling in her handbag again. "I'm blind without my spectacles." They arrived at their floor.

As she stepped into the hallway, on impulse Noel suggested she join him and Jeff for a drink. She was delighted. She wasn't looking forward to another evening alone in the small apartment to which she had exiled herself. Noel unlocked the door and gestured for

130

Millicent to precede him. Delicious odors from the kitchen permeated the air and kissed their noses. Jeff was in the kitchen performing culinary wonders. "I'm home and it smells delicious. How'd you know I wanted to stay in tonight?"

Jeff shouted from the kitchen, "Whether you did or didn't, *I* wanted to stay home."

"I have Millicent with me. Is there enough for three?"

"More than. Hello, Millicent!"

She didn't reply. She was reading about Edna Dore's murder, seated in the chair that had been her husband's favorite.

Noel shouted, "She's reading the newspaper. All about the murder. Dear boy, what *are* you cooking?"

"Coq au vin. Baby potatoes in a fresh mint sauce. Shredded string beans with burnt almonds. A delicate Caesar salad, so delicate it might expire unless subtly tossed. And then a very runny Camembert with fresh fruit. A modest Chardonnay with pretensions of grandeur. I put everything you need for martinis on the bar, including ice, lemon peel, olives stuffed with pimientos, and the baby cocktail onions."

Noel was already at the bar mixing a shaker of martinis, all the while studying Millicent's face as she read the newspaper. "I'm surprised Diana didn't phone you with the news."

"She might have tried to," said Millicent in what sounded like a bad imitation of her usually perky high-pitched voice, "but I was out all afternoon. Lunch with a friend, then the movie." She folded the newspaper neatly and placed it on an end table next to her chair. She accepted the martini from Noel eagerly and he sat on a large ottoman across from her. "Will this have any effect on the club's opening?"

"None whatsoever, and I'm sorry if I sound cold and callous. But there's so much at stake if the club doesn't open."

"I understand. I'm glad for Diana. It's her big New York City opportunity."

Jeff entered with a plate of hot hors d'oeuvres. "The chicken takes a bit of doing. This should hold us until it's ready."

"Good heavens. It looks like a volcanic eruption."

"Hot chicken livers with all sorts of wondrous accompaniments on little slices of toast, just like Mother never made."

"Dear Mother," said Noel archly, "still in the asylum, do you suppose?"

"Oh, good heavens, no," said Jeff as he placed the plate atop Millicent's twin end table, "they've let her loose on the moors where she's hacking away at traveling tinkers to her heart's content."

"Oh, you two are impossible," laughed Millicent.

"It takes nonsense like this to keep us from taking life too seriously," said Jeff as he poured himself a martini.

"Now it's death we must take seriously," said Noel, who then launched into a detailed description for Millicent's benefit of the day's events at The Cascades. He didn't bother to wonder whether he was divulging too much; he wanted her to know everything. He had decided on the spur of the moment to invite her to have dinner with them, and that spur spurred him into the garrulity usually attributed to this gracious woman who was his very attentive audience.

She was more than attentive. She was deeply engrossed. She betrayed no emotion when he repeated what he knew of her husband's infidelity with Edna Dore. He wisely avoided Linus's swindle. When he told her it was suspected that Bizet was another possible victim of the wasting sickness, she murmured a weak "Oh no," and at one junction stared at their telephone and seemed about to reach for it and presumably phone her daughter. Instead, she held the glass steady as Jeff refilled it. Noel sampled Jeff's concoction and made small noises that could be construed as either purrs of pleasure or sounds of disapproval.

Jeff said, like a judge passing sentence, "Perfectly superb, right?"

"Oh, perfectly," said Noel while chewing slowly, "do try some, Millicent."

"In a moment."

"If Noel likes it," advised Jeff, "in a moment they'll be gone." He helped himself, chewed, and then said smugly, "Absolutely delicious." He retired to the kitchen to put the finishing touches on the dinner.

Millicent put her glass on the table at her right and said, "Is there a suspect?"

"There are many suspects. The entire company. Millicent, when you were in Rhodesia, did you ever see anyone use a blowgun?"

"My son-in-law, once."

"Did you try to use it?"

"Me? Whatever for?"

"Out of curiosity, perhaps."

"I have little curiosity about deadly weapons. I loathe violence."

"Did you ever meet Edna Dore?"

"No."

"I think you've seen her."

"Yes. I was curious as to what she looked like. I knew she'd be young. Very young. But I wanted to see if there was any, well, if there was any class to her. I'd seen photos of her, Mr. Sterne had been supplied with several by his assistant, Miss Howard. She was appearing in a revue and I went one matinee. I stayed just long enough to see and hear her. She had a few lines in a sketch." She sipped her drink and, after putting the glass back on the table, laced her fingers together and leaned forward. Noel was an excellent audience. "In truth, Noel, I wasn't jealous of this woman. It wasn't the first time Linus cheated. And frankly, I was very restless myself. Linus and I had grown very tired of each other. Even when I married him, I suspected he was after my family's money, but I wanted a husband very badly. I was the last one left in my bunch. Everyone else was married. At nineteen I was an old maid." She laughed. "Can you believe it?"

"Very easily. But hard to believe that a beauty like you hadn't been snatched up sooner."

"Oh, Noel, I didn't lack for opportunity. But you see, I wanted a knight in shining armor. I was a dreamer, a romantic. There was a war in Europe and I wanted to volunteer as an ambulance driver. My mother had hysterics and my father threatened me with imprisonment in the family castle on the Hudson."

"Tsk tsk, such melodramatics."

"The only other way out was marriage, and at this time Linus wasn't the likeliest candidate, he was the *only* candidate. So we were married and a year later Diana was born. Frankly, being a wife and a mother was tiresome. I wanted romance and adventure and Linus offered neither. So I contented myself with being very social and watching my husband become a millionaire and doing my damnedest to spend a lot of it. I have led a totally useless life."

133

"Don't be so hard on yourself, Millicent."

"I'm being realistic. Anyway, I wanted the Edna Dore evidence because I was contemplating a divorce and I wanted all the ammunition necessary to assure myself a big fat settlement. Little did I know there were only slim pickings left to be divided."

Noel thought, then perhaps she wasn't aware of the swindle. Or perhaps I do not give her enough credit for cleverness. "What happened to your family's fortune, or should I mind my own business?"

"It doesn't matter. It's been written about in Sunday supplements. My own money was eaten up by Linus and the business. After my father's death twenty years ago, Mother fled to Europe and a series of lovers who left her broke and broken. Poor dear. She was such a nice lady, but oh so naive. She died in a nursing home in Brooklyn."

"Brooklyn!" She might have said Devil's Island.

"She was gaga by then. It didn't matter. She went quickly."

Like Edna Dore, thought Noel. The phone rang. Noel reached for it. "Hello, Jacob. Not interrupting at all. Just having a lovely chat with Millicent Headman. She's joined us for dinner. We've been discussing Edna's murder."

Singer had sent Wang and Abel to Gallagher's Steak House on West Fifty-second Street where he planned to join them after phoning Noel. "You getting anything useful out of her?"

"Not so far. But perhaps."

"Well, I've got the autopsy report on Edna." The report was atop his desk next to a stack of memorandums. "She was poisoned by a distillation of a deadly nightshade found in tropical and subtropical climates. Potassium chloride."

"Potassium chloride? Never heard of it." He could feel Millicent's eyes boring into the back of his head.

"It's not easily detectable. Lucky for the coroner Wang tipped him to look for it in Maxine Howard's body, because he found it there, too. Which is how he recognized it in Edna. It's very deceptive. It makes it look as though the victim has suffered a heart attack."

"Bad press notices can do that too."

"I thought you'd like to know."

134

"I most certainly did want to know and I appreciate your thoughtfulness, Jacob."

"And guess who just dropped in on me a little while ago."

"Queen Marie of Rumania."

"Big Ike and Fat Harry."

"Well! The world is full of surprises!"

"They brought me a box of chocolates."

"Poisoned, I'm sure."

"That's what Vivaldi suspects."

Noel's eyes widened. "Not really!"

"Very really. It was given to Fat Harry anonymously on the first day of rehearsal. Left on his desk."

"No card attached, of course."

"There was a card. But it was illegible. Unfortunately, Fat Harry threw it away, though I doubt it had prints on it."

"How'd they suspect the chocolates were poisoned?"

"It's Vivaldi's theory and it may prove logical. The candy's being tested in the lab. According to Fat Harry, who ate only a few pieces, Bizet the Weasel gorged himself on them and Vivaldi suspects that whatever the chocolates were doctored with might explain the Weasel's so-called wasting disease."

"That is very very interesting. Tell me, Jacob, the box in which the candy was packed. Was it very elaborate in design?"

"Why? What's the box got to do with it?"

"The box might tell us if it was purchased by a man or a woman. Women go for the fancy stuff. Men usually buy their boxes of chocolates in drugstores, places like that."

"This is Fannie Farmer."

"Oh dear," said Noel in despair, "everybody purchases that brand. That's no help at all."

"But it was smart thinking, Noel. You beat me on that one."

Noel grinned. "Let me know what the lab tells you about the chocolates. Ah! Jeff is bringing our dinner to the table. If I don't hear from you tonight, I'm sure I'll see you at rehearsal tomorrow. Dear Jacob, I had no idea murder could be so much fun!"

He didn't see the expression on Millicent's face. It was fearsome.

Electra emptied the envelope onto the plate. She set the envelope aside for future use, waste not, want not. "Cuttings of his hair?" She was handed another envelope. She emptied the hair onto the plate.

"I always give him his haircuts," explained Samantha with a becoming innocence.

"An article of his clothing?"

"I brought a jock strap, is that okay?"

"As long as it's his, sister."

"It's his, all right."

Even Nicholas was impressed by the size of the athletic support. Electra laid it on the plate. "Rather large." Samantha grinned greedily. "Now then, Samantha. This is your chance to reconsider. You sure you want to bring this grief to your man?"

Her lower lip trembled. She was considering. Finally she asked, sounding like a little girl, "Will this hurt him much?"

"This will hurt him a lot."

"It won't kill him?"

"Only if he has a weak heart."

"He has a weak head. Go ahead. Go ahead, Mrs. Priestess, you go ahead!"

From under the table, Electra brought forth lighter fluid and matches. She doused the contents of the plate with the lighter fluid and then from a bowl, also found under the table, she sprinkled the plate with a white powder. She warned Samantha, "Stand back." Samantha stood back. The boa constrictor closed its eyes, fully aware of what was coming. Electra lit a match, applied it to the plate, and the white powders exploded into a red, white, and blue flame. Nicholas rather enjoyed this patriotic touch. Then the plate was engulfed; those closest to the ritual held their noses. There was a noxious odor, undoubtedly caused by the victim's undergarment. Electra held the boa constrictor high above her head. It hung limply, blasé, bored, hungry, while Electra chanted unintelligibly in singsong. There was a hideous shriek from the back of the basement as a young man leapt to his feet, grabbing his crotch and screaming in agony.

"Oh, my God!" yelled Samantha, "It's my boyfriend! He followed me here!" She burst into tears as he ran up the stairs, out of the basement, out of the studio, ululating down the street followed by a rueful Samantha. Electra turned her back on the audience, the boa constrictor now back in place around her neck. Slowly, to the deafening accompaniment of drums and cymbals, she walked to a black cloth. Two disciples separated the cloth for her and she walked triumphantly, seductively, into the darkness beyond.

Nicholas Benson was impressed. The ceremony was finished and the babbling audience filed up the stairs and out into the street, most awestruck by what they had witnessed. Nicholas was thinking, Electra was a brilliant performer, a superb technician, a delightful fraud. He was sure the sequence with Samantha was a plant prepared for the delectation of Electra's simple-minded followers. Dan Parrish was at his side and as though reading his mind said, "If you're thinking what you just saw was a fake, believe me, it was the real thing. Come backstage. Electra was delighted you accepted our invitation. We're surprised the fuzz aren't out front. We thought Singer and his boys would be anxious to check us out. You know. The wasting sickness." Nicholas followed him backstage.

There was a surprising amount of space behind the curtain. There were a number of large dressing rooms, storage bins, and a kitchen on the left, and on the right, into which Nicholas was led, the private quarters of Electra and Dan. It was tastefully furnished, albeit spare. There were some excellent pieces of art on the walls mixed with posters of theaters and clubs in which the couple had headlined. There was a bottle of champagne icing in a cooler and Dan set to work uncorking it. Electra had settled onto a chaise longue and with a sigh of exhaustion lay back and stretched her arms. Nicholas sat on a straight-backed chair that he suspected might be a very sturdy relic, possibly attributable to Heppelwhite. They sat in silence, Electra with her eyes closed, while Dan served the champagne. After placing the bottle back in the cooler, he sat near Electra and asked Nicholas, "Did the ritual disappoint you?"

"Are you joking? I was very impressed. I'm ghoulish enough to admit I'd like to have seen an animal sacrifice; however, you can't have everything."

"We never sacrifice when there's a full moon. The witch's moon. The moon of the werewolf. When the moon causes our body liquids to ebb and flow and make some of us commit acts we will later regret. The full moon is a murderer's moon. Nice champagne,

Dan." Dan nodded. "Now my friend Nicholas, you have asked so many questions and I hope our answers have been satisfactory . . ." (Somewhat, thought Nicholas, even the artful evasions.) ". . . and now it is our turn to do the questioning. Turnabout is fair play, right?"

"Right. Not to be argued with."

"Beethoven, Vivaldi, Bizet." The names emerged like a series of gunshots. "Do the police suspect they're still in the flesh market? Do they?"

"I can't give you any direct quotes, but I think it's on their mind."

"So those three bastards could have been indirectly responsible for my sister's murder."

"It stands to reason." He cleared his throat. "Um, are you possibly responsible for Bizet's illness?"

She laughed, a very tired chuckle. "Child's play. I don't cast those kinds of spells. It's all power of suggestion anyway. If that poor fool hadn't trailed his girlfriend here tonight and heard my mumbo jumbo, he'd never have felt a thing. Being here, he fell victim to the power of suggestion and went off howling and clutching his precious goodies. Had he stayed at home, he wouldn't have known about it and he'd have been fine." She was silent and then snapped her fingers at Dan Parrish. A cigarette and a lighter promptly materialized and she took a deep drag that worried her lungs for several seconds before she exhaled. "I suggest that the Weasel is being poisoned. Maybe cyanide, maybe arsenic . . ."

Dan interjected, "Maybe potassium chloride, a distillate of deadly nightshade. Witch doctors have been using it for decades. It brings on those painful sweats, the fever, and when the victim keels over, the symptoms are similar to a heart attack."

"I'm glad somebody's trying to do my job for me," said Electra. "I don't like blood on my hands, but my mother won't let me rest until Maxine is avenged. Maxine was always a pain in the ass. There's more I need to know from you, my friend." Dan refilled their glasses. Nicholas waited for Electra to continue. "Who's bankrolling the bastards?"

Nicholas replied, "I can't help you. I don't know."

Electra sat up abruptly, a quick, clumsy movement, but without spilling a drop of champagne. "Don't lie to me."

Nicholas held up his right hand as though swearing an oath and said, "Scout's honor."

"Bullshit. All you rich ones stick together."

"Not so. I don't have any money anymore. And I don't know anything about the club's financial structure."

"Diana Headman bought her way in, didn't she?"

Nicholas shrugged. "That's fairly obvious. How did you two land in the show?"

"I'm asking the questions," Electra's voice crackled.

"What difference does it make where the boys got their backing?"

"Because I think that's why Maxine was killed. She uncovered something hot, something dangerous. The power behind the three thrones. Listen, Nicholas, you're in a position to get that information. You get it for me."

"If Jacob Singer has failed to learn that, how do you expect me to succeed?"

"How the hell do I know? Work on it. I'll give you an incentive. It's worth money to me. I've got plenty. And I know you need money."

"These days, everybody needs money."

"Stop that shit kicking!" she raged.

"Cool it, babe," cautioned Dan.

"I'm not being evasive. I don't have the information you want." Nicholas was anxious to leave. He did not know how to cope with these people. He'd had no experience with Negroes, let alone this woman with her temperamental, explosive, and potentially dangerous disposition.

"Then go out and get me that information." Her eyes were ablaze, her nostrils flared, her temples throbbed. "Now I'm tired. I need a massage. Good night, Nicholas Benson."

A few minutes later, Nicholas was out in the street searching for a telephone. He found one in a tobacconist's. He entered the booth, shut the door, placed a nickel in the slot, and dialed the number. Seated at a worktable in the window, the tobacconist skillfully created cigars, one of his own creations in his mouth. Through the window he saw Nicholas reflected, speaking passionately into the

141

mouthpiece. Ofays. Whites. He had little use for them. Nicholas shouted something nasty and the tobacconist grimaced with distaste and disapproval. Some of these ofays, he was thinking, they got no class at all.

Clara Bizet removed the castanets from her fingers and placed them in her handbag. The nurse had been firm in her demands that Clara either stop exercising them or leave the room. "Your husband is a very sick man."

"Is he dying?"

Bizet groaned.

The nurse looked appalled. "You've spoken to his doctors."

"They wouldn't give me an answer either. I got to know. I got to plan. Leave me alone with my husband."

The nurse was reluctant to obey Mrs. Bizet's command. "It's after visiting hours, Mrs. Bizet, you're the one who should be leaving."

"I'm his next of kin and this is a private suite. I'll stay as long as I like." She jerked a thumb toward the door. "Now beat it, sister." The nurse marched out of the room, out into the hallway, and toward the reception desk where she was sure to find a guard. She'd soon have the satisfaction of seeing that fat bitch ushered out of the hospital.

Clara sat at the edge of the bed and held the Weasel's hand. It was hot and sweaty. "Irving. Irving, do you hear me? It's me, Clara. Your wife, the mother of your children. Irving!"

His eyes flew open. Even semiconscious, he responded to the ominous command he'd been conditioned to for over two decades. No one could speak his name with the variety of inflections his wife had developed over the years. There was the tender *Irving* of love, the inquisitive *Irving* of the coquette who needed to buy some new dresses, there was the dangerous *Irving* when she suspected he was two-timing her again, there was the ominous *Irving* when she was about to deliver a punch to his kidney, and now there was the commanding *Irving*, the one she had just spoken, the one that caused his eyes to fly open.

"Clara?" She didn't recognize his voice. It was disembodied and weak, more like the pitiful mewing of a starving kitten.

"Clara," she echoed, "I'm Clara. Don't close your eyes, Irving,

142

and pay attention. Did you hear me? Do you understand?" His eyes were opened wide, staring at the ceiling. "Blink your eyes once for 'yes,' blink them twice for 'no,' better still, just talk plain."

"Clara," he whispered.

"Now listen, Irving, if this disease you got is fatal, promise me you won't linger."

"Clara." So soft, she thought it was a reproof.

She decided to try getting cosier. "Irv . . ."

"Yeah?"

"The safe-deposit box. Where's the key?"

"The key . . ."

"Is it in your office in a drawer? Is it at home someplace? Is it here in one of your pockets in the closet? Where is it?"

"The key. . . ."

She fretted with impatience. "Yeah yeah yeah! The key! The key! The key! Where's the frigging key?"

He licked his lips. His mouth was dry. The fever raged unchecked. His eyes blinked and his mouth twitched. "Fat Harry . . ."

Her heart sank. "Fat Harry has the key?"

"Yeah. Before . . ." he spoke with an effort, as though every breath might be his last, ". . . he was here . . . before . . . you . . . got . . . here. My vest . . . he took it . . . from . . . my vest."

"Oh hell! Well, I'll get it from that bastard, he'll come across or I'll make more trouble than he ever dreamed of. I could spill plenty to the cops, I got enough on those two bastards to put them away for not only life, but the afterlife!"

"Clara . . ."

"What? What do you want?"

His eyes were tearing. Poor Irving. Poor little Irving. She softened and thought of embracing him, but on the other hand, a cooler head prevailed, he might be contagious. "Clara . . ." she stared into the pathetic face, ". . . cremate me."

"Right now?"

After dinner, Abel pleaded fatigue and went to his sorry furnished room for some much-needed sleep. Wang accompanied Singer back to the station house, where the laboratory report waited for him on

143

the desk. He read it quickly, clucked his tongue, and handed it to Wang.

"Poison," said Singer as Wang read the report. "Potassium chloride, the same stuff that killed Maxine and Edna. Let's hope there's an antidote." He phoned the hospital. The Weasel's doctor had left for home. Singer asked for a supervisor. He advised the supervisor of what was killing Bizet and the supervisor hoped it wasn't too late to reverse the Weasel's perilous position. He wondered where he might find Vivaldi and Beethoven. Fat Harry had eaten some of the candy, nowhere near as much as the Weasel had eaten, but still, enough to give him, to put it mildly, some discomfort.

Harry was suffering discomfort. He and Vivaldi were in Vivaldi's office in the club's basement when Fat Harry felt nauseous and feverish. He lay on the couch clutching his stomach while Vivaldi dosed him with a variety of possible remedies, bicarbonate of soda, a variety of name-brand medicines guaranteed to cure all ailments including acne, boils, dyspepsia, and hemorrhoids. The phone rang and Vivaldi grabbed it. He was for the first time in his life relieved to hear from a police officer. Singer advised him the chocolates had been poisoned and Vivaldi thanked him, and helped Fat Harry off the couch, up the stairs, out the building, and into a taxi that was idling on the street corner waiting for the light to change.

"Roosevelt emergency!" commanded Big Ike, and the driver took off, wondering if the stricken man had been shot or knifed. In this neighborhood, it had to be one or the other.

Vivaldi stared at Fat Harry's face; he was glad he had taken possession of the key to the Weasel's safe-deposit before Harry was stricken. And then he realized, the situation was not without its humor. If the Weasel died, if Fat Harry died, then the whole shooting match was his, Vivaldi's.

Hard-hearted bastard, the cabbie thought of Vivaldi as he sneaked glances at him in the rear-view mirror, smiling while his buddy could be on the verge of death. Wait till I tell the missus about this; as a practicing sadist she's bound to appreciate it.

Singer phoned while Noel, Jeffrey, and Millicent were having coffee and liqueurs, and Noel was not surprised to hear that the chocolates

144

had been poisoned. "Well, then, so much for voodoo spells," commented Noel.

"I just spoke to Roosevelt Hospital again. Vivaldi has checked Fat Harry into another private suite. He's not as sick as the Weasel so he's out of danger."

"That will be a relief to the criminal fraternity, I should think," said Noel. "And the Weasel?"

"Well, now that I told them about the poison, they're coming up with an antidote. It's a drug they don't know too much about. Very obscure."

"I'm sure it'll soon find its place in the limelight. Well, it's still the full moon out there." He could see it out the window from where he was standing. "What happens now?" asked Noel.

"I continue doing some heavy thinking."

"You have someone in mind, don't you, you sly puss?" Noel was examining his reflection in the wall mirror and then noticed that Millicent was sitting quite still, her eyes presumably on the floor, as though in a trance.

"I always zero in on someone for a while, even if I know I could be wrong. But it strengthens my resolve when I've got a point of reference."

"Of course, sort of like Captain Ahab enjoying a spot of trout fishing before catching his second breath and setting out once again in pursuit of the white whale."

"Noel, I'll have that group photo on my desk in the morning. I think it would help if you dropped by before going to rehearsal and had a look at it."

"I'll be there first thing in the morning."

"I'm fascinated by your line of reasoning, someone was there who shouldn't have been there at all, or someone who should have been there wasn't there at all."

"Sounds like the cue to a very dreary novelty tune."

"Millicent Headman still with you?"

"Yes indeed."

"Get anything helpful out of her?"

"I'll see you in the morning. By the way, Jacob, there hasn't been another murder reported, has there?"

"No, not yet."

145

"You still believe there'll be at least one more killing?"

"I didn't set a number. I said I thought there might be another victim. Could be the Weasel, you know. That might fill the bill."

"Somehow, I don't find the prospect of his death all that substantial."

"But it would be murder. He *was* poisoned."

Noel was thinking. He was thinking very hard. Jeffrey saw Noel's brows were knitted and he was massaging his temples and this signaled the onset of a brainstorm, a momentous brainstorm. "Jacob, apparently Big Ike doesn't fancy chocolates."

"I don't know. Maybe he just doesn't fancy fancy chocolates."

"Jacob, Fannie Farmer aren't fancy, they're just very very plain chocolates, of interest only to children and greedy grandmothers."

"You think Vivaldi was looking to unload his partners?"

"Why not? Isn't it a fairly common practice among the underworld's lower depths?"

"Where's the connection? He couldn't have killed Edna."

"Isn't it possible for a businessman to have more than one partnership?"

"You have such a wicked mind, I love it."

Noel grinned. "I'll see you in the morning. Shall we say around ten? Fine." He hung up and returned to the others. "Is there more coffee, Jeff?" Jeff refilled Noel's demitasse cup and without being asked, refilled Millicent's.

"Of course my curiosity is piqued," said Millicent. "I gather there's much ado about poisoned chocolates."

Noel said with a sniff, "A rather commonplace touch in murder mysteries. Poisoned chocolates, poisoned biscuits, chicken soup heavily seasoned with arsenic. I know a playwright who, when his play was savaged by a homosexual critic, threatened to send him a poisoned choirboy. Yes, we are now involved with poisoned chocolates." Noel told Millicent and Jeffrey the details.

At the conclusion of his litany, Jeffrey had a bright expression on his face. "I say, Noel, doesn't Agatha Christie claim poison is a woman's weapon?"

Noel said with hauteur, "I never read cheap mysteries."

"Well, I do and I jolly well enjoy them. Miss Christie is very big

146

on lady poisoners. So who are the ladies involved? There's Electra Howard."

"I doubt if voodoo and sweets mix well."

"Doesn't matter, she's a woman. She's also a voodoo practitioner. She must know about poisons. Then there's Nancy Adman, the costume lady."

Noel crossed a leg while lighting a cigarette. "Certainly an excellent candidate as least likely suspect."

"Don't dismiss her so easily." Millicent was fascinated. Her head moved back and forth between Noel and Jeffrey like a spectator at a tennis tournament. "She's been in the theater for ages. She's been around. Maybe she's been nursing a grudge for years."

"Against Edna and the three monsters?"

"Why not? Fate brings them all together, as you yourself continue to remind me . . . *The Bridge of San Luis Rey* . . ."

"I'm sorry I ever mentioned it."

"So am I . . . but what the hell . . . here is a golden opportunity to wreak revenge on all of them in one fell swoop. Poisoned candy . . . poisoned dart and all!"

"Sounds reasonable," conceded Noel. "Who plays the part in the movie? Glenda Farrell?"

"If you won't take me seriously, I'll say no further."

"Oh please go on," urged Millicent, "I'm absolutely fascinated."

"Very well, I will. Edna's girlfriends. What's their names?"

"Trixie and Angie," said Noel, while stifling a yawn.

"How about them?"

"Well, as of today, Trixie has a logical reason for wanting to kill Fat Harry, he having infected her with crabs, from what I can gather." Millicent wore a look of distaste. "But unfortunately for your theory, dear boy, they were standing on either side of Edna when she caught it in the neck." He smiled. "We seem to have forgotten Diana. I don't think she'd like that."

Millicent agreed. "Diana gets very testy when she's left out of things."

"Oh well," said Noel dismissively, "all this will soon come to a head, I'm sure. In fact, I have this strange feeling that the answer is right here . . ." he held up his right hand ". . . at my fingertips. It's right here under my nose. So obvious that I shall feel ridiculous

147

when the riddle is solved. The obvious can be so elusive, because of its very obviousness, that one tends to nudge it aside because it couldn't be the right answer. And all because it's too obvious. Don't you agree, Millicent?"

"I guess you're right, Noel. I can't think clearly. My mind is too cluttered right now. I must go to my flat and try to sort things out for myself." Noel accompanied her to the door. "Noel, what we discussed earlier . . ."

"If necessary to be repeated, only to the proper ears. And the only proper ears are those of Jacob Singer and his associates."

"I understand." The three exchanged goodnights and when they were alone, Noel suggested to Jeffrey, "Shall we have a nightcap? Do the honors, Jeff. Please." Jeff obliged while Noel sat, staring into space and deep in contemplation. He took the liqueur and sipped it. Then he said, "You know, I feel as though I'm almost on top of the situation. And when I get there, I plan to plant a flag."

Fourteen

■ 〓〓 ■

TRIXIE Bates and Angie Murray were so unnerved and upset by Edna Dore's murder, they agreed to spend the night together in Trixie's apartment. After applying the necessary lotion to rid herself of the crabs ("Those darling little lovebugs," as Angie so quaintly put it) and reveling in a hot shower, Trixie phoned for Chinese food and poured each of them a stiff tumbler of bourbon. Trixie stretched out on the sofa and Angie settled into an overstuffed chair with her feet on the matching footstool. For a few moments they chitchatted about nothing of importance, and then Angie asked, "Shouldn't Edna's family be notified?"

"Sure they should. Where are they?"

"Somewhere on the New Jersey shore. I think Asbury Park."

Trixie sat up. "Shouldn't the cops be doing the notifying?"

"You're right. We ought to call them and tell them they should be notifying Edna's family. Is Dore her real name?"

Trixie shrugged. "I don't think so. I think she was a Polack or something like that."

"What about all her things? Her apartment? Her furs? Her clothes and her jewels?" Angie was a born scavenger. She'd always admired the loot Edna had acquired during her brief tenure as a kept woman. "You know, Trix, I'm sure Edna would have wanted us to have a couple of keepsakes or something."

149

Trixie was quick on the uptake. "You're right. She knew how much I loved that mink jacket of hers. And that cocktail wristwatch Big Ike gave her on her birthday. Oh, how she loved for me to ask her the time so she could tell me 'It's three rubies past an emerald.' I'm really going to miss Edna."

Angie said wistfully, "She always wanted me to have her Valentino ball gown and the string of pearls she was always biting. I miss her already. Trix?"

Trixie was somewhere off in dreamland. Angie repeated her name and Trixie came back to the present. "What?"

"I've got a key to her apartment."

"You do? How come?"

"She gave me one a couple of weeks ago so I could let Hattie Beavers in to straighten up the place while she went to Atlantic City with Big Ike. I kept forgetting to give it back."

"Thank God. Now wait a minute." Trixie set her glass on an end table. "We can't just go in there and steal things. Big Ike'll have our heads when he finds out."

"Why does he have to find out?"

"He'll remember what he gave her and what's missing. He'll suspect us right off."

"No he won't. He'll suspect Hattie Beavers."

Trixie mulled it over. "Forget it. It won't wash. We'll never get away with it." Then she added, "What'll Big Ike do with that stuff? He can't wear any of it."

"Knowing him, he'll probably go find himself a new girl who can wear Edna's things, give or take an alteration. Maybe you, Angie." She smiled. "You still wondering if Big Ike goes for you?"

Angie fumbled for words. After all, Bizet was still among the living and here she was discussing his possible replacement without considering the possibility he might recover from his mysterious ailment. "Well . . . you know, Trix . . . I mean you know what I mean. I sometimes find him staring at me . . ."

"Probably wondering how the hell you ever teamed up with the Weasel."

"Aw, Irving's okay. He's always been good to me. We never squabble the way you do with Fat Harry, or come to think of it, the way Edna and Big Ike used to go at it."

150

Trixie picked up her glass, stood up, and went to a window. "You got a great view, Angie."

"Yeah. Pretty nice. Listen, Trixie, who do you think murdered Edna?"

Trixie turned and stared at her. "Who do *you* think murdered Edna?"

"I asked first." Angie was at the liquor cabinet adding ice to her drink.

Trixie said, "She was asking for trouble, face it. Snooping around. Questioning everything and everyone. A regular Mattress Hari. I know Big Ike didn't like her getting so chummy with the cops and that Benson creep. I wonder if Ike ever suspected she'd been doing it with Abel Graham."

"He's real cute," said Angie. "Don't you think Abel's real cute?"

"I never give it much thought." The phone rang. Trixie caught it on the third ring. She recognized Jacob Singer's voice. "Is something wrong?"

"Fat Harry's in the hospital."

Trixie's alarm was genuine. "What happened? Who shot him?"

"Nobody shot him, he's been poisoned."

"Poisoned? How? Who did it? I'll kill the bastard."

"Now calm down, Trixie. Just calm down and listen." Angie, distressed after hearing 'poisoned,' hurried to Trixie's side. Singer told her the whole story, the poisoned chocolates that only the Weasel and Fat Harry had sampled.

"But who would want to poison them?" asked Trixie ingenuously.

"Who wouldn't?" was Singer's flat reply.

Trixie said to Angie, "They been poisoned! Irving and Harry have been poisoned! Chocolates! God damn chocolates! Oh my God! They were in that box in Harry's desk and I almost ate one. Oh my God!"

Angie put her arm around Trixie. "It's okay, Trix, as long as you didn't. Poisoned. My poor Irving was poisoned."

"My poor Harry." Trixie remembered Singer, who was patiently waiting for her to remember he was on the other end of the line. "Where's Harry?" Singer told her. She told Angie. "He's at Roosevelt, like the Weasel. Next door to each other." She couldn't believe those were tears she was fighting back. She asked Singer, "Can I go see him? Why do I have to wait until tomorrow? My Big Harry needs me. So what if it's after visiting hours, you could get me in, couldn't you?"

Singer was surprised to realize her concern was genuine. "I could, but it's not a good idea. You can visit him the first thing in the morning. Only check first and make sure his wife isn't there or on her way. Angie missed running into Clara Bizet, they tell me, and Clara's a tiger."

"Okay, okay. But wait, don't hang up. Who do you suspect did this?"

"I can't talk about that yet."

"Why not?"

Singer was getting irritated. "Trixie, don't bust my balls."

"I wouldn't dream of it. Thanks for letting me know. I would have worried if he hadn't phoned me soon. Good-bye." She hung up. "Can you beat that, Angie? They been poisoned. Irving and Harry ate poisoned chocolates." Their eyes met. "How come Big Ike didn't get poisoned?"

Angie said, "He doesn't eat chocolates. He doesn't eat candy or cake. He says it's from all those years when he was a kid working in his father's grocery store. He had his fill of eating sweet stuff then and now he can't stomach it."

"I suppose that's a good enough reason," said Trixie. "I suppose I buy it. And then, I suppose there's them that wouldn't buy it."

"You crazy, Trix? You hinting Big Ike's trying to get rid of Harry and Irving?"

"Well, it's possible, ain't it?" Trixie stood with her hands on her hips.

"Anything's possible." The doorbell rang.

"The Chinks," said Trixie, "and about time too. I'm starved." She pressed the button in the wall that unlocked the downstairs door, snatched up her handbag from the table near the door, and said to Angie, "You know something, kiddo? I think there's a hell of a lot more to Edna's murder and the boys getting poisoned than meets the eye." She unlatched the door and opened it, waiting to hear the elevator doors open.

"Trix, I'm scared."

"Yeah? Move over." She opened the door wider and said to the approaching delivery boy, "What'd you do? Send to Hong Kong for this stuff?"

Big Ike Vivaldi, alone in his office, was pondering the feasibility of hiring bodyguards. Edna dead. Irving and Harry poisoned. The relish Jacob Singer took when telling him the boys had been poisoned. Potassium chloride, whatever the hell that was. When he was a kid they used plain old-fashioned rat poison or weed killer. He remembered his cousin, Tommy "No Thumbs" Gambarelli, explaining to him how you added water to the poison, made it into a paste, and then spread it on pumpernickel bread with peanut butter and jelly. Not just a quick way to kill, but a tasty one, too.

He felt in his vest pocket for the key to Bizet's safe-deposit box. He'd get to it the first thing in the morning. He thought he heard a movement behind him. He was sitting with his back to the open door, a very foolish thing to do, and he cursed himself for his carelessness. But this had been a bad day and the night had turned even worse, what with both his partners in the hospital. He opened the top drawer of the desk very slowly, noiselessly, and felt for the automatic he'd stashed there for emergencies.

"You don't need no gun, Ike." He recognized Clara Bizet's voice. "I ain't here to kill you." Vivaldi swiveled about and faced the human pouter pigeon. "I'm just here to threaten you."

"How'd you get into the building?"

"Irving's key. I found it in his pants pocket in the hospital."

"How's he doing?"

"You know how he's doing. Lousy." Her eyes narrowed. "What'd you do to him, Ike?"

"Nothing. I didn't do nothing." He explained about the poisoned and that unless she already knew, Big Ike was also the room adjoining the Weasel's.

a foot, arms folded, handbag swinging from her ll this is yours, right?"

e okay."

deposit box key." She held out

"I'll give it to you tomorrow morning. At the bank. You meet me there at nine when it opens."

"What the hell are you up to?"

"Irving was keeping some books for me. I want those books before the cops get to them. I don't want the jewels or the cash or the insurance policies. I got my own. But I want those books."

"Books, my ass. His *diaries*. You didn't think I knew about them? I'm the one who told him to put them away for safekeeping. For insurance in case you bums decided to give him the double ex."

"Nobody's double-crossing nobody."

"Only poisoning them."

"Use your head, Clara. Why would I be dumb enough to poison them? I'd be the first person under suspicion. You know what I think? I think someone's trying to make me the fall guy and I don't like that." He quelled his rising anger. "Go home, Clara. I'll meet you in the morning downtown. Dime Savings."

"I know that. You better be there."

"I'll be there."

"You better be. I know a lot of what's in them diaries. A lot. A whole lot." She turned to leave.

"Forgive me if I don't see you to the door."

She responded with a very unladylike gesture. Vivaldi snorted. Then he went to the door, stuck his head into the corridor, and watched her as she minced her way up the stairs, handbag swinging, all the while muttering under her breath. Then Ike shut the door, crossed to the bar, and poured himself a stiff shot of scotch, which he downed in one gulp. He poured another and walked with it to the desk. He looked at Edna's framed photograph. He lifted the glass in a toast. "Kid, I'm going to give you one hell of a funeral." It was then he remembered Edna's family in New Jersey. "Damn it." H[e] sat at the desk, flipped through his voluminous address boo[k] he came to the Zs. There was only one entry, Zbernic, La[dy] dialed the operator. He gave her the number in New J[ersey] he downed the second scotch. He knew he'd b[e] lot of them tonight.

Angie inserted the key in the lo[ck]

"You getting cold feet al[l]

"Big Ike ain't going to like this." She indicated the two empty suitcases they'd brought with them. Edna's apartment was in a brownstone walk-up on West Forty-ninth Street between Eighth and Ninth. There was no doorman to worry about. There was a snoopy old woman on the first floor front who usually sat at her window, a self-styled guardian, Cerberus at the gate. But at this hour, which was just past midnight, her curtains were drawn and they assumed she was asleep.

"I'm not worried. We'll make it look like it was a robbery. We'll open the window to the fire escape. We'll scatter stuff all over the floor. We'll empty drawers and leave them laying there. Come on, we've seen it often enough in the movies." She twisted the key in the lock and then pushed the door open. All the lights in the living room were ablaze. "Can you beat that? Edna, may she rest in peace, leaving all her lights on like this. I'm sure glad I don't have to see her electricity bill. Come on. Shut the door. Don't slam it."

They looked around the room. "God, she was a slob," said Trixie. The drawers in a sideboard were open, and most of their contents were scattered haphazardly on the floor. Sofa cushions looked as though they'd been slit open with a knife or a razor blade. The desk drawers were half open, with papers scattered on the floor and on the desk top. The bookcase had been overturned and Edna's precious books were strewn about on the floor. Came the dawn and Trixie fluttered her eyelashes. "Oh my God! We've been robbed!" She grabbed Angie's hand. "I don't like it. Let's get out of here."

Angie shook Trixie's hand loose. "The bedroom. That's where she kept everything. She had a wall safe." Without thought of hidden danger, Angie hurried into the bedroom. It too looked like a human hurricane had struck. Clothes and furs were strewn about the room, on the bed, on the chairs. Someone had been in a very big, very desperate hurry. "Look. The furs ain't been touched."

"And her jewels." Trixie had opened the beautiful jewel box on Edna's dressing table, an elaborate affair purchased by Vivaldi at Tiffany's. It had five separate compartments, all bursting with sparkling wealth. "I don't get it. What kind of thief breaks into an apartment and then doesn't take anything?"

"What about her paintings? Didn't she buy paintings?"

"See for yourself. They're still hanging there."

Angie had seen them before and didn't realize they were supposed to be valuable. "This crap is worth money?"

"Yeah. Edna was always bragging about them."

Angie laughed. "What a break! It's a good thing we decided to get the stuff tonight." Her arms and hands were spread wide. "A beautiful setup. Somebody breaks in, see . . . the fire escape window is open . . . they tear the place apart but they don't take anything. Not anything valuable they don't take, so what the hell were they looking for?"

Trixie was examining the fire escape window. "This window's been jimmied. That's how he got in."

"You're sure it wasn't more than one?" She lowered her voice. "Trix, supposing they're still in the apartment?"

"Stop scaring me."

"They could be in the kitchen. Or the terlet."

Trixie's heart was beating faster. She could hear it throbbing through her skin, under her ribs. "Let's get out of here."

Angie was determined. "Not without the stuff we came to get. Get the suitcases. I'll fold the dresses and the furs."

Trixie went to the living room. She hurried to retrieve the suitcases. Then she heard a noise from the kitchen. Her heart began pounding again. She froze to the floor. "Angie!" she cried. "Angie! There's somebody in the kitchen!"

Angie hurried into the living room. She could see into the kitchen. "Well, I'll be a monkey's uncle!" She laughed. "Hey, Trix! Look at who's been playing burglar!"

Trixie turned around. In the doorway stood Nicholas Benson. She put her hands on her hips. "Well, Mr. Benson, imagine finding *you* here."

His lips moved but no sound was forthcoming. He extended his right arm and then let it fall limply to his side. His knees were bending and slowly he sank to the floor. They later surmised that what they heard was his death rattle as he fell face-forward into the living room, a carving knife having been plunged into his back down to the edge of the hilt.

Trixie opened her mouth to scream, but Angie moved quickly and clamped a hand over Trixie's mouth. "Don't scream! Don't scream or we've had it." She waited several seconds. "Can I take my hand away? Promise you won't scream?" Trixie bobbed her head up and down, heart still thumping, feeling a weakness in her knees. Angie thought of getting her a glass of water, but that would mean stepping over Nicholas's body and she had no stomach for that.

Trixie drew breath and then asked, "What do we do?"

Angie sank onto a settee, hearing Trixie breathing heavily like the threatened heroine of a turn-of-the-century melodrama. Trixie repeated her question. "We level with Singer."

"You crazy? He'll never believe us."

"Oh, yes he will. Look Trix. We have no reason to murder Benson and Singer knows that. We didn't kill Edna because we were on either side of her when she got it. We tell him the truth. We tell him we came to get her stuff for safekeeping before somebody thinks of breaking into the place and stealing it. Yeah! That's it! We had all promised each other that if anything happens to any of us, we'd go get our valuables and keep them until we could turn it over to the cops."

"You think Singer'll buy that?"

"Yeah. I think he'll buy it." She looked at the body. "Poor bastard. He must have been the one who jimmied the window."

Trixie emphasized, "Angie, he didn't come alone."

"How do you know? Maybe he didn't know there was someone else in the apartment when he got here. They didn't take any of the valuables. I wonder what they were looking for?" Angie dialed the operator and asked to be connected with Jacob Singer at his precinct.

"Do you think he's still there?" asked Trixie.

"If he isn't, they'll know where to find him." She spoke into the phone. "Can I speak to Mr. Singer? Tell him it's Angie Murray, tell him it's very important. Tell him I've got a stiff for him."

Fifteen

ABEL Graham was awakened gratefully from a nightmare in which he was copulating with Edna Dore in her coffin, and ordered to join Singer at Edna Dore's apartment. Singer gave him the address.

"Nicholas Benson? My money wasn't on him!"

"Well, somebody else's was!"

Graham was dressed and out of his furnished room in five minutes.

The operator at the Hotel Algonquin had trouble rousing Abraham Wang because he was having trouble rousing the young woman he had picked up in the bar downstairs an hour earlier. She said she was a school teacher from Montpelier, Vermont, and Wang thought she still had a lot to learn. He answered the phone on the tenth ring, lying that he had been in the bathroom. "Benson? Well, I'll be damned."

"No," said Singer, "he is." He gave him Edna's address and hung up and then dialed Noel Coward's number.

Noel and Jeffrey Amherst were enjoying a game of backgammon, sleep having eluded both of them. They sat at a bridge table wearing very expensive dressing gowns from Sulka, sipping brandy and smoking cigarettes. Noel reached for the phone while saying, "At this hour it can't be good news. It's almost midnight. Hello? Jacob? How lovely to hear from you. I'm not in the least bit sleepy and neither is Jeffrey. Shall we go dancing at Roseland?" He paused to listen. "Nicholas Benson." Jeffrey stared at him and exhaled smoke. "What was he doing in Edna's apartment with Angie and Trixie?" He thought of asking "And what are the thirty-nine steps?" but decided this was hardly the moment for frivolity. "We'll be right there." He memorized Edna's address, hung up, and said to Jeff, "Nicholas Benson's been murdered in Edna Dore's apartment. He was found by Angie and Trixie. Don't look so confused. I'm sure there's a reasonable explanation somewhere. You *are* coming with me, aren't you? You certainly don't want to sit here by yourself while the rest of us are having a whale of a good time playing detective."

Brazen, Jacob Singer was thinking, real brazen. Angie Murray looked almost angelic as she repeated her simple fabrication of why they were in Edna Dore's apartment with empty suitcases. She repeated the story again when Noel, Jeff, Wang, and Abel arrived and joined the assemblage in the living room. In addition to Singer, there was the coroner, his assistants, the photographer, and three other detectives who were dusting the room for fingerprints.

Noel studied the disarray and commented with the ever-present sniff, "Edna was one hell of a housekeeper." He looked at the body. "My goodness, clear down to the hilt. Whoever plunged that carving knife into the dear boy's back was determinedly sincere." He looked out a window. "Ah! The vultures are gathering!" He could see reporters and press photographers arriving. "How do they sniff out an event like this so rapidly?"

Abel explained. "They get a tip from the precinct."

"I assumed it was something like that." He walked into the bedroom, tailed by Jeff. "What an array of disarray. Ah, isn't that a lovely Balenciaga. And oh how dear Coco Chanel would have hysterics if she saw that number on the floor looking so sad and downtrodden. And what's this parvenu number?" He picked up a housecoat with a rabbit's fur collar. "Strictly Bloomingdale's basement, I should assume, before she struck pay dirt. Oh my my my.

159

Will you look at this assortment of rocks." He held a pair of diamond earrings to his ears. He asked Jeffrey, "How do I look?"

"They do nothing for you."

"I didn't expect them to do anything for me." He replaced them in the jewel box. "I only wanted to know how I looked." He now found the string of pearls. "Aren't these lovely! Someone had occasional good taste." He crossed to one of the closets. "Jeffrey, will you look at these shoes! I haven't seen such a collection since I pried around Jessie Matthews' bedroom last year. Everything here but Cinderella's glass slippers. I must say, there's certainly something to be said for having a benefactor. Why don't I ever have such luck?"

"Because you're always the benefactor."

"True. Much too true." He espied some papers on the floor and picked them up. "My dear boy, you'll never believe this. Our Edna was certainly multitalented."

"What have you found?"

"Some pages filled with what I presume to be her blank verse."

"Blank verse? Really?"

Noel read some and said, "Very blank. Oh dear. I shouldn't have touched these pages. I've left my fingerprints."

"I wouldn't worry. You're a friend of the management." Jeff followed Noel back into the living room. Nicholas's body had been wrapped in a sheet and placed on a stretcher. The carving knife had been removed. The police photographer was clicking away, his flashbulbs temporarily blinding the others.

Noel was lighting a cigarette. He said to Singer, "I'm afraid your boys will find my fingerprints on some pages of blank verse in the bedroom."

"Edna wrote poetry?" asked an astonished Singer.

"She thought she did."

"She wrote sweet things," said Angie in defense of her departed friend. "Mr. Coward, Edna could have been somebody important. She was smart. She was ambitious. She didn't want to be somebody's special girl forever. She read books and she went to art galleries."

"She also went to Tiffany's and Saks Fifth Avenue," added Noel.

"Well, why shouldn't she? If she didn't, some other broad would.

160

Those rocks you saw in the bedroom? They ain't the half of it. She hocked a lot of her stuff and invested it. She bought her family a house in New Jersey. She was sending her kid brother through college. In New Jersey." She said with pride, "Princerton University. You know who went to Princerton? F. Scott Fitzgerald!" Noel had a suspicion she hadn't the vaguest idea who Fitzgerald was, but he hoped that after his own death someone would rise to his defense as passionately as Angie did to Edna's.

"She could also do doilies," said Trixie, throwing that accomplishment in for good measure.

"Okay, okay," interrupted Singer, "let's get the show on the road. Ladies, if you'll pack Edna's treasures into the suitcases, we'll take them to the precinct and advise her family we've got them. I'm sure they'll put in a claim for them." The girls were watching Nicholas's body being carried out of the apartment.

"Poor bastard," said Trixie, "I guess he must have asked too many questions, like Edna."

"What kind of questions did he ask?" Singer spoke softly while Noel jammed a cigarette into his holder and was soon puffing away, eyes narrowed into slits as the smoke attacked them.

"Like did we know who was backing the club? You know, where was the money coming from? The boys had been broke for a couple of years . . ."

"According to legend," interjected Noel.

Wang asked Noel, "You think that was all a made-up story? A smoke screen?"

"Jeffrey and I know many wealthy people who cry poor when the poor darlings are down to their last million. When I cry poor, believe me, I'm poor. But there are those who claim not to have cash on hand and I'm sure one can believe them. But that doesn't mean they don't own real estate and other assets of incredible value that they are loath to liquidate. From what I've learned about the three partners, they accumulated huge sums during the twenties. Somehow I suspect they didn't lose it all when the stock market had its nervous breakdown. I'm sure they own the residences that house their wives and children. They own automobiles. They could have foreign, untraceable bank accounts. Switzerland is terribly hospitable in that area, among several other convenient locations."

161

"You might be right," conceded Singer, "but somehow I think Nicholas was onto something and that's what got him a knife in the back."

Trixie cleared her throat and said authoritatively, "The bedroom window's been jimmied. That's how they got in."

"You're sure it was 'they'?" asked Singer.

"Well, somebody had to come with him to stick the knife into him. Unless he had an itch and used the knife to scratch himself and killed himself by accident."

Noel smiled. She was so deliciously ingenuous. He hoped Fat Harry lavished expensive gifts on her the way Big Ike showered them on the late Edna Dore. He heard Singer say, "Benson might have surprised someone in the apartment."

"If he did," said Noel coolly, "I don't think it came as much of a surprise to Nicholas."

Wang had been poking about in the kitchen. He returned to the living room and announced, "She ate a lot of tuna fish. There's six cans in the cupboard." For some reason, Abel made a note of it. Jeff was staring at Trixie and Angie and wondering what he would find if he wiped the heavy makeup from their faces.

Singer said to Noel, "You think he knew positively who was behind Edna's murder and the poisonings?"

"I do," said Noel "and I'm sure you do too, Jacob, so don't toy with me. He also probably suspected the same person authorized Maxine Howard's death in Shanghai. I presume her autopsy's been completed and proved she was shot through with potassium chloride?"

"Right," said Singer. "I'll show you the coroner's report when we get back to the precinct, provided you and Jeff aren't too tired."

"I'm not too tired and I'm sure Jeff isn't either." Jeff stifled a yawn and knew better than to disagree with Noel. Noel smiled graciously at Trixie and Angie. "I believe you should be packing Edna's goodies." They took the hint and went to the bedroom. "Now then, Jacob, let's not play Parcheesi with each other. Edna and Nicholas, and Maxine before them, were murdered because they stumbled on information that was a dangerous threat to someone."

"Vivaldi, Beethoven, and Bizet," said Wang, while still wondering how anyone could eat so much tuna fish.

"But they didn't call the shots where the murders were concerned. There's someone behind them, I strongly suspect, and so do you, Jacob, because of that wicked little grin on your face and you're much too old to be cute. And that someone holds the purse strings. And what's more, I think that someone possibly fears the detection of other crimes in which that someone was involved. If I've derailed myself, Jacob, kindly set me back on track."

"You're doing fine, Noel. Real fine."

"How generous you are, Jacob, I'm tempted to indulge in an eruption of rodomontade, which means extravagant boasting or vain bluster, but somehow I'm overcome by an attack of unbecoming modesty. Now what do you suppose they were after?" He was lighting another cigarette. "Nicholas and his slayer are whom I'm referring to. Is whom correct? Who? The hell with it. Let's get on with it. What were they after? Well, I'll tell you what I've deduced. From the way the jewelry and the furs were cast aside, no robbery was planned, certainly not by Benson's murderer. And look at how the pillows and the furniture have been torn apart. So without any further beating about the bush, the killer was looking for something incriminating that he or she suspected Edna had hidden in the apartment. I think Nicholas had the same suspicion and, possibly in the false disguise of conspirator, arranged to accompany the killer here, poor thing, little suspecting he was the second target for tonight." He suddenly exploded with "Ha! Ha! Ha!" while pointing a finger at Singer. Abel swallowed hard. Coward couldn't be accusing Singer of the murders. Noel cackled, "I said the full moon would bring mischief, didn't I, Jacob? And another murder! Ha! Ha! Ha!"

"Noel, I'm beginning to suspect you practice some black magic of your own," said Singer.

"By the by," said Noel, "for what it's worth, I think Nicholas attended a voodoo rite tonight in Harlem. Electra and Dan also invited me, but I begged off. Not that I think it might have something to do with his murder."

"Why not?" It was Wang who spoke. Maxine was his case and Electra was her sister. "Nicholas told me there was an argument over Electra and Dan's being hired for the show by Fat Harry without consulting his partners."

"I know all about that," said Noel, "and I don't think it has anything to do with the crimes. It's the old American show business bugaboo of mixing black and white entertainers. It's usually taboo."

"What about your minstrel shows?" Wang asked Singer.

"I think they don't exist anymore," replied Singer.

"Anyway, in minstrel shows, it was white performers wearing black makeup. Blacks didn't start appearing with whites until the black comedian Bert Williams broke through the barrier several decades ago. Since then, of course, we've had Ethel Waters in the all-white revue, *As Thousands Cheer*, but precious little else. I think Fat Harry truly saw Electra and Dan perform somewhere . . . was it Paris? Rome? London? . . . no matter, he was overcome by their brilliance and wanted them in the show. Full marks for Mr. Beethoven, although I shall strangle him if I can find his neck. I won't have them stealing the show from me, I simply won't."

Wang asked, "Noel, is this the first time you've shared the stage with black performers?"

"Actually, yes," said Noel, "though I had the opportunity several years ago to play Iago to Paul Robeson's Othello in London. I turned it down, not because I didn't want to appear with Robeson, who, as it turned out, gave a very disappointing performance. I did want to attempt Shakespeare, but in a role more suited to me. As it is, I'm too old for Juliet and too tall for Desdemona. Hmmm." He had a faraway look in his eye, one familiar to Jeffrey Amherst. "I could be a formidable Oberon, and possibly a devastating Titus Andronicus. Hmmm. But that's neither here nor there at the moment. I wonder if Edna kept a diary?"

"I wonder if Edna was doing a little blackmailing?" Singer's suggestion tickled Noel's ear but not his fancy.

"Somehow, I don't see Edna as the blackmailing type. Not someone who's been struggling with *War and Peace*. In my experience, blackmailers are terribly unimaginative. They're also terribly foolish. Don't look at me like that, Jacob, I've been the victim of a few extortionists but fortunately I have friends in high places. No, Edna was not a blackmailer. She was more a quidnunc, a gossip, a busybody, and a snoop. That's why she was so valuable to you. Don't look so downcast, Abel. Edna was not the sort of girl you could bring home to mother."

"I don't have a mother," said Abel.

164

"Why? Can't you afford one? Jacob, I can see Abel is vastly underpaid, you must remedy the situation at your earliest convenience. Back to Edna, who probably never had as much attention in life as she's having in death. I hope she's relishing every moment, wherever she's eavesdropping. Hmmm."

"Now what?" asked Singer.

"I wonder if Big Ike Vivaldi talks in his sleep. If so, Edna could have picked up some tempting tidbits."

Trixie and Angie returned from the bedroom loaded down with furs and the suitcases. "This is most of it," said Angie.

"Okay, ladies," said Singer. He motioned to two of his assistants to relieve the girls of their burdens. He asked one, "You finished dusting?"

"They got it all," said Abel, before the other man could reply. "There's fingerprints all over the place, none on the knife hilt."

"I didn't expect any," said Singer. "The other stuff will probably be useless too. It'll be Edna, Vivaldi, our girlfriends here . . ." He made an encompassing gesture toward Angie and Trixie.

". . . and Hattie Beavers," contributed Angie. "Hattie cleaned for Edna." She explained why she was in possession of the key to Edna's apartment. "Edna didn't trust Hattie with the key, so when she was going to be out of town I had the key and let Hattie in to do the housework."

"Okay. Hattie Beavers." Singer made a mental note to question Hattie at length in the morning. Abel had already jotted down a memo to himself.

Noel had an arm around Abraham Wang's shoulder. "There's such a glacial expression on your face, Abraham. What's troubling you? Are you feeling ignored?"

"Not at all. I'm a good listener and a good listener hears things the speaker does not realize he's saying. Like from what I've heard all day, who is the murderer, why was Nicholas Benson stabbed in the back, what information did he possess that Edna Dore might also have possessed, and if he did have that information, then why did he bother breaking and entering here?"

"To help someone else," said Noel. "Which does narrow down our list of suspects, doesn't it?"

Trixie held her breath. Angie was staring at Noel. Abel stared at

Trixie. He wondered if she might be available. Singer said to Trixie and Angie, "You girls go home and get some rest."

Trixie snapped, "Rest? Are you nuts? After what we've been through tonight, I need a hot bath and a cold beer. Come on, Ang, we'll pick up some sandwiches, I'm starving."

After they left, Singer said to Noel, "Suspicions aren't worth a damn without proof."

"I know that. And our killer knows that. And I suppose it's what you call a Mexican standoff until somehow you trick the culprit into either making a confession or making that false step you need to solve your case."

"I don't think confession comes easily to this murderer. And the false step was made tonight. Nicholas should never have been murdered. Come on, let's get back to the precinct. I want you to get a good look at that group photograph. And I hope that cockamamy theory of yours works."

"Jacob," said Noel as he exhaled cigarette smoke, "you do go in for some colorful turns of phrase. Don't you agree, Abel?"

"Noel," said Abel, "you ain't heard the half of it."

Sixteen

O UTSIDE the brownstone, Trixie and Angie had been way-laid by the press. They posed for the photographers, happy to sit on the steps, cross their legs, raise their skirts above their knees, and revel in a limelight not often accorded them. A sob sister asked in a voice that had been honed by gin, "What are you girls doing at the scene of the crime?"

Trixie said, "Taking inventory." She leaned forward toward a photographer who asked for more décolletage.

"We found the body," said Angie. "It came out of the kitchen."

"Come on! Whaddya mean it came out of the kitchen, for crying out loud," asked the *Daily Mirror*, not terribly intelligent, like most Hearst employees.

"Just like what I said," insisted Angie. "He was still alive." The sob sister gasped. "For real, I'm telling you. He held out his hand to us." She illustrated graphically and several reporters moved back.

"That's when he gurgled and fell on his face," said Trixie matter-of-factly, now an authority on murder victims.

"What gurgle?" asked the *Evening Journal*. "You mean his death rattle?"

"He didn't have a rattle," said Trixie, now anxious to get away from these people who were making her uncomfortable. "He just made that awful noise and fell on his face. That's when we saw the knife sticking out of his back."

"What kind of knife?" shouted the *Brooklyn Eagle* from the rear.

"A carving knife," said Angie. She made a fist and then raised her hand and brought it down into an imaginary body. "Right down to the hilt."

"Much blood?" asked the sob sister.

"Not much at all," said Trixie, rising and straightening her skirt.

"Nothing like what you'll see when Electra Howard lops off a chicken's head in our show," said Angie with relish. She was enjoying herself immensely.

Jacob Singer emerged from the house followed by Abel, Wang, and Jeffrey. Trailing them was Noel, a fresh cigarette in the holder, his left hand in his jacket pocket, head held high, poised and ready for action. He enjoyed the murmur of surprise caused by his unexpected appearance, and flashbulbs popped as he altered his pose with telling effect.

"Hey, Mr. Coward," shouted the Associated Press, trying to elbow his way forward with difficulty, "how come you're mixed up in this?"

Noel moved forward, the portrait of a star letting his audience know, but oh so subtly, they were privileged by his presence. "I have my dear dear friend, Detective Jacob Singer, to thank for allowing me to study police procedure. As you know, one of our showgirls was murdered today and in fact," he indicated languidly an area above his head, "another murder has just taken place tonight in her apartment." He asked Singer, "Dare we divulge the victim's name or is that sort of thing withheld until the next of kin can be notified?"

"I'm sure they know it's Nicholas Benson," said Singer knowledgeably.

"Mr. Singer is sure you know it was Nicholas Benson who was murdered, a free-lance journalist specializing in true crime stories."

"Hey Jake!" yelled the United Press. "Got any suspects?"

"You know better than to ask that," replied Singer.

"No, I don't. I ain't got enough for three paragraphs."

"Then use your imagination," suggested Noel, bored with it all now that the photographers had stopped taking his picture.

"Who's the Chinese guy?" asked the *Morning Tribune*.

Singer stepped forward with his hands on his hips, now a menacing figure. He loathed the working press. Their rudeness, their cockiness, their penchant for manipulating information from truths to half-truths and insinuations. He had suffered their barbs in print in the past and knew they would continue to victimize him at every opportunity.

"The gentleman on my left is detective Abraham Wang, of the Shanghai police force. He's here as my guest. We're old friends."

The *New York Times* stepped forward. He was tall, thin, wore tweeds, and was working toward his goal to be the paper's theater critic and hold incredible power in his typewriter. He had no love for the theater whatsoever, which is why he knew he was qualified to replace the incumbent, Brooks Atkinson. "Is Mr. Wang possibly involved in solving the murder of Maxine Howard, which was reported in the . . . um . . . tabloids a few weeks ago. I believe her sister is Electra Howard, who is appearing with Mr. Coward at The Cascades."

"Yes, I am," said Wang, answering for himself.

The *Times* was not quite satisfied. "Is it possible there's a concatenation here?"

Wang was perplexed. "I beg your pardon?"

The *Times* looked superior, which was how he felt. "A linked series, sir. Is Maxine Howard's death in any way connected to that of Edna Dore and Nicholas Benson?"

Singer stepped in. "We're not sure. There's a remote possibility."

Noel said with a polished laugh, "We do hope the possibility won't remain remote." He could tell from Singer's quick glance that the detective wished he had kept his mouth shut. "It's just that it's so late, and we're all so teddibly teddibly tired"—it was now Jeff's turn to flash him a disapproving look—"and I think we all ought to call it a night. Jacob, I assume those police cars are at our disposal?" He moved forward with authority and the crowd of reporters and photographers parted before him as the Red Sea did for Moses. Noel mouthed "Good night" to each member of the press as he passed before them like the king of England reviewing his troops.

169

Noel, Singer, and Wang shared one patrol car while Jeff and Abel were delegated to the one following Noel. Settled in the backseat between Singer and Wang, Noel said, "Stop pouting, Jacob. I'm sorry if I put your nose out of joint but I recognized there's no love lost between you and the press and I feared matters were getting out of hand. I have the same problem at home with our gentlemen of the press and I call them gentlemen advisedly. Whatever I said, and I barely remember what I said, I doubt could be harmful in any way. I'm a past master at the art of double-talk. Ask any of my most recently discarded lovers. Now let's get on with it. My adrenalin's at a peak and let's make the best use of it. I want to see that photograph you had taken this afternoon. I want to know for sure that my suspicions are correct. And if they are," he added darkly, "I think there's the strong possibility that some deaths in the past could be reinterpreted as murders." He exhaled smoke. The officer at the wheel coughed. Noel said a brisk, "Sorry, old boy," and they rode the rest of the way in silence, the three in the backseat deep in private thoughts.

At the same time, Hattie Beavers was helping her Grandma Sadie polish off a pint of Jamaican rum. Although it was almost one in the morning, the two overweight ladies were as perky and bubbly as schoolgirls about to join a maypole dance. Grandma Sadie was staring into her crystal ball while making eerie clucking noises.

"You see something bad, Grandma?"

Grandma reached for her corncob pipe, which smoldered in an ashtray. She lifted it to her lips, took a long seductive drag, and then placed it back in the ashtray. She held the smoke in her lungs for over thirty seconds, and then exhaled with a beatific expression on her face. Hattie didn't have to ask what was smoldering in the pipe bowl. She recognized the tantalizing scent of opium, Sadie's long-time addiction.

"What you see, Grandma?"

"I see a dead man. He's young. He's got a knife in his back."

"Somebody I know?"

"I think so. Turn on the radio. Get WINS. They'll have the news at this hour." Hattie switched on the radio, she played with the dial until she found the station, and after suffering some dreary items

170

about Eleanor Roosevelt urging the country to buy Girl Scout cookies and New York's Mayor Fiorello H. LaGuardia addressing the graduates of the police academy in his celebrated high-pitched, piping voice, the announcer informed them of Nicholas Benson's mysterious murder.

"God have mercy on us!" cried Hattie as she crossed herself and then switched off the radio. "Mr. Nicholas murdered. A knife in his back. In my Miss Edna's apartment." Her face hardened. "I know what those two whores was doing there. They was there to rob Miss Edna's jewels and furs."

"Shit, girl, I told you you should have gone there after Edna was killed."

"I ain't no thief, grandma. You know that."

"I sure do. You're the white sheep of the family. Anyhow, you listen to me, girl, and you listen good." She pointed an index finger at Hattie, who instinctively felt something awful was coming. "You are in trouble."

Hattie took a deep breath. Was the husband who had abandoned her ten years ago coming back from the unknown? Was Electra Howard going to hex her because she suspected Hattie was on to her fakery? "What kind of trouble, Grandma? Is it bad?"

"Trouble ain't never good, honey. And the trouble is in your apartment."

Hattie was wide-eyed. "I got a leak in the bathroom?" Her apartment was in a decaying tenement across the street from where her grandmother lived on St. Nicholas Avenue in Harlem. Hattie had no children. She lived alone except for an occasional itinerant lover.

"You got something that is dangerous, Hattie." Her grandmother's eyes shifted swiftly from the crystal ball to Hattie's perspiring face. "I know you don't steal, Hattie. I believe you when you say you don't steal, but you got something valuable. You got something that don't belong to you. Well? Speak up, woman."

"I've got something of Miss Edna's, Grandma."

"And it's valuable."

"I guess it's worth something because she gave it to me to keep for her in a safe place. She gave it to me last week. But Grandma, it's just an ordinary envelope. I don't think it's got nothing more in it than a sheet of paper."

171

"You sure?"

"I'm sure. I held it up to the light."

"Hattie. Take it to the police."

"I don't like the police. I don't trust them. They don't like us black folk." She thought for a moment. "But I like Abel Graham."

"Who's he?" She took another hit of opium. Grandma Sadie leaned back in her chair. Some of her was off in another world, the rest of her was waiting for her granddaughter to identify Abel Graham.

"He's a detective feller. Miss Edna was sweet on him for a while until she got afraid Vivaldi would cotton to it and give her what for. He's a good man. So is his boss, Jacob Singer."

"I've heard of him. They's a lot of talk about him. He's a name fucker. Likes to run with famous people."

"That's right. Right now he's sucking up to our Mr. Coward."

"You get in touch with Abel Graham."

"Right now?"

"Sure, right now."

"But he won't be there this late, Grandma."

Grandma Sadie took a peek into the crystal ball. "He's there all right, honey. He's messed up in Benson's murder. There's the phone, woman, you go call him."

Hattie took a swig of rum, and so fortified, went to the phone to try and rouse Abel Graham.

Abel had just arrived in Singer's office with Jeff, joining Singer, Wang, and Noel, when Singer informed him the switchboard was holding a call for him. Abel was surprised. Who could be calling him at the precinct at this hour?

"Hattie?" He was the center of attention. "What's up, honey?" He listened. He wrote on a piece of paper. "I'm leaving right now. I'll meet you in front of your building. I should be there in less than half an hour." He hung up.

"What's up?" asked Singer. Abel told them about Hattie being in possession of an envelope Edna had given her to hide.

"Then Hattie's in danger," said Noel. "If the killer suspects this envelope exists, and I think the killer does, not having found it in Edna's apartment, then the logical person for Edna to trust would be Hattie."

172

Wang asked, "Why not Trixie or Angie?"

Noel said, "Because what I think is in that envelope is the name of the person involved with the three partners, the unholy fourth. Edna trusted Hattie."

Singer said, "Not enough to give her a key to her apartment."

Noel said, "Jacob, I think I can logically guess that Edna was reluctant to give Hattie the key because that envelope was still in her apartment and she didn't want Hattie there alone in case the murderer came looking for it. Jacob," he said the name gravely, "I think Nicholas went to Edna's apartment with the killer because he wanted the contents of that envelope to confirm his suspicion. The way we need it to confirm ours."

Singer said, "You're so sure that's what the envelope contains?"

"I'm sure." He wasn't and Jeff, smirking, knew it.

"Then why didn't Edna whisper that name to Abel?"

"Possibly for blackmail purposes, but I prefer to think it was out of loyalty to Big Ike Vivaldi. I was rather fond of Edna and her dear ambition to better herself. I prefer to think that right up to her tragic end, she was on the square. Now gentlemen, we're keeping Hattie waiting and ourselves in suspense. Shall we be off to Harlem?"

Before driving off uptown, Jacob Singer cautioned both patrol car drivers not to use their sirens. "Sirens in Harlem," he advised Noel, "are like a declaration of war." Noel found himself ensconced again between Wang and Singer, like a first edition between bookends.

"Curiouser and curiouser," said Noel.

"Meaning what?" asked Singer.

"So near to the solution, but yet, also so far."

Wang said, "Once we get our hands on the envelope . . ."

"I hope it's as simple as that," said Singer, for the first time since Noel had met him, sounding weary, tired of it all. "But I don't need to remind you, Abe, there can always be an unexpected complication."

They drove through Central Park, entering at Central Park South and Seventh Avenue. They passed a number of hansom cabs and Noel wondered why courting young couples found the conveyances romantic. He had never been inspired to heights of passion in anything on wheels. Ocean liners yes, except when there was a squall at sea. The Metropolitan Museum on their right loomed dark and foreboding. The traffic on Fifth Avenue was light and almost noiseless except for the grinding of brakes of the double-decker buses. Noel ached for a very cold dry martini and wondered if Hattie might be in a hostessy mood.

She wasn't. She was standing in front of her tenement home, trying to look like someone minding her own business. Even at this hour of the night, Harlem was far from asleep. Tourists would be arriving most of the night to enjoy the mysteries of all-night entertainments in some of the better clubs, such as the Cotton Club and Small's Paradise. Vendors were still on the streets hawking hot dogs and large hot pretzels and root beer and Cokes. While waiting, Hattie had fended off a couple of drunks and one ineffective masher. Even without sirens wailing and top lights flashing, the populace knew instinctively that the fuzz had arrived. Windows flew open and heads popped out to see what all the fuss was about. The fuss was only Hattie Beavers and everybody knew Hattie and her Grandma Sadie. Hattie was a God-fearing woman who attended church every Sunday morning and lighted candles and went to confession regularly because she enjoyed lying. Grandma Sadie was something else again, but her uncanny talent as a fortune teller was widely respected and recognized. So what was Hattie up to with the police? And two squad cars yet; two squad cars were reserved for very important people or a raid on a gambling parlor or a whorehouse. There was neither establishment in Hattie's tenement.

"I'm a nervous wreck waiting for you people!" exclaimed Hattie as the five men got out of the patrol cars. "Oh, what a nice surprise seeing you, Mr. Coward. Shouldn't you be home getting your beauty sleep?"

"I'm not acquainted with any beauties, dear girl." Noel flicked ash while Hattie led the way into the building.

"I'm just straight down the hall in the back. It's very quiet."

"It's very dark," said Noel.

"The landlord don't hold much with improvements," explained Hattie. "There's only one forty-watt bulb to a floor. Oh, Jesus save me, my door is wide open! Someone's been here!" Singer and Abel drew their guns.

"Stand aside, Hattie," ordered Singer. "Where's the light switch?"

"On the left wall, just by the door," she whispered.

Singer found the switch. It illuminated a small, sparsely furnished living room. Noel was sure that Hattie normally kept a very neat apartment, but like Edna Dore's apartment, Hattie's had been torn apart in what Noel imagined to be a frantic, frustrated frenzy. "Oh, dear Jesus! Oh, my beloved Jesus!" Noel wondered if Hattie had an autographed photograph of Himself. "If I'd have been here you'd have found me dead!" Singer silently agreed with her. "My knitting and my needlework! Look at this mess!" She gasped. "And look at the rug!" It had been pulled back, revealing a scuffed wooden floor. "Oh, Mr. Singer," wailed Hattie mournfully, "it's gone! The envelope's gone! I had it hidden under the rug!"

Noel asked Hattie politely, "Do you mind if I smoke?"

Seventeen

NOW how the hell did the killer figure out Hattie had something Edna'd given her to keep for her?" Abel voiced his frustration while running a hand through his hair.

"Quite simple, dear boy," said Noel, "process of elimination. If it wasn't in Edna's apartment, then it had to be with the one person Edna would consider innocent enough not to pry into the contents of the envelope. To wit, Miss Hattie Beavers."

"I could have been killed," muttered Hattie, "I could have been killed."

Wang asked, "How did the killer know where Hattie lived?"

Noel explained. "Either look her up in the phone book or take her address off the call sheet."

"Call sheet? What's a call sheet?" Wang was understandably perplexed.

Noel enlightened him. "The call sheet is a sheet of paper that hangs in the stage-doorkeeper's cubicle. It lists a production's personnel and their home addresses and phone numbers. In the case of the artistes, their agents are also listed and where to contact them. Actually, our call sheets were mimeographed and distributed to the entire company. Quite convenient, especially for the killer. Well, Jacob, what next?"

"Back to the precinct and the group photograph. Let's go." He started out.

Abel's voice stopped his exit. "We can't leave Hattie here like this."

"Why not?" questioned Singer. "There's no further danger. Whoever took the envelope has what he or she came for. Hattie's in no danger."

"Hattie," said Hattie, "nevertheless is going across the street to spend the night with her Grandma Sadie. I got to get up early for rehearsal. And you do too, Mr. Coward," she scolded good-naturedly.

"I promise you I'll get a good night's sleep," said Noel warmly, "if not tonight then the next night or the night after . . ." He made circles with his right wrist as he followed Singer out into the street.

Half an hour later they were in Singer's office. The group photograph, in an enlargement, lay flat on the desk. Noel sat in Singer's chair studying it closely while the others were standing grouped around him, wondering what it was that Noel was so positive was wrong with the photograph. Noel went through his usual ritual of loading the cigarette holder, applying his lighter, and inhaling deeply before concentrating on the task at hand. Singer, bone tired, shifted from one foot to the other. He didn't like the way he looked in the photograph and said so. Noel commiserated. "Well, after all, dear boy, there were no pains taken with the lighting and an airbrush hasn't been applied. I look like a beagle hound who's lost the scent. Nicholas Benson photographs magnificently. Too bad he's missing this. Electra Howard looks as if she's about to breathe fire and I'm sure if she wanted to she could. Dan Parrish is really quite an attractive man. And here's Diana looking quite bored with it all. Isn't it strange, Jeff, how unalike she and her mother are." Jeff yawned while aching for the comfort of his bed. "Chick Mason and his orchestra. They look like sixteen con men in search of a sting. They'd be better served looking for some decent orchestrations. Nancy Adman also photographs well for a least likely suspect." He stared into space for a few moments. "I wonder, I do wonder."

"What's on your mind?" asked Singer.

"I'm wondering about what's *not* on my mind. I can't find it,

177

Jacob. There's something definitely wrong with this picture, but I can't find it."

"You're too tired. We're all bushed. Let's call it a night."

Noel yawned and stretched. "I give up. Me for beddy-bye after a lovely ice cold martini." He asked Wang, "Can we give you a lift, Abraham?"

"No, thanks. It's just a short walk from here to the hotel."

"Walk alone through these dark streets at this hour of the night? Are you mad or merely feigning insanity?"

"Nothing will happen to me."

Noel took one last look at the photograph. He said to Jeff, "I'll bet if Bea Lillie were here she'd pick her spot instantly and say "Ere's what's wrong, ducks' with that uncanny instinct of hers."

"Maybe we should send for Miss Lillie," suggested Singer slyly.

"You'll meet her at the opening. She'll be there with another of our partners in crime, the unsinkable Gertie Lawrence. Opening night will be an autograph hound's dream come true. Or possibly nightmare. Come Jeffrey, let's find a taxi and wend our way home."

Good-nights were exchanged, and after Noel and Jeffrey had departed, Wang said to Singer, "Maybe it's all a figment of Noel's imagination. Maybe there's nothing out of kilter in the grouping."

Singer, hands on hips, running his wet tongue around his dry lips, merely said, "Maybe."

In the taxi, Jeff said to Noel, "Why wouldn't you tell them?"

"Tell them what?"

"What you spotted was wrong with the photograph."

"I didn't spot anything, although at the moment there are spots developing before my eyes."

"Noel," said Jeff, and Noel recognized the tone of voice Jeff used infrequently, "for a few moments back there, you stared into space. I'm very familiar with that faraway look you get when you're onto something. And I don't think you had Singer fooled for one moment."

"You really think not? I think I did. We'll discuss it later." He indicated silence was in order with a nod of his head toward the cab driver. They sat in silence until they reached West Fifty-eighth Street.

In the apartment, Jeff fixed cold martinis for the two of them. "I don't care whether I had Jacob fooled or not," said Noel as he lighted what Jeff hoped would be his last cigarette for the night. "If I told Jacob what I knew, he might impetuously rush into making an arrest. But the person would be freed on bail almost immediately. Jacob has no proof, no solid foundation on which to present his case. I can see the killer now, sitting and holding that envelope."

"It's probably been set afire by now or torn up into little bits and sent wafting into space from the back of a taxi." Jeff stirred the martinis.

"Don't bruise the gin," cautioned Noel. He settled onto the sofa while Jeff poured and served the drinks. "I'm going to trap the killer myself."

"Noel!" cried Jeff with alarm.

"Watch those bloody drinks, you fool, you almost spilled some!" He took a glass from Jeff, sipped it, made a small peep of delight, and then settled back. "It's the only way. By now I should think our killer is drifting about on a pink cloud of smug self-satisfaction. Good. I'll help keep it that way until opening night." He laughed. "I really can't resist. The idea of unmasking a murderer on an opening night is just too too marvelous to resist!"

"Noel, you sound like a fool. I've rarely said that in the years we've known each other, but now I think you're going too far."

"Oh mymymmymymy," said Noel, his left hand lifted with an effort to his forehead, his voice blasé and world-weary, "I remember the times you thought I hadn't gone far enough."

"Those times," retorted Jeff, "as I recall, were few and far between. I don't approve of this plan at all. It's risky and foolhardy and has it occurred to you that due to your smug self-satisfaction you might get yourself killed?"

"I couldn't possibly let that happen. I start filming in two weeks. Have you read the script of *The Scoundrel*, by the way? Awfully arch and cynical. It won't earn a farthing. Pour me another drink. And Jeffrey, don't you go tattletaling to Jacob about my plan. I'll deny it vociferously and you shall be sent to Coventry."

From the bar, Jeff said, "I'd rather you stopped speaking to me for the rest of my life than have you set yourself up as a sitting duck."

"Jeff," said Noel, watching his friend slowly mix the next batch

179

of martinis, "I'm genuinely touched. I had no idea you cared this deeply about me."

"You would if you'd ever shut your mouth long enough to listen to someone else."

Noel stared at the floor. "Shame on me. I had no idea you find me so self-centered. I shall do my best in the future to improve. Jeff?"

"Yes?"

"Trust in me. I know I can handle what I've set out to do. All right?"

"All right. But begrudgingly."

"Accepted. Now hurry with that martini. I parch so easily these days. And I'm not in the least bit sleepy. Let's try that new word game I bought the other day, *Criss Cross*. We're both dreadful spellers so we shall have a marvelous time cheating. You'll find the box in the bedroom on the windowsill."

Jeff refilled their drinks and then went to the bedroom. Noel set up the card table, deep in thought. Sitting duck, perhaps. Rash and foolhardy, perhaps. But it's the only way to get the goods on the culprit, and I for one shall savor the moment of the unmasking.

Alone in his office, Jacob Singer sipped from a container of luke-warm coffee and studied the group photograph. Then he said aloud, "Okay Mr. Coward, if you're planning a grandstand play, I'm going to let you get on with it. There'll be no interference from me. If it doesn't work, I'm sure your friend Alfred Lunt will deliver an eloquent eulogy at your funeral." He slammed his fist down on the photograph. Fool. Damn fool. Ahhhh, the hell with it.

At the downtown branch of the Dime Savings Bank the next morning, Clara Bizet and Big Ike Vivaldi confronted each other in the safe-deposit vault. Wearing a fur coat badly in need of hollanderizing, Clara looked like an oversized beaver in search of a challenging dam to sink her teeth into. Big Ike had been to the hospital and was genuinely glad to be told that Fat Harry and the Weasel were both on the road to recovery, Fat Harry likely to be released the next day. He shared the news with Clara, who stood with a palm outstretched. "Give me the key, Ike. I'll open the box. It's none of your business what's in that box beside his diaries."

"I've been here before with Irving, Clara. You don't have to be so touchy."

"You don't have to be so nosy." She snapped her fingers. "Come on, come on, the key." He gave her the key while whistling between his teeth, something he did when contemplating delivering a blow to a jaw. To think he once thought of seducing this woman. It must have been the bootleg booze. It rotted a lot of brains. Once in possession of the diaries. Big Ike slipped them into a briefcase and with a curt "so long" for Clara, left the woman examining her husband's life insurance policies. So he's getting better, she thought moodily. Well, she'd still outlive him. All the women in her family outlived their husbands and she was confident she wouldn't be the exception. Nice policies. Nice Irving. He would leave her well fixed. Now if he'd only leave her. There was this Good Humor ice cream salesman she was seeing on the sly.

On the phone from his dressing room at the club, Noel, with a hint of amusement in his voice, was talking to Jacob Singer and pleading temporary amnesia. "It's really most frustrating, Jacob. It's like coming onstage after playing a part for weeks and weeks and letter perfect, and suddenly drying up for no reason whatsoever. Imagine *me* forgetting my own deathless prose! Absolutely unforgivable."

Jacob was an equitable player in the game. "Don't force it, Noel. It'll come to you. I'm sure it will."

"Bless your heart, Jacob. You're such a comfort." He hadn't heard Electra Howard entering. He saw her reflected in the dressing table mirror. "Dear girl, you startled me! I didn't hear you come in."

"I hear tell you were in Harlem last night. One of my dancers saw you and your friends on the street with Hattie."

"Quite right. On the trail of the murderer."

"You expected to find the murderer in my neck of the woods?"

"Actually, if you must know, we were on the trail of a clue that we hoped would identify the killer."

"And did you find your clue?"

"No, curse the luck, it had been removed before our arrival." He was rubbing his fingers with hand lotion. "It doesn't really matter. I'm pretty sure I know the killer's identity."

181

"Well now, speak up, speak up."

"What's the point? We have no proof. My theory, I'm sure you understand, is pure supposition. After all, I've never done detective work before." He was wiping his hands with a towel. "Awfully exhausting, have you ever tried it?"

"No, but I've got some theories as to who might have had my sister killed. In fact, I've got four theories. The three bastards who are running the show and the silent partner. That ever-present mysterious X. My sister's funeral is Saturday afternoon."

"But my dear Electra, that's the day after our opening."

"So what? The show must go on."

"Ours or your sister's?"

Angie Bates and Trixie Murray were a fascinated audience and Hattie Beavers had them spellbound relating the previous night's encounter in her apartment. "My Grandma Sadie saw it all in her crystal ball too. Mr. Benson and the knife in his back and everything. Now, how about these pictures of you two in the newspapers?" They were spread across the front page of every newspaper except the *New York Times*, which obviously didn't consider them candidates for "All the News That's Fit to Print." It didn't bother them. Their friends and families read the tabloids and that was where their celebrity counted.

The girls had learned their benefactors were on the mend, but Angie was still uneasy. "Gee, Hattie, don't it scare you none knowing the murderer was actually in your apartment?"

"Son of a bitch sure messed the place up."

Trixie was cold-creaming her face. "I'll bet it was just like Edna's."

Hattie asked suddenly, "What they do with all her good stuff?"

"Confiscated it. Her family'll probably claim it."

"I cleaned out her dressing table. For the new girl."

"She ain't dressing with us," said Angie, "she's dressing with the other girls. That dressing table's reserved for Big Ike's next."

"Who's that?" asked Hattie.

Said Angie, "I don't think even Big Ike knows."

* * *

Jeff Amherst had invited himself into Millicent Headman's apartment for coffee, on Noel's instructions. He knew he wouldn't survive the day on just four hours' sleep, but they'd gotten so caught up in *Criss Cross*, in which one formed words and crisscrossed them much as one did in a crossword puzzle, that they found it hard to stop playing, even when Jeff insisted there was no such word as "humongous." Millicent was absorbed in Jeff's tale of the previous day's and night's adventures and then finally said in despair, "Oh, when will this killer be apprehended? I do so fear for Diana's safety."

"Why would Diana be in jeopardy?" asked Jeff before taking a bite of cheese danish.

"I should think she's in danger just being on the scene! This killer sounds thoroughly deranged to me. Whoever it is might take it into his head to kill at random just for the hell of it!"

"Noel disagrees with you, I'm happy to tell you. He thinks the killer has a brilliant mind."

"Really!" The very idea of Noel Coward paying a killer a compliment.

"This is strictly confidential, Millicent." He leaned forward. "I think Noel has a suspicion as to the killer's identity."

Millicent's mouth formed an O. "Noel is really too clever. Has he told the police?"

"Not yet." He sipped some coffee. It was weak. It needed chicory added to it the way they made it in England. "He has the suspicion but no support for it."

Millicent placed her cup and saucer on the table. "You mean if he made an accusation arrived at solely by deduction, he couldn't make it stick?"

"Well, let me put it this way. Knowing Noel and his superb talent for brazening things through, I'm sure he could point an accusing finger hoping to unnerve the murderer into making a slip and thereby a confession. But knowing another side of Noel, he does tend to overact, thereby diluting the effect, and his effort would go for naught and he'd be left on the wrong side of an action for slander." He attacked the pastry ferociously. Millicent stared out the window while Jeff chewed.

"Such a lovely morning," she said. "Too lovely to be talking about murder." Her eyes had misted.

"Millicent? Have I said something to upset you?"

"Oh no, no. It's just that Nicholas was like a son to me. When Diana phoned to tell me he'd been stabbed in the back, it was as though I too had suffered the attack. Nicholas wanted so badly to survive." She dabbed at her eyes, blew her nose, and took a sip of coffee. "He would have inherited a small fortune if his father hadn't been ruined in the crash. His father's suicide was a terrible blow and I feared for Nicholas's sanity. He was a good lad. I always hoped he and Diana would marry. I think he would have been a stabilizing influence on her."

"You consider Diana unstable?"

"Diana is what we call 'a free soul.' She hears a different drummer. She always did. She was a handful as a child. A little demon, but smart as a whip. She dispirited and exhausted over a dozen nursemaids. She was an impossible student in school. I don't mind telling you her father and I breathed a collective sigh of relief when she married. She was sixteen and too young, but we thought then she'd settle down. But it was hopeless. I don't know what she expected marriage to do for her. And he committed suicide. The next one, too. And then my husband." She poured more coffee for herself after Jeff refused a refill.

Jeff said, "I thought he died of a heart attack."

"It was suicide. He drank potassium chloride, a distillate of a deadly nightshade. It's not easily detected. Unless a doctor knows what to look for, he could very easily misdiagnose a heart attack. That's what happened with Linus. The nightshade is indigenous to Africa. I suspect he got it when we were there to see Diana through her ordeal with her husband's illness. What a terrible time that was."

"How's Diana taking Nick's murder?"

"She's terribly broken up. I begged her not to go to rehearsal today. I hope she didn't go. I wish she'd give up this nonsense of being a society singer. She has so little talent. But that's my daughter. Willful, headstrong and oh what the hell!" She slammed her hand down on the table. "An absolute bitch. Why in God's name we chose to adopt *her* . . ." She gasped. She sank back in the chair. "I shouldn't have told you that. I . . . oh hell." She rolled her handkerchief into a tight little ball and let her hand fall into her lap. "I couldn't conceive. Linus so hungered to be a father. So we decided to adopt. What a game we played!" She threw up her hands and the balled handkerchief flew across the room. "We wanted it to be a secret, to make it look as though I had, on doctor's orders, gone to my aunt's home in Palm Beach for the necessary months of bed rest and nursing care in order to ensure a safe delivery. So I lived in exile for some six months when the agency in Chicago through whom we arranged the adoption informed us they had an infant girl for us. She was four weeks old when we got her and brought her to New York. I should have guessed then she'd be trouble. She was colicky. She screamed and screamed and poor Linus moved into another wing of our apartment. The truth is, he never really cared for her. She wasn't his own flesh and blood. He wanted his very own. I suppose I did too, if I can be honest with myself. I tried hard to be a good mother, whatever that is. And I worked hard not to lose Linus." Jeff was a wonderful listener, a fine art achieved by few people. He knew Noel would applaud verbally when he repeated it all to him.

Millicent was lighting a cigarette. "I loved Linus very much then. But it wasn't easy sustaining that love. There were bitter arguments over Diana, she was a hell-raiser, absolutely uncontrollable. I wish I'd been able to trace her natural parents to see if there was anything in her heritage to give us a clue as to how to control her. Her sudden rages, her instant likes and dislikes."

"You seem to get along well enough now."

"It's easy when you conduct your relationship by telephone. I rarely see her."

"I thought you two had dinner the other night."

"What? Oh yes. We did." She changed the subject rapidly. "Do you think the club will be a success?"

"Noel tells me the opening night is sold out. What happens after that is anybody's guess. They've got a Cordon Bleu chef, so that's a huge plus. They're reasonably priced, keeping in mind the state of the nation's pocketbooks. They have a classy entertainer in Noel, and I think Electra Howard and Dan Parrish are going to make a big hit. Of course, right now there's the notoriety, the murders, and

New Yorkers I'm told are a bloodthirsty lot. Have you an escort for the opening? If you don't, may I volunteer?"

"Why, Jeffrey! You're so kind. You and Noel are both so kind, I'm so fortunate to know the two of you, I really am."

Eighteen

■ 〓〓 ■

NOEL was thoroughly astonished when, the afternoon of the opening, Jacob Singer asked him to come to see him at the precinct. "You're terribly out of order, Jacob," admonished Noel. "You must never disturb an artist the day of his opening night." He saw the group photograph laid out on the desk. It now had numerous notations in various colors of ink. Jacob had been working hard. Undoubtedly pressing Abel and Wang into service above and beyond the call of duty.

"Sit down, Noel." He indicated a chair next to him. "I didn't want you to think you were putting anything over on me."

"I wasn't doing that at all. I admire and respect you and I'm sure you're as positive as I am who's responsible for these murders, but I'll bet my bottom shilling you don't know why. Well, let me tell you something interesting." He repeated the information Jeff had gleaned from Millicent at breakfast a few days earlier. In conclusion, he said, "I suppose if I were Sigmund Freud I could come to some interesting psychological conclusions about a weakling of a father, a milksop of a mother, and a hellion of an adopted daughter. Well I am not that brilliant doctor, I am a mere worker in the theatrical vineyards who happened by circumstance to become involved in a very nasty murder case. And very nasty it is. We know who the murderer is and you know as well as I do that we don't have a thing on her. Diana Headman is a very shrewd creature, I hope she's willed her brain to the Smithsonian. I see you've put a big pink star in ink over her image in the photograph. I thought you'd soon guess that was what was wrong with it."

Singer chuckled. "You'd be lousy in a poker game, Noel. Your face was a dead giveaway when you saw this picture. I knew you spotted someone who'd placed themselves in the picture when they weren't onstage at all."

"Exactly. And she placed herself next to Nicholas, which doomed him right then and there. He knew she wasn't onstage but he kept his peace until he could discuss it with her. I strongly suspect she promised to marry him at last. Then he would be her number four, and Millicent's wish would come true. And Nicholas, being only human, lusted for a share of Diana's wealth, especially if he might have guessed that a good deal of it had once been his father's." He had jammed a cigarette into his holder and was now lighting it. Singer waved a hand back and forth in an unsuccessful effort to keep the streams of cigarette smoke from attacking his eyes. "While of course, actually, Diana was backstage during the rehearsal taking aim with the blowgun, an art we may safely assume she mastered in Africa while other ladies were concentrating on golf. Although Millicent finally admitted to Jeff that her husband was a suicide, I think it's far more likely that Diana administered the potassium chloride. What's more important, I'm positive Diana murdered her husband, death in small doses. If I were you, I'd advise the proper authorities in Rhodesia to exhume Coleridge's body and search for the poison."

"I already have," said Singer, hands folded over his stomach. "I'm hoping to have their report in time for the opening."

Noel beamed. "Full marks for you, Jacob. Although come to think of it, you're the detective and I'm merely a guest star. Oh, I do thank you, Jacob. This has been such fun. Now to start at the beginning, I suspect Linus Headman got himself into a financial jam long before his pharmaceutical firm began to go bust. Burst? No, bust is right. I should say that would be about two or three years before the stock market aborted. I think at that time he met and became involved with Vivaldi, Beethoven, and Bizet. I think he gave

188

them the facilities to process drugs for a nice fat percentage. Do I make sense?"

"Very much. I think they borrowed heavily from him in return for which they let him in on their other rackets, bootlegging and white slavery."

"I wonder if Millicent knew any of this."

Singer shrugged. "If she did, we'll never prove it."

"It's of secondary importance if at all. So here's Linus making money on his own while his business is failing. Diana meantime is marrying and disposing of two husbands."

"You think she killed them?"

"In for a penny, in for a pound. You'll never prove it, but if she doesn't get the chair, I'm sure she'll write her autobiography and tell all. And the film will star Carole Lombard. Along comes Coleridge and his deal with Linus to help sequester a lot of his money. And here's where Diana gets truly greedy. Coleridge, probably when in his cups, lets Diana in on his and her father's financial plot and the wheels of evil start clicking away and then meshing in Diana's feverish brain. She sends for daddy and mummy, which should have made at least Millicent suspicious. But Linus, of course, was very anxious to get to Rhodesia for apparent reasons. I think it was there Diana began his diet of potassium chloride, in small doses, of course. So Coleridge dies, Diana is the sole heir, and no matter how hard Linus fumes and frets Diana denies him the return of the money that belongs to him. She has that agreement he signed with Coleridge to hold over his silly head. Keep in mind over these few years the unholy partners have gone into a decline. Prohibition, the collapse of Headman Pharmaceuticals, probably problems in shanghaiing young ladies to the Orient."

Singer interrupted. "If a mere mortal may speak . . ."

Noel said archly, "You have our permission."

"I suppose it was in Rhodesia Diana learned of her father's association with the three bastards."

"As good a time as any. Also remember, Linus has been having an affair with poor, ill-fated Edna Dore. Edna must have learned a great deal from him and that's why Diana marked her for extinction. Back in this country and widowed again, Diana decides on a career in show business. She knows nothing about the business but gives

189

some serious thought to contacting three of daddy's old chums who do. Hence, she is the fourth partner in The Cascades, also assuring herself a position on the bill. The envelope Edna left with Hattie Beavers must have contained much of this information condemning Diana, and hence Diana's frantic search for it. She knew she had to be rid of Nicholas, so always a gal quick to seize an opportunity, she conned him into helping her raid Edna's apartment, and when the envelope couldn't be found, she dispatched Nicholas with a well-placed thrust of the carving knife. Then deducing Hattie had the envelope, made her way to Harlem and triumphed. If that mind and energy of hers could have be harnessed, I think Diana could rule the world."

Noel was lighting another cigarette. "Now then, how the hell do we prove any of this?"

"If we hit the bull's-eye with the autopsy on Coleridge, we've got her nailed. On the other hand, if Electra Howard learns that our Miss Headman is part of this gang that murdered her sister, she might have special voodoo means of her own to force the lady to fess up."

"Do you suppose it would help if we placed a headless chicken in Diana's dressing room?"

"Noel, you are truly evil."

"By the by, where are Abel Graham and Abraham Wang?"

"Out renting tuxedos. It's a big night, tonight."

"Of course. Any night starring Noel Coward is a big night. There'll be quite a turnout, Jacob. The cream of society, the cream of the cinema, and the cream of the theater, though the way the Broadway season's been going, I suspect much of that will be curdled. And who's your date for tonight?"

"Mrs. Parker. She got in from the coast last night and phoned me this morning. She left her husband behind."

"She's always leaving him someplace. Poor Alan Campbell. Why anyone would marry Dorothy Parker I do not know. Why a homosexual would marry any woman, let alone Mrs. Parker, is beyond credulity. But then Alfred and Lynn, my darling Lunts, they married each other . . ." he flicked ash on the floor, ". . . and soon fell madly in love with themselves. I'm off, I suppose my dressing room will be festooned with flowers and congratulatory wires and cablegrams and all sorts of gifts and I shall have to dress in the hallway. Fame is so exhausting."

"Come to think of it, Noel, I'm bringing you a present."

"How sweet." He had the door open for his exit. "I'd prefer you brought me a future." And he swept out.

Singer pressed a button on the intercom. "I want that report from Rhodesia on my desk thirty seconds after it gets here, if not sooner."

Though still in a weakened condition, Bizet joined his partners for the opening night of The Cascades club. Beethoven, also not fully recovered, nursed a glass of milk. Bizet was also nursing a fit of pique upon learning from Vivaldi his diaries had been consigned to the flames in the club's furnace. "You had no right, Ike, you had no right. That was my whole life in them diaries."

"Some life. If you had croaked, what do you think would have happened to Fat Harry and me if your wife got her hands on them?"

"Aw, Clara wouldn't make no trouble."

Vivaldi asked him, "You been married to Clara how long?"

"Too long," he said with a scowl. "Who do you think sent those poisoned chocolates? Don't the cops have no leads?"

"Boys, you know as well as I do who left that box of chocolates and we're going to have it out with that bitch after the show."

"Why not before?" pleaded Fat Harry, "She's so fucking awful."

"She's got a lot of her society friends out front. And there's every newspaper and news service out front. And listen, you two, I had to pay off the fire department this morning. There was two inspectors here and they were going to close us as a firetrap until I opened the safe. God, there's a lot to be said for corruption."

Bizet sounded forlorn. "Why would Diana want to kill us? Ain't we been on the up-and-up with her, like we was with her father?"

"I could think of a couple of reasons. She wants out and we've got too much on her. Or she's greedy and she wants the whole operation to herself."

"She wouldn't know how to run it," snarled Fat Harry.

Vivaldi said thoughtfully, "Or she's just plain off her rocker. I sent her a nice bundle of flowers."

"Oh yeah," growled Fat Harry, "what kind?"

"Lilies."

It was a beehive of activity backstage and even busier out front. Chick Mason's orchestra was doing yeoman duty, its repertoire leaning heavily on selections from Broadway and Hollywood musicals. The tables were slow to fill up, the opening night celebrities stopping on the sidewalk out front to pose for pictures, give interviews, sign autographs, wave wildly at each other while making snide remarks under their breath. A cordon of police had put up lush velvet ropes provided by the club in order to hold back the great unwashed who were clamoring for a sight of celebrities, giving out a roar when someone especially famous stepped out of a limousine. There were roars when Joan Crawford arrived with Franchot Tone, soon to be her ex-husband, and cheers for Constance Bennett when she slithered out of her limousine followed by Gilbert Roland, soon to be her ex-husband. Jeffrey and Millicent arrived in a taxicab in time to hear Mexican-born actress Lupe Velez ask her handsome escort, "Don't you want to come to Mexico and sit on my hacienda?"

He said, "Wouldn't it be less expensive if I sat on it here?"

Jacob Singer helped Dorothy Parker out of the taxi and then paid the fare. "I still think you could have been a bit daring and devil-may-care about tonight, Jacob, and brought me here in a squad car with the siren screaming and the lights flashing."

"The taxpayers wouldn't have liked that."

"I didn't expect you to ask them to join us. Oh look, there's Ogden Shoemaker, the archeologist."

"Who's the woman with him?"

"His wife. Something else he dug up."

Nancy Adman was in Diana Headman's dressing room, making some last-minute adjustments to her purple evening gown trimmed with monkey fur. "I can't get this right when you're fidgeting. Why don't you take something for your nerves?"

"I need a drink," said Diana. There was a knock at the door. "Come in!"

Noel entered with a big smile on his face, the inevitable cigarette holder and cigarette in his left hand, and in his right hand, an open box of chocolates. "I have come to wish you good luck, my dear. My, but aren't you enchanting! What kind of fur is that? Lynx?"

Nancy Adman shot him a look. "It's monkey fur."

"Oh dear." He held out the box of chocolates to Diana. "Have a chocolate. It'll steady your nerves. It's a lovely assortment and they're all filled with liqueurs."

"I don't eat chocolates." Noel wondered if her face was pale under all that heavy makeup.

"Good for you. Fat Harry and the Weasel wish they hadn't eaten chocolates."

Nancy Adman got to her feet while asking, "Why, for crying out loud?"

"Because that's what put them into the hospital. Poisoned chocolates left on Fat Harry's desk."

Nancy Adman was shocked. "Poisoned chocolates?"

"Indeed," corroborated Noel, "would you like one of these?"

Nancy waved them away. Noel said, "I've had a peek out front. The club's beginning to fill up. There are those who will be blinded by the jewelry, real and paste. I do hope Jacob Singer isn't delayed. He's escorting Dorothy Parker, but he might be held up waiting for an important paper from abroad." He caught Diana's eye as she sat at her dressing table and saw his reflection in the mirror. "He's waiting for something from . . . for heaven's sake . . . *your* Rhodesia." The hairbrush she was lifting slipped and fell back onto the table. "Good luck again, darling, may this be the most memorable night of your life."

In an area just beyond Diana's dressing room, Electra and Dan's six dancers were dousing torches with lighter fluid. They would be set aflame and held aloft for the number they danced to "Stormy Weather." Noel wished them luck when he emerged from Diana's dressing room. As he passed Electra and Dan's dressing room, he heard a chicken clucking. He stuck his head in the room. "Best of luck, my dears. I suppose it's pointless to wish any for the chicken."

"You're very jaunty," commented Electra. "Have you got nerves of steel?" She held out her hand, "Look, it's trembling."

"Why don't you cast a spell over it?" With which he was gone.

Out front, Tommy Manville, a very wealthy playboy who was celebrated for his numerous marriages and divorces, was paying court to a young redhead who was telling him about a promiscuous girl-friend. "She goes to bed with anybody. She's a regular elevator the way she goes up and the way she goes down. My mother thinks she's a nimblemaniac."

Jacob Singer and Dorothy Parker had a prime location. At the next table were Noel's two special friends, comedienne Beatrice Lillie and the sophisticated singer-actress Gertrude Lawrence. Mrs. Parker introduced Singer to the two glamorous British stars who had become equally popular in the United States, and Miss Lillie, who was immediately intrigued by Singer's rough-hewn good looks, said, "I've been telling my table about this strange German actor I met who told me in foreign films he dubs Harpo Marx. Oh la, but isn't he the mad one! Gertie, how's that niece of yours who married that dreary lawyer?"

"His parents treat her like one of the family. Miserably."

Jacob said something to Mrs. Parker. She nodded and waved him off as he left her to go backstage in search of Noel Coward. Beatrice Lillie induced Mrs. Parker to join their table, which she did with alacrity.

Bea Lillie leaned forward cosily. "Now then, Dorothy . . . I may call you Dorothy, mayn't I? I mean if I have to call you Mrs. Parker then you have to call me Lady Peel. But since I'm long estranged from Lord Peel, I prefer you call me Bea, but oh the hell with it. So where's your husband tonight?"

Said Mrs. Parker, "Christ knows, and I hope He keeps His secret."

The maître d' was leading Abraham Wang and Abel Graham to their table. They chose to eschew female companionship for the opening as an unnecessary encumbrance should there be fireworks more lethal than the Fourth of July variety. Wang was lavish in his praise of the club's interior with its torrential cascades craftily constructed to seem to be flooding the room, but actually directed into pipes that led to a disposal unit under the basement. Abel concurred, "No expense spared. Look, there's Walter Winchell with orchestra leader Ben Bernie. They're supposed to be feuding. I guess it's all for publicity. And look! There's Jean Harlow with William Powell. What a knockout!"

194

Wang agreed. "She'd be a knockout back in a Shanghai sing-sing house. They pay a lot for blondes. Swedes and Germans are top dollar. There's Mrs. Parker, but I don't see Jacob."

"Probably backstage giving Noel his present."

Noel was saying to Jacob, "If I was given to tears, there'd be a flood in this dressing room! Wait till Jeff sees this." The dressing room door was open and Dan Parrish materialized. Noel was holding up Jacob's present, an honorary police badge.

"I can't say that's a pretty sight," said Dan, who'd had his skirmishes with the police as a youngster.

"I think it's the most beautiful sight in the world," said Noel. "I shall treasure it always."

Dan asked Singer, "Do you give those badges away to anybody?"

Noel said huffily, "Noel Coward is not *anybody.*"

Singer explained to Dan, "It's his reward for his invaluable service in helping to solve the murders."

"Are they solved?" Diana was standing outside the door, unseen by them.

"We think so," said Singer, as he retrieved a paper from his inside jacket pocket and handed it to Noel. "This arrived a little over an hour ago."

"Ah!" cried a delighted Noel. "Rhodesia came through at last." Diana leaned against the wall, her hands clasped together, seemingly transfixed by the black dancers on her left who were lighting the torches they would soon be using onstage. "So it *was* potassium chloride. Oh dear dear Jacob, does this mean the show is canceled? I don't get to open?"

"Not at all. I've got the place ringed with my boys and they're poised for action once the curtain comes down. Give us a great show."

Dan said, "We'll do our best," and hurried away.

Singer said, "He's going to tell Electra."

"I thought it was Electra for a while, especially the blowgun touch. But remember when after Edna's murder I asked to examine the mouthpiece for traces of lipstick and I found none? Well, Jacob, right after the murder when Diana suddenly reappeared onstage, she was lavishly applying lipstick. The smart lady had wiped the lipstick off her lips before using the blowgun."

Diana had left her position outside Noel's dressing room when she heard Singer say the club was surrounded by his men. She went in search of the partners and found Fat Harry coming out of Angie and Trixie's dressing room. Diana grabbed his wrist. "I need help. I'm in trouble, and if I'm in trouble, the three of you are in trouble!"

Fat Harry said with a snarl, "You got another box of chocolates for us?"

Diana backed away from him, a look of fear on her face. She turned and ran.

The show was beginning. The orchestra was playing the overture, a medley of Noel Coward favorites that brought about a smattering of applause from the audience, most of whom were still craning their necks spotting celebrities. Tallulah Bankhead was ferociously attacking her hair with an oversized comb while her escort, a wet-eyed import from London, was devouring her with his eyes. She growled at him, "Montmorency, should I ever be overcome by a deplorable lack of taste, I'll consider you for a lover. Until then, grab a waiter and show him no mercy. I need another drink. Dahling, doesn't Noel write the loveliest ballads? They're almost singable."

Over the loudspeaker they heard against a drum roll Chick Mason announcing the introduction Noel had written for him. "Ladies and Gentlemen, welcome to The Cascades club and welcome also to one of the world's greatest performers. The one, the only, the inimitable who needs no introduction . . . the Master himself . . . Mr. No—ell Coward." Impeccably groomed and suited, Noel emerged from the wings, arms outstretched overhead while the audience was on its feet applauding wildly. There were shouts and whistles while the orchestra vamped behind him. Noel was proudly wearing his honorary police badge, which led Mrs. Parker to suspect he might be having an affair with Jacob Singer. Noel was waving and blowing kisses and mouthed "Hello Bea" and "Hello Gertie" and "Darling Tallulah," and then almost wept with joy at the sight of Eleanor Roosevelt at a front table with the Fiorello LaGuardias and J. Edgar Hoover. He held his arms out for quiet and in his delicate, fragile, yet thoaty voice, began to sing:

196

Big parades,
All lead to Club Cascades . . .

On the various levels behind him, Trixie and Angie and the other showgirls appeared wearing vulgar headdresses that simulated waterfalls, cataracts, and cascades.

Charades . . .
Are divine at the Club Cascades . . .

Backstage, Electra Howard, carrying the machete she used in the act, was stalking the cleverly elusive Diana Headman . . .

Even butlers and maids . . .
Delight to splurge at the Club Cascades . . .

Onto the stage high-kicked the chorus girls dressed in scanty maids' uniforms, holding feather dusters and waving them in the air . . .

Straight and gay blades . . .
Come directly to the Club Cascades . . .

Backstage, a wild-eyed Diana wielding a lighted torch was setting fire to the dressing rooms. Hattie Beavers ran shrieking into the alley and into the arms of a policeman. "Fire! Fire! The club's on fire!"

Smoke was soon pouring out into the club. Noel whisked a handkerchief from his breast pocket and swished it around in the air, determined to finish his song.

Cas . . . (cough) . . . cades, Cas . . . (cough) . . . cades . . .
Where all the world . . . (cough) . . . masque . . . (cough) . . .
rades.

He was alone onstage. The musicians had fled. Tables and chairs were overturned as celebrities and lesser folk fought their way to the inadequate exits. Jeff was leading Millicent backstage when he saw

197

Noel make a dash for the wings. Mrs. Roosevelt did her best to look dignified as she rode J. Edgar Hoover piggyback, he seeking an exit, visibility almost impossible due to the heavy smoke.

Montmorency pleaded with Tallulah Bankhead to abandon their table. "As soon as I finish this martini, dahling. It's damned good liquor, especially for a nightclub. And besides, look at the crush at the exits. Might as well die happy as by suffocation."

Backstage, half a dozen policemen were herding Vivaldi, Beethoven, and Bizet out the stage door to one of the several paddy wagons parked there for the occasion. Trixie and Angie were climbing out of their dressing room window to what they hoped was the comparative safety of the back alley.

Backstage, Noel was found by Jeff and Millicent, and they held handkerchiefs to their faces. Millicent cried, "Where's Diana? Where's Diana?"

"I'm afraid she's about to be the victim of a voodoo spell." Singer and Mrs. Parker came stumbling onto the scene, Mrs. Parker muttering obscenities about a torn dress she had not yet paid for. From above them in the flies they heard Dan Parrish shouting, "Don't, Electra, don't! Let the fuzz handle it!"

Wielding the machete with horrifying menace, Electra was pursuing Diana along a catwalk. Diana reached an iron-runged ladder leading down and started a descent. Electra was too quick for her. Millicent screamed and fell into Jeff's convenient, albeit reluctant, arms. Jacob Singer put his arms around Mrs. Parker, who watched with bloodthirsty fascination as Diana Headman's head landed near them, spinning briefly like a top. "If it's any consolation, Dottie," said Noel as he nonchalantly lit a cigarette, "in their act they decapitate a chicken. Oh dear, Jeff's having trouble balancing Millicent Headman . . ." In an aside he said to Dorothy while indicating the head, ". . . her mother."

On the catwalk, Electra surrendered the bloodied machete to Dan and then, with head held high, descended the ladder. She may not have liked her sister Maxine, but she knew her mother would be proud of what she had done. Maxine, of course, had been the baby, her mother's favorite.

They made their way out to the back alley where they found Wang and Abel helping minister to the injured. The fire engines had arrived with a clamorous roar and the firemen with great gusto and enthusiasm went to work with their powerful hoses and axes and in short time demolished what the dreadful flames had not already destroyed. A short time later, from the interior of the Hell's Bells bar across from the destroyed nightclub, Noel stood at the window, martini in one hand, cigarette in the other, and said, "What a shame. What a damned shame." He turned to where Singer and Mrs. Parker sat with Nancy Adman, Millicent Headman, Jeff, Wang, and Abel. "I suppose now I shall never collect my fee."

Millicent's shoulders shook, her hands flew to her face and she burst into uncontrollable sobs. Nancy Adman put her arm around Millicent's shoulders and patted her gently. "There, there dear, there there. She would have gotten the chair anyway." Mrs. Parker looked disapproving. Noel and Jeff exchanged amused glances. Singer downed his whiskey, anxious to get back to the precinct with Wang and Abel, Wang equally anxious to quiz the three partners about the Shanghai operation. Nancy Adman was saying, "I know what it is to lose a daughter. Many years ago in Chicago . . . I was a very . . . I knew a very foolish teenage girl who gave her daughter up for adoption . . . and regrets it to this very day."

Noel flashed a heaven-help-me glance at the ceiling and then said, "My dears, I think we'd better get going. There's so much still to be done." Jeffrey seemed to have fallen asleep. "Jeff! Jeff! Wake up, dear boy. We're leaving. I think this is where we came in."